BEYOND CORISTA

Other books by Robert Elmer

The Shadowside Trilogy:

Trion Rising (Book One)
The Owling (Book Two)

The Wall series:

Candy Bombers (Book One)
Beetle Bunker (Book Two)
Smuggler's Treasure (Book Three)

Visit Robert Elmer's website at
www.RobertElmerbooks.com

THE SHADOWSIDE TRILOGY

BEYOND CORISTA

ROBERT ELMER

ZONDERVAN.com/
AUTHORTRACKER
follow your favorite authors

We want to hear from you. Please send your comments about this book to us in care of zreview@zondervan.com. Thank you.

ZONDERVAN

Beyond Corista

Requests for information should be addressed to:

Zondervan, *Grand Rapids, Michigan 49530*

Library of Congress Cataloging-in-Publication Data

Elmer, Robert.
Beyond Corista / by Robert Elmer.
p. cm. — (The shadowside trilogy ; bk. 3)
Summary: When, after an arduous journey, fifteen-year-old Oriannon and her blinded enemy Sola are brought to the Gamma project as condemned prisoners, Oriannon has little left but her faith, courage, and the Pilot Stone given to her by her mentor, Jesmet.
ISBN 978-0-310-71423-1 (softcover)
[1. Good and evil — Fiction. 2. Christian life — Fiction. 3. Science fiction.] I. Title.
PZ7.E4794Bdw 2009
[Fic] — dc22 2008045534

Published in association with the literary agency of Alive Communications, Inc., 7680 Goddard Street, Suite #200, Colorado Springs, CO 80920. www.alivecommunications.com

Interior design by Michelle Espinoza

Printed in the United States of America

09 10 11 12 13 • 24 23 22 21 20 19 18 17 16 15 14 13 12 11 10 9 8 7 6 5 4 3 2 1

BEYOND CORISTA

Because you are the last asylum, spread the light
so they will hear beyond Corista — even where the Trion
is but a faint glimmer in the night sky.
~ Codex 101:3

1

"What's going on?" Just after the impact, fifteen-year-old Oriannon Hightower of Nyssa pulled herself hand over hand out of the back room of the shuttle, making her way forward to where her friend Margus Leek had been thrown to the floor in the control room. Eye-watering black smoke made her choke on her words and gasp for breath before a burst of chilling argonite gas snuffed the fire out.

"Did we hit a mine?" she asked.

Their spacecraft shuddered and tipped to the side. Gravity stabilizers must have taken a hit.

"You mean, you don't know?" came a low, mocking voice from the back of the control room. Huddled in the corner, a defiant Sola Minnik waved her arms for balance as an even larger explosion ripped through the underbelly of the craft and the overhead lights flickered out. The darkness made no difference to a blind woman, however.

Oriannon ignored Sola's question and glanced up at the Pilot Stone—which still glowed a faint gold and blue from its place next to the directional displays. The array of multicolored screens still glowed steady as well, taking their coordinates from the Stone. Or so Oriannon assumed.

"Ori!" their Owling friend, Wist, shouted from the darkness of the passenger area. "You guys okay up there?"

"Um ..." Oriannon gripped a handhold to keep from being thrown about. "Can't say for sure."

Oriannon couldn't be certain if their craft might explode at any instant, or if they'd been less fatally wounded. She flinched at the sound of grinding and twisting metal all around them; the smack and shudder of raw impacts as something hard hit the outer skin of their craft—three, four, then five times. The engines shrieked in protest, and she felt their forward momentum slow, then come to a complete stop with a rude jerk. Margus struggled back up to his chair, holding his forehead.

"What's happening now?" asked Oriannon, rushing to help him.

"It's like a huge hand just closed around us." Margus pointed at zeros on a screen that normally marked their forward speed. "I don't know how, but we're being pulled backward!"

Never a whiner, Margus ignored the blood trickling from a gash above his eye, focusing on the ship. He throttled back so the ship lurched and they leaned to the other side. If anyone could pilot them through this, he could, though his signature grin had long since disappeared.

"Backward?" Wist struggled forward to join them as the ship jostled from side to side like a hooked fish that knows it's going to die. But looking out the forward viewports revealed nothing except the emptiness of space. Then slowly, the nose section of a dark, silver-black Coristan Security cruiser pulled into view. It might have blended into the blackness if its windows had not been brightly lit from within. Oriannon groaned.

As emergency lights flickered on, she wondered how long they had left before this escape was all over—before they were dragged back to Corista to be executed as rebels and insurgents.

"They're all around us," reported Margus. "Five cruisers. They've caught up."

"But how?" Wist looked around the control room as if black-suited securities might step in through the skin of the shuttle. Another metal-on-metal impact shook them nearly off their feet, and Oriannon worried about her father resting in one of the two tiny passenger cabins aft of the control room. Margus checked his instruments once again.

"Grappling hooks." He didn't need to yell. "They're using grappling hooks!"

That would explain the grinding noises as large metal hooks burrowed their way more deeply into the ship's outer skins. Since the hooks had certainly been fired from several of the Coristan Security vessels at once, there would be no way to shake free.

"Ah, I see they've finally arrived. Have they?" Sola smiled as she felt her way forward, turning her head each time a new hook penetrated their hull with a sickening shudder. Even if the shuttle was built with multiple skins and air locks in between, they could not survive this kind of brutal attack for long. From her own twisted perspective, Sola had reason to smile.

However, that didn't mean she was easy to look at. The woman's eyebrows and eyelashes had been singed completely away, while her once full head of red hair had been reduced to ugly, twisted wisps here and there. Worse yet, her face looked as if someone had blackened it with a blowtorch, while angry red blisters rose across her nose and cheekbones, framing sightless eyes still wet with rheumy, coagulated tears. It could have been worse, considering the flash bomb that had blown up in her face only hours before back on Corista. In an instant, she had gone from someone who prided herself on her well-kept good looks to a snarling, helpless apparition.

Now Sola blindly reached out and grabbed Oriannon by the collar of her tunic. "You didn't answer," hissed Sola.

"Let me go!" Oriannon tried to pull away, but she literally had nowhere to escape. Maybe it didn't make any difference if they reached the way station ahead of the pursuing Security vessels. Maybe it was better to end this way.

"Why don't you just enjoy what little time you have left?" Sola challenged her again. "Have a snack. I've stocked plenty of supplies. A cup of clemsonroot tea?"

"Why don't you shut up!" Margus yelled in her direction. "Why don't you just keep your mouth shut and mind your own business!"

"Oh, but that's just it." She returned another crooked smile in the direction of his heated voice. "This *is* my business, just like this is my shuttle. My beautiful shuttle."

"You stole it," answered Oriannon. "It belonged to the Assembly."

Oriannon couldn't think of anyone she wanted on this "borrowed" interlunar shuttle less than Sola Minnik, who had served as the former Security advisor to the Ruling Elders of Corista before promoting herself to First Citizen. Or, dictator, to put it bluntly. Why would anyone want to travel with the fiery woman who had deceived and then nearly killed Oriannon's father—and probably all six of the other elders as well?

"I'm very sorry you feel that way, Oriannon." Sola's sarcasm dripped through her words. "There's so much you don't know."

Oriannon didn't answer. Oh, Sola was probably sorry, all right. Sorry they had caught up with her and destroyed the death camp, where hundreds and thousands of the Owling people (Wist included) had been imprisoned while being prepped for forced labor all over the planet. Sorry the Owlings had escaped. After all the work Sola and her Security forces had put into setting up the camp, she would naturally be very sorry about that.

Sola might also be sorry they'd saved her life by pulling her into the shuttle as they took off from the chaos of the camp, probes blowing up around them. She would be sorry they'd had to escape in the same luxury craft Sola had once used to travel around the planet.

But most of all she would be very sorry the flash bomb had exploded in her face, blinding her completely and instantly. Yes, she would be very sorry about that.

"Dear Oriannon." Now Sola shook her head. "You simply have no way of understanding. Neither does your common friend, Margus. And besides, who's left of the Assembly, aside from your father?"

"Because you killed them all!" Margus yelled at her again. "You had no right!"

"But that's just it. I do indeed. That's exactly why we've been pursued all the way from Corista, and that's why this little game is going to end in my favor. Because it's my right to decide what happens next for Corista, and it always was."

By this time, Wist stepped forward to face their unwelcome passenger, and the short-statured girl tried to push Sola away. "You be leaving her alone!"

"How noble of you to defend your friend." Sola finally released her grip on Oriannon but didn't move away. "And you know, I should thank you for saving my life back there on the planet. Quite unexpected. I did get a good look at your lovely Owling face, by the way, before the explosion. I've always admired your people's distinct eyes and that wonderful olive tan of yours. But then, you're probably already regretting what you did for me, aren't you?"

"Are you being okay, Oriannon?" asked Wist. Oriannon didn't know what to say as Sola went on with her tirade.

"In fact, by this time you're probably thinking, *I should have just let that red-haired monster drop off the side of the shuttle back when we had a chance*. Isn't that what you're thinking, sweetheart? Well, it's a little late for that. Even if you dumped me now, you still can't get away, and I imagine that must be a lovely, sinking feeling."

Her laugh cut short just as a bright flood of light suddenly illuminated them from outside, and a tremendous shockwave knocked them sideways. At first Oriannon thought the light came from one of the Coristan vessels.

A moment later, she knew this was no searchlight and not from any other vessel. This light shone bright as any sun in the Trion system, and Oriannon had to turn away as it poured in through the observation window.

"What in the world?" Wist cried as she shielded her eyes. Margus ducked his head to the side. Even Sola would most certainly feel the overpowering force that had gripped them.

Now their ship trembled as if caught in an awful, confused tide, much stronger than before. One of the Coristan ships scraped past them in front of the observation ports before tumbling away like a stray toy. That couldn't be right.

Neither were the powerful explosions that rocked them. Oriannon wondered how they had not yet been shredded or destroyed. Then something else exploded inside their own ship. The ship yanked and spun as if someone was pulling all the grappling hooks into a tangled ball, while shockwaves from a firestorm of explosions rocked their world, pummeling them from outside.

This would certainly finish them off, Oriannon knew, and she whispered a last word to the Maker as she gripped the back of Margus's chair to keep her balance.

"If this is what you will," she whispered, falling to her knees and bracing herself, "then I'm your servant."

She squeezed her eyes shut, fully expecting to open them up and see her Maker, or perhaps even the Maker's Song, Jesmet, standing before her. She wondered if it would hurt to die. She hoped not.

Only her ears hurt. Every warning buzzer on the ship sounded at the same time, screeching an unholy symphony to rattle her eardrums.

"Please, no!" She held her ears and peeked through tears to see her first view of heaven, which looked surprisingly the same as the control room of the interlunar shuttle in which they had been riding. She gagged on a toxic blend of smoke and sickly sweet argonite gas.

I'm still alive? she wondered, unsure whether she should be relieved or terrified, or if she could be both at the same time. A quick glance confirmed that if she was *not* alive, then Sola Minnik had come with her. That was not a good development. She ducked her head, searching for air to breathe closer to the floor.

"Ori!" Margus shouted through the confusion. Beads of sweat lined his bruised forehead as he struggled with his controls. He must have been doing everything he could to control their craft, pushing buttons and pulling up star charts on his viewers. "I need help with this!"

Though Oriannon had no idea what to do, she swallowed her terror and worked her way around the chair. The shuttle writhed and turned, buffeted about like an insect swatted by an unseen hand. Artificial grav came and went, pulling them in all directions.

Together they managed to silence the alarms, though that should have had no direct effect on their survival. But as the alarms quieted, so did the rough ride and the explosions.

"Is everybody okay?" asked Oriannon, after several long moments. By "everybody," she mainly meant Wist, who nodded slightly. Sola had slithered off to her spot in the corner, while Margus kept himself glued to the shuttle controls.

"Look at this," he told them. "Asylum Way Station 1 was there on the screen just a minute ago — before all this — and now it's not there. No station, no Coristan ships ... nothing!"

"You sure your sensors are working?" Oriannon shaded her eyes as she gazed out the viewport. For a moment longer they could see nothing but that brilliant white light. Then solar filters finally kicked in and shaded the window. "There has to be something. The Securities?"

"Just debris," he answered, looking for himself, "and that crazy bright light. It doesn't show up on the scans. But the ships are gone for sure, and so is the asylum station. Very weird."

Oriannon wasn't sure what he was saying. Gone? Where would they have gone all of a sudden? But as quickly as the bright light appeared, it faded, flickering one last time in the distance like a sideways bolt of lightning, leaving them alone and drifting in the cold expanse of space—as if nothing had happened.

"It can't be *gone.*" Wist pressed her nose against the viewport as the grav field kicked in again, only several degrees crooked this time. "Like I said," Margus replied. "That was weird. Very weird."

Weird, yes. But that didn't explain what had just happened to them, or why.

"Maybe it was some kind of black hole," suggested Wist.

"Only it wasn't dark," added Oriannon. "It was light."

None of this made any sense.

With the shaking seemingly over, Oriannon hurried back to check on her father, finding him still unconscious and tied into his bunk. He'd missed all the excitement, which was a good thing. She returned to the control room.

Meanwhile, Margus rested his cheek in his hand as if trying to figure it all out. "The thing is," he said, "if that ... that light—whatever it was—did something to the asylum station, it took five big Coristan Security ships with it."

"Only not us," added Wist.

"That's what I don't get." Margus scratched his head, and green light from the primary nav screen made his face glow as he leaned closer. "They had ten or fifteen grappling hooks in us, and we're the ones who got left behind. We should have been dragged away with everything else."

Maybe so. But when Oriannon looked at the Pilot Stone, still glowing in its place near the main control panel, she thought she had a clue.

"We're moving again," she said. "Aren't we?"

Margus raised his eyebrows when he noticed a new set of numbers changing by the second on velocity gauges.

"After all that." He whistled in disbelief. "I'm amazed we're moving at all."

"And let me guess." Oriannon didn't even need to look at the nav screens — just the Pilot Stone. "We're headed to the next asylum station instead?"

It took Margus a moment to confirm his numbers, and he checked several screens to be sure, but finally he squinted at Oriannon.

"Asylum 2. Looks like it. I'd ask how you knew, but I have a feeling it has to do with that Stone of yours."

He didn't really need an answer.

"Anyway," Margus continued, "we're pretty beat up. So if we want to go anywhere else, it's going to take awhile, and we'll need to do some patching. Looks like point two five is as fast as we're going to go — quarter-speed."

Wist pointed to a monitor, cocking her head to the side.

"What's that?" she asked.

A view cam trained on the outer tail section revealed shredded chunks of titanium outer skin, gaping holes, and miscellaneous pieces of hardware peeling away.

"Oh no." Margus groaned, bringing the focus up a little and panning the cam around to show ten sharp grappling hooks still partly embedded in the outer skin. Several hooks still trailed hundreds of meters of braided cable, strangely frayed at the ends. If wind existed in space, the cables would have been flapping like flags.

"Just be telling us what to do," said Wist.

For the next several hours the three of them shut off systems and made repairs as best they could. While Margus rerouted power and electronics from dead systems to backups, Oriannon checked for hull breaches with a handheld meter and Wist fetched tools and equipment from storage cabinets. Through all this, Sola seemed to have fallen asleep in the corner.

Margus inchwormed out from under a control cabinet with a grunt. "Duct tape." He held up a roll. "Don't leave home without it."

Oriannon couldn't help smiling, despite the danger that clung to them. No, the situation did not look promising, and she knew very well they might not make it to Asylum 2 in one piece. Margus couldn't duct tape all the gaping holes in the skin of their craft, and what systems remained online couldn't be trusted. He tapped at the deep amber warning light of an atmosphere monitor and frowned.

"Not good?" asked Oriannon.

He shook his head. "Looks like we're leaking life support air faster than onboard generators can produce it."

"It's still going to be okay, though," Wist said hopefully. "Right? We'll be fixing it somehow."

"You go right on believing that, dear." Sola called over to them, her eyes still closed. "I can hear every word you're saying, by the way."

"Then you can hear this." Oriannon lowered her voice to a near-whisper. "Jesmet cares about what happens to you, no matter what you do. Even if I don't. Even if you never see the gardens of Seramine again or the way the Rift Valley sparkles in the sunlight or the orange flowers of a flamboyan tree. Even if you never look up into the sky again and see the Trion with your own eyes. Even then, Sola, he cares."

Oriannon felt a twinge of guilt for reminding Sola of her blindness in a way she would never have done to a friend. But if it did some good, maybe it was okay to rub that kind of salt in this pitiful woman's wounds.

Sola just grunted and brushed the sleeve of her dirty green tunic to her cheek as she stepped out of the room and felt her way aft to the second of the two small sleeping rooms. She kept her face pointed away from them, perhaps to shield the tears ... or not.

"I think she's had enough of our company for now," said Margus.

"Or maybe she doesn't like where we're going." Oriannon checked the nav screen to make sure they were still headed for Asylum 2 and glanced at the Pilot Stone as it glowed. She wondered if it would really guide them all the way.

Margus tapped the atmosphere monitor again and frowned, but said nothing.

Wist straightened up with a hopeful smile. "Maybe when we be making it to Asylum 2," she told them, "they'll be explaining to us what just happened."

When, not *if.*

She is the optimist, thought Oriannon, ripping off a piece of duct tape to patch a run of wiring back into place. She tried not to keep staring at the rapidly declining numbers on the atmosphere monitor, even as she tried not to wonder what would happen if more Coristan ships took up the chase.

When, not *if.*

2

Oriannon didn't sleep well at all—not with the thought of duct tape holding their ship together. Twice she got up to investigate strange grinding noises. Both times, she woke Margus, who slept wrapped in a foil blanket on the floor next to the controls in the forward compartment.

"Would you please stop worrying?" he told her for the second time as he pointed the beam of a little flashlight at her face. "We did everything we could, and we'll keep working on the life support. I promise."

"I just wanted to see if—"

"I told you the long-range com still isn't working. I don't know if it's interference from that thing we hit or if the circuits got fried—along with everything else."

"But you'll keep trying?"

"Sure I will." He sighed and snapped off the light. "But you know, Ori, I need to sleep for a couple of hours. You should too."

"I know, I know."

"And even if we could call ahead to Asylum 2, we still can only do so much for your father. We're not healers."

"Still, I would feel better if we could get through."

"So would I. I promise you, I'll let you know if anything changes. Now go back to sleep."

Easy for him to say. She nodded her head weakly and padded back down the dark aisle, past the tiny galley and several rows of comfortable seats. The shuttle had been designed for passengers and short VIP trips between Corista and its nearest lunar outposts — not for extended space voyages like this ... and not with half the systems down. Well, at least they had plenty of room to stretch out. In addition to the main cabin and a downstairs cargo area, two private (but tiny) cabins opened into the short amidships corridor from either side.

One cabin — occupied by Sola Minnik — she had no intention of looking into. But she paused a moment in front of the other, bringing a hand to her forehead. "Jesmet," she whispered, holding back helpless tears, "please help my father."

She should check on him one more time, just to see if he'd regained consciousness. So she straightened up and took a deep breath before tapping a green button on the side to open the sliding door. But like so many other systems on the shuttle, the door opener didn't work.

"Stupid ..." She jabbed viciously at the opener several more times and then wrestled it open manually.

Inside the closet-sized cabin, she could barely make out the shape of her father resting in a fold-out bunk. Still he slept, after all they'd been through! She crept a little closer just to be sure his chest moved up and down, and she hovered with her cheek above his face so she could feel his labored breathing.

It's all her fault! Oriannon felt anger rise up as she remembered the beating her father had endured when he'd come to the death camp looking for her. The securities had beat him with their stun batons over and over, while Sola presided over it all.

"How could they do this to you, Father?" she whispered. She clenched her fists so hard they trembled. But then he caught his breath for a moment, as if she had disturbed him, and she backed away quickly.

Okay, she thought. *Okay for now.*

She thought of staying with him, keeping watch, but it seemed better to give him quiet space for now. So she slipped out of the cabin and retreated to the mat she'd set up between two rows of cushy seats toward the back of the shuttle. Margus was right. She should get some rest. She snuggled into her little nest, pulled a foil blanket up around her shoulders, and listened to the creaking and moaning of the injured spacecraft as she drifted off into an uneasy sleep.

Suddenly Oriannon found herself sitting straight up, looking in vain for her blanket. Her head swam for the briefest of moments, and then the dizziness left her. Though she felt no fatigue, she couldn't decide how long she'd been sleeping, or even if she was quite awake. In the strangest way she felt neither asleep nor awake, but just more alert than ever. As if all her senses had been fine-tuned, and turned to high.

She blinked her eyes hard to clear her vision. When she opened her eyes, colors seemed far brighter, only not in a way that hurt. She hadn't noticed before how the royal blue patterns on the fabric illuminated the chairs around her. And though she'd turned off the circuit herself, the overhead lights shone bright and cheery, just as they should have. Maybe this was a dream after all. If it was, though, she'd never enjoyed a dream like this before ... complete with ... breakfast?

She breathed deeply the wonderful, heady fragrance of clemson-root tea — tangy and earthy. At the same time, the aroma of freshly baked cinnamon doan biscuits — her favorite — made her stomach growl as she looked around to see what was happening. This could not be real, though she had never before experienced anything so vividly.

And her hearing! The creaking and groaning of the wounded shuttle had stopped, and she could make out the slightest of sounds — the tinkling of a spoon in a glass, stirring. The shuffling of feet coming her way on the rich purple carpet. The unmistakable sound of a man singing!

Only, who? Surely her father wasn't well enough to be up and around, and Margus couldn't carry a tune if his life depended on it. That accounted for both males on this shuttle. She peeked over the tops of the surrounding high-backed passenger seats.

"I hope I'm not disturbing you." The familiar-looking man walked down the aisle with a breakfast tray in hand and set it down in front of her. The stainless steel teapot steamed deliciously, and the biscuits had been wrapped in a proper white linen napkin and set in a woven delfwood basket. "I thought you might like some breakfast. It's been a longer trip than you expected, hasn't it?"

Oriannon couldn't take her eyes off the man's piercing, deep blue eyes and dark, neatly trimmed beard. He wore the freshly pressed, forest green robe of a mentor. Actually, he looked a lot fresher than she felt at the moment.

The strangest thing was that she knew she should know this man—sort of like she should recognize a picture of her own father. Still no matter how hard she tried, she could not place him. Finally, she got up the courage to ask.

"I'm sorry." Her puzzled voice came out barely above a whisper. "But how do I know you?"

He smiled as he poured her tea into a fine cup. The horrible scars on his face and hands stirred her memories even more.

"Oriannon."

Hearing him speak her name turned the key, opening a floodgate of memories. How could she not have known Jesmet ben Saius, the one the elders of Corista had killed?

"Mentor!" She could hardly breathe the word, even as the questions swirled in her mind.

How did he get here? Was he on the shuttle this whole time? Did he come from another ship?

"No to all the above." He shook his head.

"Then ..." She looked around, and the unsettled *otherness* of the moment threatened to overwhelm her. Still, she had to ask.

"How real is this … are you? I'm pretty sure it's not a dream, but that still doesn't explain—"

"You're not dreaming, Oriannon," he assured her, and she tried to remember if any characters in her dreams had ever made such a claim. She hardly dared to look at him, afraid now that her panic and confusion would show.

"Then what? Mentor, I don't know what this is."

"Ori!" His eyes flashed, and he took her by the wrists. "Feel my scars!"

He pulled her trembling hands to the back of his hands, and she dared not disobey. The scars were real, though she pulled her hand back as soon as he released her hands. She lowered her head.

"I'm sorry, Mentor. It's just that …" She struggled for words that didn't sound utterly foolish. "Well, you being here on the shuttle and everything, I mean, what am I supposed to think? You have to admit …"

"I know what you're trying to say, Oriannon," he interrupted in a commanding voice, "but please just hear me now. The Pilot Stone is taking you to Asylum 2, and there's a reason why you're going there."

"I know." She nodded, waiting for the rest of the story. "I mean, I know where we're going. I just don't know why. I thought we were escaping from Corista to save my dad's life."

"That's just the beginning. Now listen."

She nodded as he went on.

"You saw what happened to Asylum 1. The Troikans will do the same thing to all the way stations—from Asylum 2 to Asylum 12. They'll do anything to expand their territory, even steal the way stations and deport the people who live on them. I want you to warn the scribes who live on each one, before it's too late."

Oriannon tried not to let her jaw drop as she nodded her head. Now her tongue would hardly move to force out the words.

"Do I tell them what to do? Or what a Troikan is? I mean, *who* a Troikan is? I've never heard of a Troikan before."

Finally he lightened up with a small smile. "Ah yes, details. You'll be finding that out soon enough. For now, just warn the scribes. Some may listen. And when they ask how you know what's to be, tell them about me. You'll know what to say."

Oriannon nodded slowly, trying her best to understand.

Tell them they're being invaded by someone I've never heard about, she thought, *and the news comes from a man who was dead and now isn't. I can't do this.*

"Not on your own," he said, pouring himself a cup of tea. She'd forgotten that Mentor Jesmet seemed to not care if she spoke or thought—he could understand her either way.

"Then how?" she asked. "How can I do this? I don't know where we're going or what's going to happen tomorrow."

"By design, Ori, by design. If you knew exactly what was going to happen tomorrow and the next day, you'd think you controlled your own destiny, and you'd spend all your todays worrying about tomorrows."

"I guess I would," she whispered, almost wishing for the opportunity.

"So please don't worry. I'm going to be there for you, one step ahead of you, at all the remaining way stations. You just have to go."

"Wait. Did you just say to *all* of them?"

"One day at a time. Just go, warn them, tell them what you know. That's all you can do."

She sighed and looked away, not saying anything for a moment.

"I know you do." He answered her unspoken thought. "I'd be worried if you *didn't* miss them."

Of course he knew she was thinking about Brinnin and Carrick, the friends she left behind on Corista.

"I ..." Now she stumbled over the words. "I still don't think I can do this."

"Not by yourself. But you can and you will. You know much more than the scribes on these stations. Believe me."

More than scribes? She didn't see how, but Jesmet's words eased her worries … for now.

"And one other thing." He took a bite of a biscuit, held it up, and looked at it. "Actually, this is quite good, you know. It'll remind you of home. You should have some."

He smiled at her and swallowed before continuing.

"I meant to say, Oriannon, that you need to keep Sola Minnik with you during this entire journey. That's very important. No matter what happens, she must go where you go. I need you to keep her with you every step. Do you understand?"

She chewed on that idea for a moment, but didn't like the taste of it at all.

"I understand what you're saying," she finally answered. "But I don't understand why."

"In time you will. For now, just know that you need her, and she needs you."

Perhaps he saw the shocked expression she tried not to show.

"Trust me for now," he told her. "Please. You saw what happened to Asylum 1. Now there isn't much time for you to get to the next way station."

"Okay, but can I ask what *did* happen to Asylum 1?"

He sighed and nodded.

"It's a long story, and you'll find out when the time is right. Just remember, keep moving, and I'll be there. Don't stop. Warn them of the danger; tell them what you know. People always listen to an eidich."

That was the first time he'd mentioned the word, and Oriannon wasn't sure what her photographic memory had to do with anything.

"I know, Mentor, but … that's the problem. Just because everything sticks in my brain doesn't mean I understand it. Couldn't you explain—"

"Soon enough, Oriannon. You don't need to understand everything right away. Oh, and one other thing."

"Mentor?"

"Tend to your father, would you, please? He's just waking up, and I believe he'd appreciate some tea."

Oriannon looked at the tray Mentor Jesmet had brought her, and once again her head swam momentarily in that peculiar way. When she looked back, Mentor Jesmet had disappeared, and in an instant everything returned to the way it was—dull and all too real.

Most of the overhead lights had dimmed out once again, and the ship's engines once again labored beneath her feet. But, the tray of clemsonroot tea and cinnamon doan biscuits remained where Mentor Jesmet had left it, now barely visible in the flickering lights from the control room.

I believe he'd appreciate some tea.

She remembered her mentor's words, picked up the tray, and made her way into her father's cabin to stand before his bunk. Though she didn't make a sound, her father blinked his eyes, grimaced in pain, then looked up at her and managed a smile.

"There you are." He closed his eyes while the weak smile remained. His breathing sounded ragged, and he seemed to fight for each breath. "How did you know I was just dreaming about tea?"

She lowered her tray and sat on the edge of his bunk by his feet, nibbling on a biscuit. Jesmet was right; somehow the taste reminded her of home, of sunny courtyards where she and her friends spent hours after school, laughing and eating. Or the terrace behind her house, where she and her father sometimes ate their meals, and where she could look out over the emerald-green valley toward the distant Plains of Izula. She wondered if she would ever see Corista—or the people she knew—again.

"And doan biscuits!" His face lit up as he interrupted her thoughts. "I dreamed about them too. Something about your … your mentor."

Pain crossed his face as he recalled the dream.

"Jesmet?" she asked, afraid of how her father would react when she mentioned the name.

"Yes. It was very ... strange. Very real." He finally nodded, but didn't add anything else, so she poured a cup of cooled tea for her father and held the cup for him as he took tiny sips in between bites of biscuit. He nodded his thanks.

"I have to say, Ori, that was one of the most vivid dreams I have ever experienced."

Her mind raced as she helped him, trying to sort out what had just happened to her, and how her father's dream fit in.

"Father," she asked, pouring him another sip of tea, "have you ever heard of a Troikan before?"

Either he didn't hear her question, or it startled him so much that he began coughing over and again.

"Father?" She pulled the tray away and gently tried to turn him on his side, but he only heaved and coughed worse than ever.

"Wist!" she called over her shoulder through the open door. "Wist, could you help me please? My father needs help!"

Oriannon wished she knew what to do — anything! But instead of Wist coming to the rescue, Sola Minnik filled the open doorway. Before Oriannon could object, the woman made her way to the side of the bed as Oriannon's father continued to gasp and cough.

"Move aside," said Sola.

Oriannon paused for a moment, unsure whether she should trust the one who had brought so much evil to Corista.

"I said, move aside!" This time Sola shoved Oriannon out of the way and grasped Tavlin Hightower by the shoulders. Oriannon watched, torn between wanting to protect her father from someone who had already badly hurt him and wanting someone — anyone — to help him.

Unfortunately, Sola Minnik was both of those persons.

Oriannon obeyed and watched as Sola first felt her father's pulse on either side of his neck, then massaged a spot behind the small of his neck, and finally turned him on his side and slapped him—hard—right between the shoulder blades.

He gasped several times as if they might be his final breaths, then sighed and nodded before Sola allowed him to slump back on his bunk. Whatever had caused him to choke was gone now, but so was his strength.

"Thank you, Oriannon," he whispered without opening his eyes, and no one corrected him.

Sola stepped back without a word and made her way out of the room, but Oriannon followed her out into the hallway.

"Why did you just do that?" Oriannon wanted to know, holding the woman back by the shoulder. "My father doesn't need your help. He—"

"He needs more help than you can give him." Sola turned and pinned Oriannon to the wall, her face only centimeters away and her breath hot on Oriannon's cheek.

"Let me go!" Oriannon cried out in surprise as she struggled against the woman's fiendish strength. "I was just asking you a question."

"All right, so you want to know why I just did what I did? Honestly I have no idea. We're just prolonging the agony. Do you hear what I'm saying? Your father is going to die very soon."

Oriannon struggled, but Sola would not back away.

"You don't know anything," Oriannon finally whispered.

"I know a lot more than you think, girl, even with these blind eyes. But there's one thing you're going to help me with, or I'll strangle you right where you stand. You're going to tell me where you heard about the Troikans!"

3

You be letting her go!" Without warning, Wist rammed into Sola and Oriannon, sending all three of them tumbling to the floor. Oriannon rolled away from Sola's grip, not quite knowing what to do next.

Wist apparently knew exactly what to do, and with arms flailing she screamed and pulled at the surprised Sola's hair. Who would have thought?

"Taking advantage of a blind woman?" Sola grunted as Wist kept up her pummeling.

"Wist!" yelled Oriannon. "No!"

Wist just kept screaming and pounding, and she didn't seem to care that she was only half the other woman's size.

"Stop it!" yelled Oriannon. "Wist, that's enough! Please stop!"

By that time Margus had arrived to pull the two apart, placing himself between them, arms extended. Still they both crouched like a couple of fighting yagwars, gasping for breath and facing each other with equally savage looks.

"What is *wrong* with you?" he asked Wist.

Oriannon wasn't sure whether Sola's swollen, puffy eyes were caused by Wist or by her earlier injuries.

Sola had inflicted several angry red scratches across Wist's face. Wist put a hand to her cheek and backed away from the fight, as if realizing for the first time what had happened.

"Wist?" asked Oriannon. "What got into you?"

Finally Wist paused, as if gathering her senses.

"I—I'm sorry, Oriannon," she gasped, her chest still heaving. She didn't look up. "I saw her threatening you, and something inside me just kind of snapped."

By this time Sola had regained her composure and was standing upright, hands on her hips in a renewed challenge. A smile spread slowly across her puffy, disfigured face.

"Well, it doesn't surprise me. I told them the Owlings weren't as meek and mild as everyone thought."

"She was just trying to help me," explained Oriannon.

"Oh, I doubt it. When it comes down to it, in fact, the Owlings operate only on base instinct, not higher reasoning. I told them the Owlings would be more than suitable for their purposes."

"Them?" Oriannon wondered who the woman was talking about, but Sola seemed far off as she continued.

"In fact, I told them ... I said, 'Just give these Owlings something to get worked up about, and they're little animals.' Which is what we just saw here."

"You can't call our friend an animal," said Margus.

"No? You saw how they acted when I kept them afraid, before we had a chance to deliver them." She rubbed the back of her neck, apparently where Wist had given her a good knock. "Animals."

"You're just evil," replied Margus.

"Evil! Now there's a good one. And what do you know of evil, boy? I'm afraid that betrays your lack of sense. Either way, I knew they would be good workers, despite the fact that they're such tiny things."

"Is that why you had them all put in your prison camp?" asked Margus, his arms folded in position as a referee between the two.

"*My* prison camp?" Sola laughed again, and it made Oriannon shiver at how close to insane the woman sounded, closer and closer to the edge. "You don't understand the importance of what I almost accomplished back on Corista. Don't you realize I was saving the planet? No, of course you don't. Even now, you still don't."

"You saved nothing," said Wist, and the anger flashed in her eyes once again. Though she couldn't seem to catch her breath, she very much looked as if she could launch into Sola at any moment. "I had friends who died there."

"My heart is bleeding." Sola pressed her lips together and shook her head, as if they were little kids who couldn't recognize a twisted mind when they saw one. "You still think you've made things better by destroying the camp I worked so hard to establish. You think you've done such a noble thing by letting those misguided Owlings loose and then stealing this shuttle. But you know what? You've accomplished just the opposite."

"You don't know what you're talking about," Margus challenged her. "I think you're crazy."

"Am I? What happened to the asylum station you'd hoped to find? Where did it go?"

"We're not sure," Margus said. "But we'll be at the next station in a few hours."

"Maybe and maybe not. The same thing will happen to the rest of the stations, if it hasn't already."

"You don't know that," said Margus. He turned aside to cough, and it sounded so painful Oriannon had to wince.

"You believe whatever fantasy makes you feel good," Sola went on, "but we'll find out soon enough. And then where will that leave you? Wishing you'd stayed home and out of my business, I suspect."

"Out of your business? Oriannon and Wist saved your life."

"They're probably wondering right now if that was such a good idea."

"So am I. But we still did the right thing back in the camp, no matter what you say."

But what if Sola's prediction about the way stations was right? Oriannon couldn't imagine the power it would take to destroy so many way stations — some of them not much bigger than her school, Jib Ossek Academy, and others the size of a large city like Seramine, the capital city of Corista. Oriannon shivered at the thought of them disappearing the same way as Asylum 1. But Sola wasn't done with her lesson, and she wagged a finger at her unseen pupils as she continued.

"The right thing? Go ahead and deceive yourselves, but you don't have the faintest idea of what's right. Because, thanks to you, Corista will meet the same end as the way stations. By poking your little do-good noses where they didn't belong, you've condemned all of Corista. All of it! I'm talking both sides — not just Shadowside. Did you hear me? The entire planet."

"No, I don't hear you." Margus set his jaw. "I don't hear anything you're saying, because I think you're making it all up."

"You're so naïve it's painful, young man." She sighed loudly, turned from side to side, and ran her fingers through wild, tangled hair. "So you want me to spell it out for you? You want specifics? All right then. Listen carefully. They needed workers who could handle extremely cold conditions. Think. How well do you do in the cold?"

Margus didn't answer, and she didn't expect a response. Coristans experienced constant blazing heat from their three suns, the Trion. They weren't used to the bone-chilling cold and twilight of Shadowside. The answer was obvious as she went on.

"I assumed that in the world they're building, minus zero conditions would be an issue. Well, once I learned of it, I took advantage of their needs. I made them a deal, which is something nobody else was willing — or able — to do."

"Wait a minute." Oriannon began to object, but Sola held up her hand and raised her voice.

"You want an explanation? I'll give you the explanation. While the Elders were posturing and pontificating, I was the only one who knew what to do. I made a deal with the Troikans. I promised to deliver at least fifty thousand Owling workers, Owlings who were used to living and working in an environment without sun and heat, and they agreed to leave the rest of the planet alone. Do you know what they would have done to Corista without my intervention? Well, you saw what happened to Asylum 1."

"The one that disappeared?" asked Margus. He unfolded his arms and his jaw dropped as the full weight of Sola's words hit him.

"Exactly!" She smiled, but in a soulless sort of way that made Oriannon shiver. "They would have done the exact same thing to our planet if I hadn't stepped in and saved us all."

"You were willing to sacrifice every Owling on the planet," objected Oriannon. Now Sola's evil was clear, and it made her stomach turn. Wist stood silently, fists clenched at her sides, as Sola proudly went on.

"Yes, and if it weren't for you three, people would be building monuments to Sola Minnik right now, naming parks and streets after me — cities even!"

Oriannon did all she could to guard her mind from the pollution of Sola's lies. She didn't believe a word of it. Still, she had to know …

"But if you really believed you were saving the planet," she said, "why didn't you tell anybody? My father never said anything to me about it. If this was all true, why didn't the Assembly know?"

"They didn't know because they didn't want to know," Sola snapped back, her eyes flashing. "They didn't know because they were stupid fools whose greatest achievement was changing the color of their robes for ceremonial occasions. The entire Coristan Assembly of Elders, including your dear father, was incompetent, timid, and indecisive. If Corista was going to survive, I knew that I had to remove them. I had no choice."

"No choice ..." Now Oriannon could hardly stand to listen; she thought she might be sick. "You're twisted if you really believe that."

"My dear Oriannon." Sola shook her head. "You're so much like your father, I'm sad to say. Everything for you is always black and white. You don't recognize shades of gray."

"I recognize them," countered Oriannon. "But they don't fool me, the way they fooled you. Your problem is that you really believed the Troikans would live up to their end of this ... this deal. But people like that never would and never will, even if you had succeeded."

"Hold on," said Margus, regaining some of composure. He held his hands up again like a referee although Sola could not see him. "You two keep talking about these ... these Troikans, like you actually know who you're talking about. But who are *they*?"

By this time Oriannon already knew the answer to his question, and felt the full weight of what she knew. But as she'd told Jesmet, knowing and understanding were two very different things.

"The Troikans?" Sola paused for effect, knowing that she was still the lead storyteller. "Oh, yes. I keep forgetting your level of comprehension is disgustingly low. But Oriannon Hightower here, that's another story. Here's an eidich, who remembers all she sees, hears, or reads. What a wonderful gift that would be, and to live as the privileged daughter of a former Coristan elder besides. So why don't you explain to us, Oriannon, about the Troikans? It seems you already know something of them."

The fact that Sola mentioned the name again confirmed everything. The vision of Jesmet, the talk of Troikans ... it had been real after all. Everyone turned to Oriannon.

"The Troikans," began Oriannon, wondering what to say. "All I know is what Jesmet told me."

"Jesmet!" screeched Sola, and her cheeks turned bright, raging red. "Don't you dare mention that dead man's name in my presence! It makes me ill!"

"You asked." Oriannon backed off to a safer distance. She still had no idea what Sola would do. She might very well attack again, like someone possessed. How could a person look so evil, and not be controlled by the Evil One? For now Sola's sightless eyes seemed to search the room, her puffy crimson face twitched in unspeakable anger, her hands balled into fists.

"I did not ask you to bring up that dreadful man's name again." This time she spat her words like darts, and Oriannon could see Wist and Margus back up in fright from the spray and the barbs as well. "He's dead, I tell you, and he's not coming back. It's only feeble minds and fools like you who continue to dredge up his memory! It won't do you any good."

"You know better than that." This time Oriannon kept her voice soft and low, watching carefully to see what Sola would do next, the way she would watch a yagwar from the opposite side of a fence, unsure whether the wild animal would jump over it. "You saw him yourself back on Corista. Or did you forget already?"

"No!" Sola rocked from side to side, gripping her face in terror. "No! I most certainly did *not* see him, because he's dead! Do you hear me? Do you think I talk to ghosts? He can't bother us again. *We killed him!*"

Even Sola seemed to recoil at the ugliness of her own stark admission. Blood trickled from the lower lip she had bitten, and she looked from face to face as if she actually saw them, desperately seeking help. But no one answered for a long, tense moment as Sola regained a small measure of composure.

"I've had enough of this," she mumbled, drawing the back of her hand across her mouth. "You kids have no idea who you're dealing with."

And without another word she stumbled across the hallway to her cabin, pulling the door shut behind her. Oriannon stared at the closed door, trying to understand the depth of evil they had just seen. Maybe she didn't understand. She slipped an arm around Wist's shoulders.

"Does that mean we're not going to hear about the Troikans?" asked Margus in a low voice.

Oriannon didn't answer; she and Wist took another step backward, as if Sola had a deadly disease they did not want to catch. At the same time, Oriannon was the first to see her father's hand wrapped around the edge of his cabin doorway.

"Father!" She came to his aid, catching him before he fell into her arms. "You shouldn't be up!"

"A fellow can't sleep with all this noise," he answered with a throaty whisper.

Oriannon wasn't sure what he had heard or if he knew what he was doing, but with an arm around his waist she guided him gently back to his bunk. Margus helped swing his legs onto the bed while she helped with the pillow.

"I'm sorry, Father." Oriannon adjusted his pillow a bit more. "We shouldn't have been so noisy."

"Yeah," added Margus. "Sola is insane."

With a shake of her head Oriannon tried to signal Margus not to go there, and she wished he hadn't mentioned Sola's name. Still her father had something to say.

"She might be insane," he agreed, "but she's right about one thing, you know."

"Shh." Oriannon tucked a blanket under her father's chin. "We can talk later. Just rest."

"What was she right about?" Margus wanted to know. The exasperated look Ori sent him had no effect, as Oriannon's father cleared his throat and straightened up. His grip on Oriannon's arm felt weak and clammy.

"Please, Father," she begged him. "You really don't need to talk. Especially not now."

"You heard her." Her father looked Oriannon in the eye when he spoke, and she knew he would not settle down until he'd said what he wanted to say. "She said I'm going to die soon."

"Daddy." Sudden tears blurred Oriannon's vision, though she tried to hold them back.

"I'm sorry, Ori, but she's right about that. So listen to what I tell you."

"Please don't talk like that." She forced out the words. "You're going to be all right. You're— "

"I told you." He interrupted her with a shake of his head. "Now listen to me, because I don't know if I'll have a chance to say this again."

She looked to Margus and Wist for help, but they had already retreated to a respectful distance out into the hallway. She would have preferred they stay close.

"You are the last survivor," he whispered. "The last surviving son or daughter of a Coristan elder. Sola killed all the rest. There are no more. Do you understand? You know what the Codex says about that?"

Yes, of course she knew, but she had never dwelled on it, and shook her head. He tried to squeeze her hand, but she could barely feel it.

"You must return to Corista," he whispered. She had to lean even closer to hear the words that cut her soul. "After all that's happened, you're the only one who can lead Corista back to ... back to the old ways. Promise me you'll do this ... what Codex requires."

She swallowed hard, trying to keep her head from swirling. Honestly, he could not be saying this! Finally she whispered her answer.

"Even if I wanted to go, there's no way."

"You can and you will." He closed his eyes again and smiled faintly at her. "You're an elder's daughter. The last one. It's what you were born for."

But how? Her mind screamed a silent protest as panic clawed at her. There had to be a way to back away from this, to pretend she'd never heard. She watched him for a few minutes as he lay his head back down and closed his eyes. She prayed that he would keep breathing, that these would not be his last words to her. Just in case, she brought an oxygen mask to help him breathe more easily. Perhaps it would help.

"Promise me," he told her through his mask, but she could not. Instead she leaned down and kissed his forehead, listening to his ragged breathing mix with the soft hiss of his mask.

Please, she prayed again, her head spinning. *Not yet.*

4

"Are we there yet?" Wist walked around the tiny forward control center, back and forth, like the tiny clipped moordove Oriannon had kept in a cage when she was little.

"You're driving me crazy, Wist." Oriannon tried not to let irritation creep into her voice, but after three days cooped up with each other and a crazy lady, that was getting harder and harder. "You think maybe you can sit down for a while?"

"Done that, done that." Maybe Wist was going a little crazy too. Not that Oriannon blamed her. At least Sola hadn't shown any interest in leaving her room for the past seventy two hours. "Want me to be checking on your father again?"

Oriannon shook her head.

"He was okay a few minutes ago. Thanks anyway."

So what else was there to do but watch the nav screen with its slowly circling view as they closed in on their objective?

"It's still being there, right?" Wist asked again. "We're going to be making it?"

Margus gave his standard answer—again. He pointed and nodded his head. "Getting closer." But he also coughed once more, and Oriannon wondered how much he knew that he wasn't telling them.

"Are you guys feeling lightheaded?" she asked the others, and tightness gripped her chest as she spoke. Wist finally sat down.

"I'll be admitting that I'm feeling a little woozy," she replied, folding her arms across her chest and looking pale in the dim overhead lights. "Like I can't be getting enough to breathe."

Oriannon knew exactly what she meant. Margus coughed again, and they both looked at him for the answer.

"I'll go check downstairs again," he finally responded. That didn't make Oriannon feel much better. Neither did the ominous groaning sounds coming from the cargo area below. While Margus went downstairs and Wist left to go lie down, Oriannon tried to doze. As soon as she felt herself nodding off, the tightness in her chest made her jerk awake, as if someone had clamped a hand over her face. She awoke each time in a panic, gasping for air as her heart beat wildly.

"Margus?" she called toward the back of the shuttle, hoping he would hear. No answer. The groaning sound below her feet grew louder and louder, as if the damaged parts of the ship were seriously close to coming completely apart.

Finally Margus hurried back to his seat, but the look on his face warned her not to ask too many questions, and a loud groan from below made her jump.

"That doesn't sound right," she told him.

He kept his eyes focused on a control screen but shrugged and shook his head.

"If I could fix it," he replied, "I would. It's a rebreathing filter of some kind, plus the O_2 generator, but I don't have any spare parts. Wish my dad were here."

She nodded and wished she could say something that would make him feel better, but knew that she could not. What words helped after losing someone you loved? Especially after he lost them both in Sola's brutal camps. She could hardly imagine, since she really didn't remember her mother much.

"I'm sorry, Margus," she finally whispered, not sure if he heard her over the noise from belowdecks. But he pressed his lips together and nodded.

"Thanks. But I guess right now the only thing we can do is keep going."

"How much longer?"

He checked the screen. "Ten hours and a few minutes."

Normally that would not have seemed too long, but the odd rumbling sound suddenly became completely quiet. Oriannon gulped, and they looked at each other.

"Is that good," she asked, "or what?"

At first Margus didn't look too sure as he checked several readouts.

"I can't tell, Ori. Half the controls don't have power, so I can't trust what I'm seeing. Maybe we'd better go down there ourselves and take a—"

His words were swallowed by a loud but muffled *thump* that nearly lifted them out of their seats, followed by a rush of air that whipped Oriannon's hair behind her like a banner.

"What's happened?" she gasped, grasping a handhold and shivering from the instant chill—as if someone had sucked all the air out of the ship and replaced it with cold, empty space.

"Downstairs!" cried Margus. "We've got to ..."

But his words fizzled as he grabbed Oriannon and they stumbled aft toward the spiral staircase that led down into the cargo hold. Air masks dropped by their umbilical cords, and bright red warning lights blinked on every bulkhead. Oriannon tried to yell at Margus to wait for her, but nothing came out of her lungs. All she could do was grab for a mask and gasp for air.

"Margus!" she yelled into her mask as Margus collapsed on the floor in front of her. Clearly he didn't hear her. She grabbed the nearest mask and pressed it to his face.

What was happening to her father and Wist?

When Margus came to a moment later, his mouth moved, but Oriannon could hear nothing. Before blacking out again, he pointed downstairs, and she thought she understood. Whatever had exploded down there had likely opened a major hole in their hull, sucking out most of their air and dropping cabin pressure to dangerously low levels. She nodded and took several more deep breaths inside her mask.

She had to seal it off—now—before they all died. Only how?

Margus tried to get to his feet but collapsed again. She held him down and signaled that she would try, though he shook his head.

Boys! With three more deep breaths she left her mask behind, shook off Margus, and headed for the stairway. If she closed the floor hatch, she might be able to seal off the lower level and save their oxygen supply. Only problem was, the floor hatch was stuck in the open position. She fell to her knees, tugging with all her strength, but the hatch only moved a few centimeters and no more.

She did not expect the power assist to work, but was it really this heavy? She would have to go back to where she could breathe better while she figured out what to do. Just then the hatch slipped back upon her, sending her sprawling with her legs caught underneath the hatch.

Now her lungs felt as if they were on fire. At the same time, she shivered at the sudden draft, feeling like she had just been thrown into a deep freeze.

Air! She gasped in what was left and felt as if she were standing on the top of Mount Seram, back home, gasping in the rare atmosphere. *I have to breathe!*

The nearest emergency air mask dangled from the ceiling three meters away. She had thought she could hold her breath a little longer than this. Now a flickering darkness pressed around the edges of her sight, and she couldn't stop shaking.

The last thing Oriannon remembered was the sight of Wist throwing her shoulder into the hatch. She thought she felt it finally give way, though she could not be sure. The floor spun beneath her feet and she felt nothing more.

●●●

"Oriannon?"

She heard the man's voice before seeing anything else, and right away she grabbed for a handhold. What had happened to Wist?

"Oriannon," came the voice once more.

She opened her eyes, and it was just like the vision before. Her hearing was sharper. Colors appeared achingly bright, from the royal blue shuttle seats to the gray non-skid floors and the sparkling yellow lights. She imagined she could smell cold and ice, and in a strange way it reminded her of the arid, open plains of Shadowside, where she first met Wist and where the Owlings had taken her in. It reminded her of space—if the airless expanse of space had a smell.

Visiting Shadowside seemed so long ago. Here and now, her mentor Jesmet ben Saius helped her to her feet.

"What ... what happened?" she asked, looking around at the now-empty spacecraft and the breathing masks, still dangling from the low ceiling. She breathed deeply, and realized that she didn't need a mask.

"You're almost to Asylum 2."

She wished he would tell her something she didn't already know. But if this vision was anything like the time before, she would have some explaining to do. Surely the others wouldn't believe that she had seen Mentor Jesmet. Or would they?

She looked around. On the floor a meter away, the hatch to the lower level was closed tightly.

"So we got the lower level sealed off?" she asked.

"We?" he asked with a comfortable little chuckle. He wore the same green flowing mentor's robe as he had the time before and the same amused look on his face. Sort of the same expression he had when Oriannon answered his music questions back at the academy.

"I couldn't get that hatch closed," she admitted. "Then Wist came, and ... hey, where are they anyway?"

"You remember correctly, and it's just like everything else, Oriannon. Just don't try to do it alone, and you'll end up fine. Look for help—and no matter what happens, don't turn back until you know you've done what you came to do."

She remembered his words clearly—as an eidich she remembered everything clearly, even the tiniest details. When she looked away to check the hatch once more, her head swam—but she didn't think it was from a lack of oxygen this time.

The puzzling part was how she suddenly went from speaking with Mentor Jesmet to lying across three passenger seats, the armrests folded back, the breathing mask on her face, and so many reflective silver blankets piled on top of her she could barely move. She tried not to yelp in alarm as she peered up at the two faces looking down at her, both wearing their oxygen masks and bundled up in blankets and parkas.

"It's okay," she told them, though it was hard speaking through her mask. "We don't need these any more."

Margus shook his head and mouthed some words that only sounded garbled and far away, while Wist produced an e-tablet and scribbled a few words for her to read.

"Keep ... your ... mask ... on," read Oriannon. She nodded and motioned for the tablet so she could answer.

"Have ... you ... seen ... Jesmet?" she wrote, hoping they would not think her crazy. But she had to know if she was the only one.

When Wist and Margus looked at each other, she knew she was. She grabbed the tablet back before they could answer.

"Never mind!" She erased her first question and replaced it with another: "What ... about ... my father?"

Margus gave her an okay sign and pointed to the front of the shuttle with a nod. Apparently her father—and probably Sola—were okay ... for now. The lower level had been sealed and some degree of cabin pressure restored, as Margus explained in a quick message. But their oxygen was limited to the masks, which they hoped would last until they made it to Asylum 2.

Oriannon was afraid to ask whether Margus knew how much longer that would be, or if he was certain they would have enough emergency oxygen. But she couldn't help asking about the way station itself.

"Is the way station still there?" she wrote. Margus thought for a minute before he answered.

"Instruments ... don't work, just ... Stone."

Oriannon shivered in the frosty chill as another bank of overhead lights flickered and blinked out. A dimmer emergency light came on instead, but it left them in cold shadows. She wondered about the new hole in the bottom of the ship that had just sucked out so much of their oxygen. Officially, they didn't know if they were moving in the right direction. Would their destination even exist by the time they arrived? *If* they arrived.

But the Stone still glowed with promise. For now, that would have to be enough.

5

Five hours later, Oriannon sat curled up in one of three swivel chairs in the control room, covered with blankets but unable to keep her teeth from chattering — her jaw was getting sore. Her eyes had adjusted to the pitch dark inside, punctuated only by the tiny, ice-blue nightlights of far-off stars. Which ones they were, she no longer had any idea. Nothing looked familiar; nothing looked like the star charts she had once memorized back home. But right now, all she could think of was getting a hot shower and a nice cup of steaming clemsonroot tea.

I wonder if they have clemsonroot tea on Asylum 2, she asked herself. *I wonder if Asylum 2 still exists.*

They would find out in a matter of minutes. In the meantime, ice had formed around the edge of her oxygen mask, chafing uncomfortably. It was all she could do not to yank it off with a scream.

Margus looked over at her as if he knew. He pointed out the forward observation port and gave her a "little bit" signal with two fingers, his way of saying, *we're almost there.*

She hoped he was right, though it could only be a guess on his part. Perhaps they were flying toward a station that was no longer there. Perhaps they would keep flying and flying until they all froze to death or the emergency oxygen ran out. Perhaps they were headed in the wrong direction. Out here, there were plenty of those.

Once in a while she dared to reach out a hand and rest it on the faintly glowing Pilot Stone, and that helped warm her just a bit. But the glow and the Song seemed more faint and far off than usual, so she pulled her hand back and did her best to keep it warm by tucking it under her arms. Still she shivered ... and even more when she crawled out of her cocoon to check on her father once again.

What else could she do? She remained at her father's side long enough to watch his chest rise and fall, rest a cold hand on his forehead to see if he was warm enough, and make sure his blankets covered his shoulders. He didn't even move at her touch. Across the hallway, Sola huddled in her own space. She had refused their offers of extra blankets and wrapped survival snacks of sweetened hezet nut bars.

Let her. Oriannon took one last look at her father before returning to the control room and crawling once more under her own pile of blankets. Margus kept an eye on her.

"Still ... ok?" He wrote on their pad. She adjusted the hose of her air mask, nodded, and scribbled back her own message.

"Sleeping," she wrote on the tablet. "Can't we ... try again ... call ahead ... about him?"

He shook his head no, and showed her that the com was still down by tapping a black screen several times, as if to say "see?"

Not that it really mattered, she knew. Even if they could get through to Asylum 2, there wasn't anything that could be done for her father over a com line. Despite the glowing Stone, they were now flying blind. They would come upon the way station blind, and they would have to dock at the station—blind.

Now I know how Sola feels, she thought, and a part of her didn't want to know—didn't even want to think of the woman who huddled in the cold, behind the aft bulkhead wall, just a few meters away. It would have been so much better, she imagined, if Jesmet had not allowed Sola to be here. So much simpler. But now Margus's wild gestures brought her back to the present.

What? She followed the direction he pointed out the viewport. A craggy, irregular small asteroid now filled their field of view, and its lights made Oriannon blink in surprise.

Asylum 2!

She recognized the remote outpost from photos she'd seen on databases back home. Even from this altitude she could make out four domed enclosures, each one dotted with dozens of skylights, and each one large enough for a small settlement. Each would be linked to the others through three airlock tunnels, one large enough to drive a shuttle through, and two of a smaller size. Most of the domes covered large craters on the surface of what was actually a large, dead, gray asteroid. Inside the domes, according to what she'd read, a learning community of scribes and their families numbered around 4,000—twice as many as Asylum 4, the only other asylum settlement she'd visited. Here they had apparently mastered the art of survival as they lived their monastic, separate lives of Codex study and prayer.

Margus signaled for her and Wist to sit down and hold on, since the grav-locks on each chair didn't seem to be working well enough to hold them in place during the docking procedure. As best he could—if any of the docking controls still worked—he would try to navigate them into one of the three large hangar bays at the end of the nearest dome.

He hit his fist against a bank of instruments on his right; they blinked for a moment but went dark. Good thing Oriannon couldn't hear what he was saying inside his air mask. But he kept trying, massaging the instruments until several finally seemed to come to life.

You can do it, Margus. She would have told him if she could.

She felt a mild jerk, perhaps a good sign that some of their maneuvering thrusters still worked, and she prayed. At the same time, Wist reached over to grip her hand. Oriannon wasn't sure whose hand was colder. She was afraid to look at the dome dead ahead, but even more afraid not to. Wist held onto her hand tightly.

"If we crash," she whispered, mopping nervous beads of sweat from her forehead, "we crash."

No one heard her, but Margus held up his hand again as if waving to get the attention of someone down on the surface. Oriannon assumed people in the way station were trying to contact the approaching shuttle on their com, and probably wondering why the shuttle didn't respond. Would they open their doors without knowing who they were? The shuttle jerked again as Margus fired thrusters to slow their progress. It wasn't enough. He slammed his open palm on the controls in front of him. If he was trying to bring their crippled ship to life, it wasn't working. Oriannon sat on her hands to keep them from shaking and felt every muscle in her body stiffen.

"Open up!" she called out to no one but herself. "Please open up!"

She wished she could shout across the empty expanse, and guessed Margus wished the same. Wist gripped the armrests of her chair, her eyes closed tightly as if bracing for impact. The dome grew closer and closer, filling their forward viewports.

Finally the nearest set of doors in the dome began to open—slowly at first, then wider and wider, like the pupil of an eye in a darkening room.

"Come on," shouted Oriannon. "Come on!"

Margus steered straight for the middle of the opening; maybe their craft could slip inside without tearing anything apart. And they nearly did. They heard a screech of metal on metal—probably their tail section. A jolt sent Sola sailing halfway across the room, sliding the rest of the way on her stomach. She ended up at their feet, still clutching her oxygen mask, though it had broken free of its tubing. She scrambled to her feet, a look of panic written on her face. Wist pointed to another working mask she could use.

Meanwhile, artificial light streamed in the windows, turning their skin blue. Oriannon felt the various bumps and thuds that told her they had landed safely inside the hangar. She closed her eyes and breathed out a sigh of thanks.

We made it!

Over in the pilot's chair, Margus slumped back in obvious relief, while Wist jumped up and slapped them both on the back in celebration. Oriannon could see the Owling girl's wide smile even behind her oxygen mask. They all jumped when the main cabin door wrenched open from the outside and a rush of wonderful, beautiful, incoming air hit them.

Air! The moment Oriannon felt it on her face, she pulled off her uncomfortable mask and gulped in the sweet luxury of atmosphere, laughing, despite herself. Never mind that it smelled a little dank and recycled with a tinge of phosphor. She could breathe again!

Just outside the door a welcoming committee of three long-faced scribes stepped up as a loading ramp brought them to the door. Oriannon quickly slipped the now-cold Pilot Stone into her pocket as they approached.

The first scribe, an older man with a paunchy chin, clean-shaven head, and a faded chocolate brown robe, planted himself in the doorway as if he was preventing their escape.

"You will kindly explain this unauthorized landing and your purpose for being here," he said, his voice tight and controlled.

He offered no "Welcome to Asylum 2" and certainly no smile. Oriannon caught her breath and looked to her two friends, wondering where they should start, when Sola stepped forward without warning.

"Don't you people know who I am?" This almost sounded like the old Sola speaking to a huge crowd back on Corista, only now a touch of desperation had crept into her voice. "I've been brought here against my will."

Oriannon realized they probably should have said something first, and right away, before Sola took control of the conversation. Perhaps they should have kept her locked in her room for a while—if they could have done that—until they could explain everything that had happened back on Corista. No doubt the reports these people had received over the past several months were biased or garbled at best. But the scribes startled her with their cold welcome, and the confusion that followed was completely unexpected.

"The woman is lying," came another weak voice. Oriannon turned to see her father ... on his feet! She brushed by Sola and rushed to her father's side in time to catch him before he crumpled. Even so, he held up a wavering hand.

"She sought to kill us all," he told them. "We escaped with our lives, saving hers in the process."

Now the scribe looked from Oriannon's father to Sola, squinting in confusion.

"And you are ...?"

"Tavlin Hightower of Nyssa, last surviving member of the Coristan Assembly of Elders. I need ... I need—"

"He needs medical attention right away," cried Oriannon, her arm around his waist. "Please! Do you have a healer here?"

"Don't listen to them," said Sola, stepping forward. "I've been blinded, and these people have stolen an official Coristan government shuttle. Check the manifest records. This was not an authorized trip."

"Authorized trip?" Now Margus stepped up. "What are you talking about? We barely get away alive, and—"

"And you had no right to kidnap me." Sola finished his sentence, her words heating up as Margus and Wist both tried to interject their arguments. By this time Oriannon couldn't blame the three scribes for looking confused. But she also knew that Sola Minnik wasn't going to talk her way out of this one.

"My father." She brought him forward with Wist's help. "You can check our stories and do what you think is best, but he needs your help immediately!"

"Our ship was damaged," explained Margus, "and our electronics ... our com was down. This was the only place we could land."

"Damaged because my securities had to take drastic steps!" Now Sola nearly screamed her protest. "Damaged because of your criminal actions!"

"I've heard enough." Finally the lead scribe held up his hand for silence. "I do not wish to become involved in your controversies. However, you will all remain in our custody until we can determine the truth."

"But my father— " began Oriannon.

"The truth is that I am Sola Minnik!" Sola's voice elevated to a painful whine. "And you people are under my authority!"

The scribe simply turned to go, while his two silent companions took up positions behind their haggard little group. Not one to be left behind, Sola had no choice but to hold onto the hem of Wist's tunic and stumble along, complaining the entire time. Oriannon, meanwhile, placed herself under one of her father's arms, while Margus took the other.

"This is outrageous!" complained Sola. "I must insist that you detain these people!"

But the scribes paid no attention as they crossed the polished stone floor of the landing hangar. A partially disassembled vessel of quite a different configuration was parked nearby, along with the bare hulks of two more, stripped to their carcasses of titanium bones. Margus looked over his shoulder at them and stumbled as they headed through a series of airlocks and narrow tunnels. Several steps ahead, their reluctant host paused for a moment.

"We'll be taking you to a temporary holding area, where you'll be processed and positively identified. As you'll soon learn, we are not accustomed to receiving this volume of refugees. In any case, stay close by me, don't speak to anyone, and you'll be all right."

Oriannon wasn't sure what he meant until he led them through a set of double-glass doors and out into the way station's huge open reception area, a sort of great hall resembling the lobby of the largest hotel, only much larger. She thought it rude that he did not introduce himself, but she quickly lost the thought as she craned her neck to take in the grand world into which they had just stepped.

Above their heads, the ceiling lofted perhaps thirty or more stories to the distant underside of the dome. It seemed far taller than she imagined from the outside. Continuous overhanging balconies, covered in climbing green vines, snaked around in graceful sculpted lines that reminded her of ever-expanding ripples in a pool of still water. Only in this case each ring of balconies grew progressively smaller as it reached toward the distant ceiling.

On the far side of the great hall a three-pointed bronze tower reached to an unlikely height more than halfway to the dome's ceiling. Its sheer height raised the obvious question: What kept such a tall spire from toppling over? It reminded her of the temple back home in Seramine.

She knew, however, that they were a very long way from home.

She stared at a wonderfully sculpted model of the three-star Trion that seemed to float high above their heads. Outside of Seramine's graceful architecture, Oriannon had never seen anything quite so pretty.

"I said to stay by me," the scribe warned them, and she soon understood why. An ocean of several hundred bedraggled travelers parted before them, very few of whom appeared to be scribes. Many looked Coristan, like herself, with a light olive complexion, dark hair, and small dark eyes that followed their every step. Oriannon tried not to stare back at their dirty-looking faces and disheveled clothes.

"They act like they've never seen strangers before," mumbled Margus. He stepped around a huddle of stooped little people with braided bluish hair who gestured and pushed at each other as they rattled off an incomprehensible string of sounds with klicks and interspersed whistles that must have been their language, but reminded Oriannon more of a chattering bird. Some seemed to be actively trading items — mainly slender jugs of amber liquid, but also brushed silver cylinders and bright red and green bundles. Others rested on small bedrolls with closed eyes and ignored the commotion.

If these are all refugees, wondered Oriannon, *what have they escaped from?*

She gazed around the great hall at people and races she had never before seen. Wist gasped and huddled a little closer to Oriannon as they stepped by a man — if he was a man — with icy, translucent skin. His dull red eyes looked them over, but he said nothing.

"Where are we going?" asked Sola. At least she couldn't miss hearing the chaos and noise of the crowds. "Where are they taking us?"

Sola must have been able to hear and smell the crush of people around them — the odd garlicky scents and the occasional unpleasant yelp or smell of small caged animals, mostly reptiles who were not at all content. One of the translucent women held a collection of four tiny wooden cages housing dozens of terramole lizards, each crawling over the backs of the others, many spitting and displaying their teeth. Sola pulled back.

A few steps later they nearly ran into a couple of small children with blotchy orange complexions, both clutching luggage under their arms and looking as if they wanted to find a way out too. The closest one looked up at Oriannon and blurted out a rush of words that sounded more like a waterfall than anything she could possibly understand. If she had heard it before, she would have known, but this language was not registered in a Coristan database.

"I'm sorry," replied Oriannon, shaking her head. "I have no idea what you just said."

Her father seemed not to notice his surroundings much. He winced as he took small, shuffling steps. Mostly he relied on Oriannon and Margus for balance, and it seemed a good thing that the scribes couldn't make much progress through the mass of people.

"You're doing fine," she told him. He would have done better, she knew, with some kind of stretcher. But the scribes offered none, so she hoped they could get him to a healer before he collapsed once again.

"Hang on," Margus told her. "We'll make it."

Oriannon wasn't quite so sure. But they continued through the crowd, through scores of odd languages and accents. She wondered what brought so many different refugees together. Some spoke a dialect of Old Coristan she had only read about, with odd trilling *r*'s and guttural klicks.

"Oriannon." Wist seemed the most overwhelmed by it all, and stayed close. "I'm thinking this was supposed to be an asylum way station?"

Oriannon knew what she was asking. As far as they knew, asylum way stations were run by peace-loving scribes whose only thought was to lead quiet, contemplative lives of Codex study and prayer. On occasion they welcomed the wandering pilgrim or refugee from outside worlds.

This time, however, the outside worlds seemed to have invaded, leaving little room for the quiet and peace of the scribes. Off to the side a tall translucent man stood on a box and entertained the crowd with a sort of acrobatic act, contorting himself by standing on his hands and then twisting his arms and legs together in a rather repulsive way. His companion taunted the crowd in different languages and urged them to come closer. Oriannon wrinkled her nose, but Margus slowed down to stare.

"Margus," she scolded him. "That's really gross."

"Yeah, I know," replied Margus, "but how does he do that?"

To Oriannon, it really didn't matter. She wondered how long it would take to get her father some help — if any existed here — as their scribe guide paused to argue with a couple of others. She couldn't fully make out what they were saying, but judging by the angry glares and impatient gestures, she thought it might have something to do with finding a place for them to stay.

"Why are we waiting here?" asked Sola, still clinging to Wist as if her life depended on it. "What's the holdup?"

"I'm thinking it won't be long," offered Wist. The blind woman frowned and batted away a small girl who offered to sell her a pair of moordoves in a tiny cage.

"Moordoves!" she sputtered, waving her hand. "What would I want with pests like that? Get away!"

"Young lady!" A voice called out to her from the crowd, and Oriannon instinctively turned to see who had called to her in her own language. A Coristan man with short-cropped golden hair and dirty black coveralls pushed through the crowd to catch up with them. "I see you've just arrived at the way station?"

She nodded, unsure what to tell the stranger and wondering if the scribes would notice they lagged behind. He looked friendly enough. Her father didn't open his eyes.

"How did you know?" she asked.

He chuckled. "Newcomers always have the same lost expression."

"Actually, we did just arrive, mister . . . ?"

"Fram." He bowed only slightly, not as much as a polite stranger would have done. "Malek Fram. I'm a bit of a poet actually. A programmer and a businessman. And a shuttle mechanic when the need arises. I assume you'll be needing my services sooner or later. Preferably sooner."

His hands looked pink and soft as he rubbed them together. He didn't look to Oriannon like someone who worked with his hands much, and she wasn't at all sure how one person fit all those job descriptions.

"I see. Well, I have to say we're a little puzzled about this place. I thought it was an asylum way station, just for scribes. Perhaps you could tell us why all these people are here?"

"Oh, these?" He waved his hand around as if just noticing the crowds for the first time. "Ah, yes, well, Asylum 2 has become a meeting place for traders. People on their way to ... well, you know. There are also a few expatriate Coristans, like myself. I've never actually been to the planet, though my father was from Corista. What's it like ... since the axis shifted and you don't have daylight all the time?"

He paused for a moment, but not long enough for anyone to give an answer. Behind them, Sola was still fussing with moor-doves, while Wist was trying to keep her from knocking over a pottery display.

"Never mind," continued the man. "My mother ... well, that's another story."

"But these people?" asked Oriannon. "Aren't they refugees?"

"Oh, yes. Some. You'll find a few scattered refugees here and there."

"That's not quite how the scribes put it," she said, eyeing one of the families with translucent skin.

He shrugged his shoulders as if it didn't matter. "Opinions vary."

"Do you know why they're here?"

"Translucents, you mean? I don't speak their language much. It's very strange. Perhaps they're here for the same reason as you." He eyed them a little more closely. "Whatever that is."

Oriannon decided she wasn't about to explain anything else to this con man, so she turned to Margus and whispered for them to go.

"Wait." Margus held them up. "You said you were a mechanic. Do you know where to get spare parts for a Coristan shuttle?"

At that, Malek Fram's eyes lit up like a salesman striking a deal, and he rubbed his hands together all over again. A glimmer of titanium showed on his front tooth.

"Spare parts, new parts, used parts ... naturally! I'll even have them installed for you. You'll find I'm quite reasonable to work with. Where's your vessel?"

“I’m sorry,” Oriannon interrupted. Her father had slumped even lower and it appeared the scribes had finished their discussion. “We really have to get going. I’m sure the scribes are wondering what happened to us.”

“They’re always wondering.” He smiled for a moment longer and seemed to study her face in a way that made her flush with discomfort. “And you’ll do. You’ll do very well.”

Do? For what? Before she could object, Malek Fram took her free hand and pressed it between his in a way that many people shake hands.

She knew right way this was different. She felt a slight tingle and jerked away, finding a red mark in the center of her palm.

“What in the world was that?” she cried, shaking her hand with disbelief. “What did you just do?”

“Simply my calling card,” he answered, again bowing slightly. “It’s the custom here on Asylum 2. Please calm yourself. Nothing to be upset about.”

She wiped her palm on the side of her tunic, but the red mark remained. A strange custom she would have to get used to? She’d had quite enough of this Mr. Malek Fram.

“By the way.” His eyes went to Oriannon’s father, sizing him up as well. “Your friend’s robe. Gold trim? Quite valuable … and not the usual.”

“My father’s a Coristan elder,” she sniffed, hoping that might satisfy him.

“Oh, really?” His eyebrows raised with interest. “I’d heard the elders were done away with back on the old planet. Perhaps I was mistaken?”

Oriannon frowned, not wanting to answer, and he went on.

“But he doesn’t look too well. Does he ever speak of the future? Perhaps a prophetic gift that could be put to … pardon the pun … *profitable* use?”

By this time Oriannon had no idea what the man was getting at, but she knew she didn’t like it.

"Look, I don't know what you're after," she told him, "but some other time, perhaps, Mr. Fram. We're on our way to see a healer."

"Oh, yes, by all means. You have my, er, *card.*" He followed them a little way to get in the last word. "I'm sure we can do business!"

I doubt it very much, thought Oriannon as they followed the scribes once more through the bewildering crowd. A couple of loud Translucents ran into them from the side, nearly bowling them over. They may have apologized, but Oriannon couldn't be sure. They simply stared at her, sputtered a string of their peculiar grunts—high-pitched and then low—before hurrying on their way.

"He seemed like a nice enough guy," said Margus, prompting Oriannon to wonder if her friend was really that dense. "Malek Fram, I mean. Sounds like he might be able to help us get the shuttle back in shape."

"I don't think so," she replied, looking back down at her palm. Over to the side, she noticed Malek Fram speaking earnestly with the performer who had been entertaining the crowd earlier. The contortionist pointed their direction before listening again. Finally he folded his hands and bowed to Malek before slipping back to his stage.

The red mark remained.

6

Ten minutes later they arrived in a great room of sorts — a lofty-ceilinged auditorium with a plain metal floor lit by rows of spotlights and filled with row after row of cots. Each cot was occupied by a surly Coristan, an Owling, a Translucent, or one of the strange smaller people with the blue hair. The scribe stopped and nodded at five open cots, each one topped by a small folded blanket.

"You'll be sleeping here," he told them, his words clipped and precise, as if the speech had been offered dozens of times before this. "You're allowed in the main holding area — where we just came through — and here, but forbidden in the rest of the way station without the accompaniment of a scribe. Should you have any — "

"Pardon me," interrupted Oriannon, "but what about a healer? My father needs attention."

She and Margus helped her father lie down on the cot, and she covered him with two blankets to keep him from shivering any more than he already was.

"Someone will look in on your father shortly." The scribe acted as if this was the first time she had mentioned it instead of the tenth. "In the meantime, our welcoming committee will want to ascertain the purpose of your visit."

He studied them with his head tilted slightly to the side, waiting for an answer.

"You mean why are we here?" asked Margus.

"Simply put, yes."

"That's easy." Margus nodded. "Our atmospheric generator blew out and we were on emergency O_2 for the past few hours. A lot of our power was out too, and since the cabin pressure was so far down, the heat wasn't working, so—"

"I meant the purpose of your visit," said the scribe, "not the minute details of your vessel's failure."

"Oh." Margus looked to Oriannon. "Well, we sort of had to leave Corista in a hurry ..."

His voice trailed off as the scribe frowned.

"And you chose this station because ...?"

"Uh ..." Margus fumbled for words. "It actually wasn't our first choice, but it was a good thing we had Oriannon's Stone, so—"

"Pardon me?" The scribe interrupted with sudden interest. "Certainly you don't mean a Pilot Stone?"

A couple of burly Coristans two cots away stopped their conversation and turned their heads to stare. They wore the same black coveralls as Malek Fram and gave Oriannon the same ill feeling. This could not be good, not in a place like this.

"It's a long story." Oriannon stepped in before Margus said something he shouldn't. She still wasn't so sure about the scribes at this way station or what they were all about. She would tell them about the approaching Troikans, but did she have to give all the details right here? The scribe crossed his arms and looked from one to the other.

"Are you telling me you are in possession of a Pilot Stone?"

Oriannon caught her breath as she felt in her pocket just to be sure.

"We escaped Corista because my father's life was in danger," she finally explained, avoiding the question. Very well then. Anyone who wanted to hear this part could hear—even the neighbors who now made no effort to hide their curiosity. "But we came here because of Jesmet's command, not because of any stone."

"Jesmet?" The scribe narrowed his eyes. "What do you know of Jesmet?"

She took a deep breath before continuing, her heart racing. She would tell them.

"Jesmet ben Saius. He was ... is my mentor. But he's also the Maker's Song. You know, in the Codex, chapter two, how the Maker created the universe with a Song? Well— "

"You don't need to quote Codex to me, young lady."

Oriannon almost bit her tongue.

"Right," she told him. "I didn't mean to offend."

Margus held up his hand to add, "She's an eidich," which only served to sidetrack the conversation more than it already was.

"Is that true?" asked the scribe.

"Yes," she admitted. "But Jesmet, my mentor, sent us here to warn you about the Troikans. That's why we're here."

By this time a cloud had descended on the scribe's face, and he looked around the room to make sure that no one heard a word of their conversation.

"They're the ones responsible for the disappearance of Asylum 1," she added. "And we think— "

"No, no, no." The scribe interrupted her, lowering his voice as he took her by the arm. "You're making accusations here. You know these Troikans? You've met them? Spoken with them?"

Oriannon sighed. She'd apparently mentioned something he didn't want to hear.

"Not exactly. But— "

"There, see? If you haven't seen them or spoken with them, we can safely assume there's room for misunderstanding."

"Oriannon doesn't misunderstand things," said Margus, coming to her defense.

"In this case I'm afraid she has, and I would warn you both not to discuss your ... misunderstandings with others."

"Seeing Asylum 1 disappear was no misunderstanding," Margus countered, but by this time the scribe's face had turned crimson as he faced them both down.

"We'll discuss this some other time. Right now I have some urgent details, some other arrivals to tend to. If you need anything else, please don't hesitate to contact me."

"But wait!" Margus waved at him before he could get away. "How can we contact you, if you've never told us your name?"

"My apologies." He paused, then bowed, and almost tripped over another cot in his efforts to leave. "I've had to deal with so many refugees in the past several weeks, perhaps my manners have suffered. My name is Stratus. Stratus Main. Up until the latest, er, influx of visitors, I was deputy chief scribe of this way station. Of necessity I have been drafted into service as a sort of innkeeper."

"Main?" asked Oriannon. That reminded her of another scribe, perhaps older, and on another way station. But now that she thought of it, he showed a striking resemblance. "You're not related to Cirrus Main, are you?"

"You know my cousin?" Stratus stopped, his eyes wide. "We haven't heard from him."

"I met him a few months ago on Asylum 4," she replied, "before it was ... destroyed."

"We'd heard only sketchy reports," he told her. "Nothing definite."

"It wasn't the Troikans, though." Oriannon didn't want to muddy the main issue, but she had to explain what she knew. "It was by order of Coristan Security."

"Hmm ..." His face drained of color, and his voice was quieter now. "Perhaps you should share your story with several of our other scribes after all. And if you actually do have a Pilot Stone, they would be highly interested in this, as well. I'll, ah ... let you know."

Sola must have been following along, but by this time she had apparently lost patience.

"This is all very touching," she said, thumping a fist on the cot, "and I hate to interrupt the pleasantries here, but am I to understand that you actually expect me to sleep here in this room, on this dreadful cot, and in full view of anyone passing by? You know I have special needs, and I cannot tolerate this kind of accommodation. I demand to be placed in a suitable single room."

To emphasize her point she flung her blanket to the floor in a petulant challenge. Stratus Main, however, simply stepped over to the blanket, picked it up, folded it carefully, and replaced it on the cot next to her. He pressed his lips together for a moment before answering.

"I regret our hospitality doesn't meet your expectations. However, you should understand that our purpose for generations has simply been to study the Codex and preserve its sacred teachings. This is a community of scribes and academics temporarily overrun by people such as yourself."

"Overrun?" She ground her teeth. "You don't know what the word means."

"Forgive my bluntness. However, even though our protocol compels us to welcome strangers among us, they do not require that we permanently house them. With that in mind, you are always welcome to continue on your way."

And with that he turned to continue on *his* way, but not before he nodded at Oriannon.

"I'd like to hear more of what you know about my cousin," he told her, his voice trailing off. "Perhaps also ... about this mentor of yours."

With that he left them to themselves — or rather, to themselves in the midst of several hundred other refugees, many of whom had obviously not bathed in a long time. Some openly stared with curiosity, as if Oriannon and her troupe had just put on an interesting show, while others huddled together whispering in strange sounds. A baby fussed on the other side of the room, its cries echoing again and again throughout the auditorium. Still others lay quietly, staring blank-eyed at the ceiling or trying to sleep. Oriannon thought it was probably a good thing Sola could not see the strange menagerie of people here, or she might have been even more put out than she was.

One man in particular studied them from across the room, his arms crossed, his glare unmistakably hostile. Although he looked very much like many of the other Translucents they had seen — with elongated features and an ice-blue tint to his strange, see-through skin — she knew they had seen him before. Oriannon tried to look away, to ignore him, but Wist noticed it too.

"Don't be looking now," she whispered to Oriannon, "but were you seeing the scary-looking guy?"

Oriannon nodded and checked to see if Margus noticed too. He was sitting on his hard cot, and Oriannon tapped him on the hand and quietly motioned a warning with her eyes.

"Over there," she whispered. "It's the same guy I saw talking to Malek Fram just a few minutes ago. He was doing a contortionist act."

She couldn't help shivering as the Translucent approached them, stepping on blankets and shoving aside people on their cots as he did. Margus, bless his brave heart, stood up to meet the challenge while she looked for an escape route. But when the Translucent came within a meter of their cots, he stopped and drew himself up to address the curious crowd, raising both hands over his head for attention. Oriannon could see, as if looking through an X-ray, the shadow of twin hearts beating through the skin of the man's neck, and she tried not to stare in fascination.

"Welcome the newcomers, everyone!" He spoke their language with a distinct accent, strange to Oriannon's ears. But his words pierced and carried, making her wince, and there would be no doubt that everyone in the room could hear him. "Five more Coristans, or, pardon me, four Coristans and an Owling. The little people with the big eyes."

That got him a laugh from the audience, or at least from the non-Owlings.

"And now they've come here uninvited in a stolen shuttle, no less. Well, that I can appreciate. I have a friend who's going to enjoy the spare parts, thank you very much."

Another laugh. If that was an inside joke, Oriannon didn't think she liked it very much.

"Er, pardon me— " Margus tried to interrupt, but the Translucent, at least a head taller than Oriannon's father, just talked over him.

"So now they come with warnings. Did anyone hear that? Warnings about a coming danger. As if you didn't know about *that* already!"

No doubt this man was used to entertaining the crowds, and by the way they reacted, the crowds knew who he was. The frightening part, however, was that he seemed to have heard them talking to Stratus Main from all the way across the room. Oriannon made a mental note to be extra careful around Translucents.

"I heard it too, Alymas," said a small blue-haired man sitting nearby. "I heard them try to tell Stratus Main about Troikans."

"There, see?" When Alymas the Translucent laughed, his long nose seemed to buzz. But the meaning was clear, and others in the room laughed along in their own way. "Troikans! Has anyone ever seen a Troikan? Of course not. It's just one more rumor to frighten us, one more Coristan lie!"

Now Alymas turned deadly serious, but he had the crowd following every word. Oriannon thought she could see bluish blood coursing through the veins in his neck.

"Now just wait a minute," Margus began. "These are not— "

"And you know what I see?" Alymas wasn't letting anyone else take center stage, now that he had it firmly in his grasp.

"Tell us what's going to happen with them!" shouted someone from the back of the room. Alymas looked as if he relished the attention, turning slowly with his arms extended. His awful red eyes seemed to roll back into his head in a way that turned Oriannon's stomach. But people all around her watched him, transfixed, and she or Margus or Wist could do nothing to stop this performance.

"What do I see?" he said again. "These people have brought trouble with them to this way station. A curse."

That brought the expected gasps from the crowd, which had closed in around them. Alymas only raised his voice even more.

"And the blind one here?" He pointed out Sola. "Before three months are up she's going to die a horrible death. I know this! Wait until you see it! It will be more entertaining than my acts. And you know what else?"

"That's enough!" Oriannon's hands shook as she stood to face this fortune-teller. Her entire body shook, for that matter. She didn't look to see how Sola had reacted to the man's words. But Ori knew she had to stand up to him now, or things would only get worse. And when she saw the surprise on his face, her fear drained away, to be replaced by an unexpected calm.

"What did you say?" He coughed and scratched his head nervously. In so doing, he showed glowing red marks on both his palms, much like the one Oriannon had received. Calling cards?

"It doesn't matter what I say." She spoke loud enough for people around to hear, but did not strain her voice. Let them listen more closely. "What matters is what Jesmet would tell you if he were here. He would say— "

"Who is this Jesmet that I should care what he says of me?" The man sneered as if he thought Oriannon could do nothing to stop him. "Let him come and complain himself."

"He's not here at the moment. But since you asked, he's the Maker's Song, the Music that created the Trion and Corista, the moons and beyond ... and every one of us. Even you, Alymas."

By this time Oriannon had no idea how she stood up to this tall stranger, or where she found the courage to say what she said. She only opened her mouth, and it came out.

"Oh, come." Now Alymas sneered again, showing stained teeth. "Don't they teach you on Corista about the progression of the species? Here, let me tell you what's going to happen to you and your two friends. For a slightly higher charge, I'll tell you down to the very last detail."

"No, Alymas." She interrupted him. "And since he sent me, I'll tell you the same thing: *That's enough. No more of this future-telling.*"

Alymas pulled back at the pronouncement, as if she'd slapped him in the face.

"What's the matter?" he whispered now, suddenly deflated. "You don't like my predictions? Everybody on the way station comes to me to hear the future. Even some of the scribes. No one else can see the future as I can."

He looked around him for support, something like the way he'd done when he first approached them, but this time people seemed to pull back.

"Isn't that true?" he asked, looking more and more desperate as he looked first from one person, then to the next. Each one avoided his eyes. "I'm right, am I not? You all come to my shows."

But this time no one spoke up, and his words echoed in a silent room. The baby cried in the back, again. Someone coughed nervously.

"A circus act is one thing," answered Oriannon, and a part of her hoped her words didn't fatally wound him. "But the Codex forbids divination. Not for fun and games, not for any reason. The Maker doesn't want us to foretell the future."

"Why not?" Now Alymas looked more hurt than anything else. "Because he's afraid—"

"The Maker is afraid of nothing," she told him. "He forbids future-telling because it's only for him to know. Because he cares for you. It's for your own good."

"My own good," he echoed the words, as if such an idea was completely new to him.

"Your owner knows that, and I think you probably do too. But that's not the only reason I'm telling you to stop."

"My owner ..." His eyes narrowed, as if in fear, and now he seemed to shrink back several more degrees. "How would you know about my owner?"

Oriannon was surprised, but it all added up. Even Margus and Wist stared at her as if she was out of her mind. Not to mention the crowd all around them.

"Listen, Alymas. Just because you have spots on your palms doesn't mean you have to be a slave. Don't you see? That's the main reason you're going to stop what you've been doing. Malek has no rights to you."

"No, you don't understand." Now Alymas faced her with fresh tears in his eyes. "The things I do, the things I say ... they earn him a lot of privileges. You can't take that away."

"That's the way you want it? You want Malek to use you?"

"But you don't know Malek. When he finds out, he's going to—"

Alymas didn't finish his sentence, or couldn't, as he winced in obvious pain and held up his shaking hands. And once more, she knew what to do ... without knowing.

"Alymas, look at me." She took his hands in hers, and he let her. By this time, the marks on his palms were glowing bright red. And a burning sensation on her own hand told her that her own red mark was beginning to respond in much the same way. She ignored the pain, swallowed, and went on.

"Something like this happened to me before, back in Corista. Fear implants. Trust me; they weren't any fun."

"What ... did you do?" he whispered.

"That's just it; I didn't do anything. Jesmet shut them all down—for me and for thousands of other people. This is no different. I'm telling you he'll do the same thing for you—for us—again. Right now. Do you believe me?"

She didn't have time to tell him the entire story of how Sola and her Security forces had installed fear implants under the skin of thousands of Owling conscripts, and into her as well. All she could do was offer the only solution that made any sense.

"I don't know," he answered. "I think yes, but I'm so tired."

Finally he nodded and collapsed to the floor—quite a change from the one who had challenged them just a few minutes earlier. As he kneeled, sobbing, he held his hands out in front of him, and together they watched as the throbbing red welts on his palms slowly but surely gave way to the normal pale blue coloration of his skin. Oriannon noted, when she looked at her own palm, that her mark had faded as well.

"I'm frightened," whispered Alymas in between sobs, but his voice had changed from haughty and high to a soft ghost of what it had been. Oriannon could hardly believe this was the same person who had strutted up to them a few minutes earlier.

"You don't have to be," she answered, holding his hands in hers as the pain from the red spots faded completely. She took a deep breath, amazed at what she had just said and seen, as if it had all happened to someone else, and she felt as if she might collapse. "Not any more."

He nodded as if he understood, took a deep breath, and straightened up to his full height. When he did that, Oriannon had to bend her head back to see his face.

"You're not angry anymore?" she asked.

"I was never angry," he whispered, so softly no one else could hear. "That was someone else, not me."

And with that he bowed low to her and kissed her hands, which was a little awkward, but she understood. He paused, then looked to her with a shy smile and a soft "thank you" before fading back into the hushed crowd.

"Whoa, Ori." Margus came up beside her to see for himself. "I don't know how you did that."

"Me neither," she admitted, turning her hands around. She looked at their audience, returning to their cots. Several glanced nervously at the entry doors, as if expecting Malek, the slave owner, to enter and reclaim his living property.

Well, not if I can help it, Oriannon decided, resting her hands on her hips. She felt as drained as Alymas looked, yet felt ready for whatever happened next. But her father still needed help; he'd slept through the entire confrontation with Alymas. They still needed to convince the scribes of the coming danger—somehow.

Is this why Jesmet brought them here?

She couldn't say for sure. But when she looked around, she noticed something—someone—was missing.

"What happened to Sola?" she asked.

7

He does not appear well," pronounced a middle-age scribe as he bent over Oriannon's father several hours later. It had taken that long to find out the way station would not provide him with a healer. They had to find a healer on their own.

If this actually *was* a healer ... He pushed up the threadbare brown sleeves to his elbows, rubbed his bald dome, and pulled an older handheld scanner from his crowded shelf as he repeated the prognosis.

"Not well at all."

No revelation there. As he traced the blue light of his scanner over Tavlin Hightower's closed eyes, Oriannon could have said exactly the same thing without his expertise. Her father lay still on the gleaming stainless table, shivering even in his elder's robe and under a small blanket.

"Let's see. Perhaps ..."

He did not seem entirely comfortable with the workings of the scanner as he fumbled with the adjustments once again, then set it down. But Oriannon said nothing as he consulted an ancient book with actual paper pages, yellowed and brittle with age. He held it up to the overhead bank of lights as half the page disintegrated and drifted to the floor.

"You *are* a healer, aren't you?" asked Margus.

"Healer?" The scribe straightened up. "Heavens, no. I'm just another scribe, Pset Much, and I've been studying Codex all my life. We haven't had a healer here on Asylum for ... well, I don't recall we've had one as long as I've lived here."

A soft pink light filled the room, casting shadows on the examining table and a glass-fronted cabinet that filled the far wall. The case featured odd medical instruments of a vintage and style Oriannon could only recognize as old, very old. Perhaps this windowless little stainless steel room had been decorated when the way station was first founded many generations ago and ignored ever since. The bottles in the cabinet must have been filled with ancient remedies. Each was marked with faded notations in flowing old Coristan, difficult to read from a distance.

Margus cleared his throat. "So then ... How long have you lived here?"

The scribe scratched his head. "Let's see. I was born on Asylum 4, but my father brought us here ... I suppose it's been seventy-three years and three months now. Time passes, does it not?"

Oriannon looked more closely at the scribe; she would have guessed he was no older than half what he just told her. No wrinkles ... How? He smiled knowingly at her before returning to his patient, mumbling something they couldn't quite make out.

"I think we'll just wait outside then," said Margus, standing just inside the door, an arm's length away.

Oriannon held out her hand. "No, please," she told him. "Stay here with me. I— "

I need you both here, she would have said if she could. He nodded as if he understood, while Pset Much seemed to ignore their conversation and consulted his book again.

"It says here," said Pset, fumbling with the book, "that with the kind of readings I'm getting, he should be ..."

He paused and flipped a couple of pages.

"No, sorry," he went on. "Wrong section. We don't often encounter these kinds of injuries, but I believe it's telling me there's extensive tissue damage here, subsurface burns, vital organs compromised, along with a high-grade infection. Are these injuries from weapons of some kind?"

"Back on Corista, yes." Oriannon choked out the words. "You can help him, can't you?"

"Hard to say actually." Pset shook his head and returned the instrument to a cracked leather case before replacing it on the shelf next to the rest of his ancient-looking instruments. Everything he did and said seemed measured and careful. "I can give him something for the fever, but we're not equipped to treat his kind of injuries here."

"In other words," said Margus, "you don't know what to do."

Pset frowned but continued.

"We're equipped to offer the most basic forms of medical attention for headaches, stomach ailments, ingrown toenails, and the occasional sprained ankle. Not life-threatening stun baton wounds, as this appears to be. So if you keep him here, I'll do what I can, but . . ."

When Pset's voice trailed of, Oriannon looked once again to Margus and Wist for help. Wist stayed in the corner, her arms crossed. If this was the best help they could find here on Asylum 2, they would need to try something else — before it was too late.

"We're actually on our way to someplace else," Oriannon told him. "We weren't planning to stay long."

"Good. Then perhaps you'll find better treatment for him at another way station. I do know he seems to be in and out of a comatose state, so his nervous system is affected."

"What do you mean, *affected?*" asked Margus.

"I mean, he may not recognize you all the time, or be fully aware of his surroundings. Or he might act normal, though weak and in pain. I will pray for your father."

Oriannon bent over to touch her father's cheek, but pulled back as it burned cherry red. He groaned softly. Margus frowned as he paced the tiny dispensary, then threw another question at the scribe.

"That's the best you can tell us?"

"Margus!" Although Oriannon might have said the same thing.

"I wish I could do more," Pset told them as he straightened his equipment. "But I have to admit we've been overwhelmed by all the refugees in the past several months. I'm sorry."

Oriannon didn't expect the catch in his voice as their scribe pulled down a blue bottle from the shelf above their heads. He poured a small amount of thick liquid into a tiny glass vial, cocked his head to the side, changed his mind, and went looking for something else.

"You'll assist me," he told them as he returned with another bottle. "Please."

Now they sat her father up so he could swallow his medicine, and the scribe explained how often they should give him another dose, and how much.

"Although ..." he hesitated, then consulted his book again. "No, twice a day would be fine. Thrice."

"Which?" asked Margus.

"Three times a day. Yes. But I do recommend you take him to an actual healer, perhaps Asylum 3. They have a much better facility. Unless you choose to return to Corista."

"Not right away," Oriannon answered. "It's not safe there for my father."

The scribe glanced back at her father's wounds as he washed his hands, rubbing them thoroughly beneath a spigot of oscillating green light set into the wall.

"I understand," he said, looking around as if someone might overhear them. "But you've already caused quite an uproar here at the way station with what you did to Alymas."

Oriannon flinched at the sudden change of subject. "Malek wasn't too pleased?" What else could she say?

"No, but most of the scribes understand that you did what we did not have the courage to do. You must be careful from now on."

"Why?" she asked, puzzled now. "What would happen to me?"

"That I cannot say. But you do realize Malek had a substantial business going, with Alymas telling futures? Many of the scribes themselves were some of Malek's biggest customers. Now that's been terminated. Why did you get involved?"

"Jesmet says if we knew what was going to happen tomorrow, we'd think we controlled our own destiny. The Maker doesn't want us to know futures."

"Perhaps. But the name you used ... this Jesmet ..." He paused to think, rubbing his chin.

"My mentor."

"Yes, and you said you knew the Maker's Song ..."

She felt the Pilot Stone in her pocket, knowing that she should explain the Song to him, but it was like trying to describe a scent. It would be much easier for him to hear it for himself.

"I've read of him," he explained further, "but none of the scribes here can agree what kind of a Song he's to be. Everyone has a different opinion. You say you've actually seen him?"

Oriannon wasn't prepared for his thirsty questions, as if he might lap up answers like a tremonian leech that hadn't tasted water in weeks. But she couldn't help glancing at her father again, and then out the door at the lineup of refugees, all waiting for help.

"I'm sorry," he said. "Perhaps another time you can share your story with my friends and me. There are a number of scribes seeking answers, you know."

Oriannon could have kicked herself for hesitating, for not telling him now, *Yes, I know him!* Instead she thanked him as she slipped her shoulder under her father's limp arm, and Margus took up the other side. It was going to take the help of Margus and Wist, as well as all her strength to ferry him back down the hall and through the waiting crowds.

"By the way, your blind friend has been out making her case," he told them as they left. "Our leadership is taking her words into account."

"Don't believe a word she tells you," said Margus. But by that time Pset Much had already disappeared back into his little clinic with the next patient. When they turned back, their way was blocked by a Translucent woman holding a small child. Oriannon and Margus were forced to pull up short.

"Pardon me," Oriannon told her, looking up. "Could we please get by? We need to get my father back to his cot."

The Translucent woman had other ideas, as her dark expression broke into a storm and her tongue let loose, burying them in a cyclone of red-eyed fury. She held up her little child—who looked every bit as frightened as she looked enraged—and gestured to him as she spoke, as if the child was enough evidence to convict a person of murder or worse.

"I'm sorry," Oriannon tried to tell her, "but we don't understand your language."

At least not the spoken part. The body language was clear enough, and so were the blood vessels in her forehead, swelling like balloons. The woman shook her head wildly and continued her lecture, not slowing and not letting them by. One way or another, it seemed, she was going to unload her complaints.

"Back off, lady!" Margus held up his free hand, but that only seemed to enrage the woman more. "We don't even know you."

"Margus," said Oriannon, "you're not helping any." She turned to the people in line for help. "Can anyone tell us what she's saying? Does anyone understand?"

By this time several other Translucents had gathered closer, encouraging the upset woman with nods and angry agreement even as they gave Oriannon and her friends fierce, cold stares. It was probably a good thing that Oriannon's father didn't appear to notice it.

"I do." A soft voice came from behind them, and they looked to see a familiar face: Alymas! Oriannon wasn't sure which way to run now, and she checked for signs of his master. Probably the only thing worse than being caught in the middle of an angry mob was being caught in the middle of an angry mob with an even angrier former slave owner.

"He's not here," Alymas told her, perhaps guessing her thoughts. "And I'll help you if you let me."

He looked entirely different from the person who had confronted them earlier. Though his shoulders still seemed to slump in exhaustion, his eyes held none of the wildfire they'd seen before, and his voice matched the shy smile on his blue lips.

"Ori?" Wist couldn't hold up Tavlin Hightower's other side for much longer. What choice did they have, trapped here in this little hallway? More people now gathered around and behind the angry woman, blocking their way ahead and behind. Oriannon looked from Alymas to the woman and the crowd and back again. Several young men began pumping their fists and chanting something that sounded like a war cry.

"All right." Oriannon finally nodded to Alymas. "Can you tell her we don't know what she's angry about, and that we mean her no harm?"

Even if that sounded like a weak defense, Alymas nodded and slipped in a few words before the woman released another angry diatribe. He nodded as she spoke, holding up a hand to try to calm her. Finally she settled enough to let him relay her words.

"She says your stories have terrified her young child." Alymas chose his words carefully. "He will not stop crying."

"My stories?" asked Oriannon, thinking back over the past several hours since they'd arrived at the way station. "I don't—"

"Your stories of the invading Troikans and the magic stone," he added. "She says you have no right to come here with such lies. She says the blind woman brings death."

"Alymas?" she asked, feeling a chill up her back and a danger in the air. "Tell her the stories of the Troikans are not lies. Tell her I'm sorry her little boy is scared. Tell her ..."

She paused as he relayed her words.

"Tell her I didn't mean to bring fear," she added. "I am only trying to help."

The mother didn't seem to follow. She wagged a long blue finger at them. The jeering crowd followed her example and didn't let up their verbal attack. In any language, Oriannon could taste the flavor of the insults and the unmasked anger.

"Go now," Alymas urged them with a nudge to the shoulder. "I will show you a safe place."

Oriannon checked on Wist and saw the fear in her friend's eyes, but Margus nodded as he kept her father from falling.

"They don't understand," Alymas replied, leading the way. When he yelled out a few commands in his language, the crowd slowly parted to either side of the hall.

"What did you just say?" asked Margus.

Alymas hardly slowed down but called over his shoulder.

"If you go to sleep in the room with all the rest of them, you will not wake up. Do you understand my meaning?"

Unfortunately, Oriannon did. Alymas led them through a maze of narrow, darkened corridors where utility pipes, hissing steam in all the wrong places, lined a ceiling that was low enough to bump their heads. Margus ducked as they rounded a corner, but too late.

"Ouch!" said Margus, rubbing his head.

"Don't slow down," Alymas warned them. They followed him to a series of service rooms filled with vibrating air vents, humming machines, and electronic equipment. She felt herself sweating through her tunic.

"You did tell that mother I was sorry," she said, breathing hard to keep up with Alymas. "Didn't you?"

The thought crossed her mind that perhaps his new, softer personality had simply been put on for the occasion, or for the chance to lead them into a trap. He didn't answer right away.

"Alymas?" she asked again. "Did you hear me? What exactly did you tell her?"

He stopped to hold open a round steel door and waved his hand for them to enter a dark little room.

"Watch your step. I told her that if they touched you, they would catch a horrible disease and lose their sight as well, and that this man had nearly succumbed."

"Oh no." Oriannon helped lower her father to the floor in the corner of the tiny utility room. She had to raise her voice to be heard above the humming of some kind of generator. "You shouldn't have said that."

"I'm sorry," he replied, clearing a place for them between packing crates. "It was the best I could think of at the time."

Oriannon waited for her eyes to adjust to the dark. Meanwhile, it was hard to miss how the humming generator radiated more than enough heat to keep them warm, and then some.

"You really think we need to hide in here?" she asked. "Maybe you could tell people we're okay."

He shook his head.

"You didn't understand what the the crowd was saying," he told them, heading for the door. "Just believe me when I tell you that you must stay here for now. I will bring you some food. And don't open up the door for anyone but me."

Oriannon stopped him for a moment before he left.

"Why are you doing this?" she asked, and he turned away before answering. "You're a Translucent too."

"You freed me," he said, choking up. "All my life I was property, performing for my master. No more. I can't tell futures any more, no matter how much Malek beats me, and he knows it. You and your Jesmet freed me."

"But ... Malek?"

"Yes, I know. But even if Malek decides I am worthless now and has me killed, I die free. Now, please lock the door when I leave."

Oriannon did as he told her, still shaking at what Alymas had said. After what they'd already seen, she didn't have a hard time imagining what Malek could do. Alymas knew what he was capable of, more than anyone.

So she leaned back against the heavy door with a sigh as they settled into their new hiding place. Margus found her father a place to sit next to the door, and he held up a small glowstick to cast a faint circle of light around them.

Surely they wouldn't stay here for long. What if the darkness hid hungry little muren or other nasty rodents with sharp teeth and hungry appetites? As if to confirm her fears, a shuffling sound made her freeze.

"Is anyone there?" she asked, grabbing Wist's hand. At first they heard nothing, but then she made out a figure huddled in the corner.

8

Sola didn't apologize for startling Oriannon and the others after they walked in on her in the dark utility room, but that surprised no one. The blind woman kept to herself in the far corner, grumbling about their latest accommodations.

Meanwhile, Oriannon tried to pretend she was sitting in the leafy shelter of the Glades back home on Corista, enjoying a cool evening breeze on her cheeks and the sweet smell of lonicera blossoms. If it were only real! But she couldn't relax, and she certainly couldn't sleep. It wasn't on account of the hard cement floor, the unforgiving heat, or the constant buzz and hum from the generators. Oriannon had even recovered from the fright of meeting Sola in their dark little hideout. But now her mind refused to stop spinning.

Wist, on the other hand, seemed to sleep peacefully through it all, and so did Oriannon's father. Oriannon could make out his constant snore above the noise.

Sleep! She commanded her eyes to remain closed, but it didn't help, and she couldn't keep her mind from drifting to thoughts about home and her friends there. Sleep . . .

Hours later she still could not sleep — especially not when she realized someone was sitting on the floor not a meter away. She sat up straight and fumbled for the glowstick to see who it was.

"Margus?" she whispered. "What are you doing up?"

Strange that she hadn't heard him approach from the other side of the room. She had been awake after all. Hadn't she?

"Sorry," said the man, and Oriannon gasped at the sound of his voice. "I didn't mean to startle you, Oriannon."

By the dim light of the glowstick, Oriannon could now easily make out the sleeping form of Margus over on the other side of the room, while her father slept by the door — which was still locked. However, she could no longer hear the rumbling of the ventilation equipment. And now there was no mistaking Mentor Jesmet's voice, and if he said anything else, he would surely wake everyone else in the room.

"I'm not startled." Oriannon blurted out the first thing that came to mind. "I mean, maybe a little. But ... what are you doing here?"

The room lightened a bit as her focus sharpened.

"I just came to encourage you to keep moving ahead, Oriannon, no matter how discouraged you feel. Please don't forget that you're doing the right thing."

"It sure doesn't feel like it sometimes. Especially when everyone on the station is ready to kill us for trying to warn them about the Troikans."

"I know. Wait until you tell them who sent you."

"It's going to get worse?"

She could clearly make out his gentle smile in the vivid green light as she told him what had happened earlier, and how they'd been taken to this hiding place.

"I don't know how long we're going to have to stay here," she told him, "hiding."

"Not long, Oriannon. You'll need to leave for the next way station very soon."

"We'll know when?"

"You'll know." When he rose to leave, Oriannon wondered if he would bother to use the door, or if he would just fade into the fuzzy edges of her vision as he had before.

"Mentor?" She held out her hand, wishing he would stay just a little longer. "Are things going to change? Is anything going to get easier? What about my father?"

"You want me to tell you the future?"

"No—I mean, I'm sorry. I didn't mean it that way."

"I know you didn't." Again he smiled, and he looked down at Margus, sleeping through it all. "He certainly snores, doesn't he?"

So Mentor Jesmet wasn't going to answer her questions. He did rest his hand on her shoulder though, the way her father would have if he had been well, and it made her look up.

"I can tell you this much, Oriannon," he said. "The Troikans want every asylum way station, not just one or two. That's why it's so urgent for you to keep going. They've already taken the first, and they're working on the second as we speak. It could happen any minute now. And if they succeed, they'll go on to Asylum 3 within days, and then ultimately, they'll want to take Corista itself."

Take it? She wasn't sure she understood, but she didn't know how to respond.

"I'm not telling you the future, Oriannon," he assured her. "Just what they want to do. You understand the difference. But I can tell you this without a doubt: It's going to get harder before it gets easier."

She swallowed hard. That didn't exactly sound like encouragement, but she nodded her understanding as he reminded her again to keep Sola close, and the Pilot Stone closer.

"I have been," she told him. She reached into her tunic pocket to pull it out, and it nearly burned her hand.

"Warm, isn't it?" He chuckled. "But the Stone is just one more reminder that you're not alone in all this. Even if it gets worse before it gets better, you're not alone."

"Right," she answered quickly, trying not to sound as flustered as she felt. "I knew that."

"Really? Then don't forget what this is all about." That seemed like an odd thing to say to an eidich, but she nodded anyway. "You must tell the next way station of the danger, or they'll all die."

She nodded as the weight of his words settled on her shoulders.

"I'll tell them," she said. "I promise."

"Good," he replied. "Oh, and one other thing? Please don't be afraid to tell them about your mentor as well."

Oriannon flushed a little, since he must have known how little she had told people up to now. But the hand on her shoulder never left her, and he said nothing more as she sensed the lights fade and felt a sudden touch of dizziness. The next thing she knew the hand on her shoulder belonged to Margus, and she instinctively pulled away when she recognized his face in the green light.

"Okay then," he told her. "You keep promising ... whatever. I don't have the slightest idea what you're talking about."

"Margus!" She looked around, but nothing had changed except he was awake. Wist and Sola still slept, and so did her father. She held out the Stone. "Feel this."

He did and jerked his fingers back immediately.

"What are you trying to do, burn my fingers? How did you do that?"

"I didn't do anything. The Stone sort of wakes up when Jesmet is here."

"He was here?" Margus groaned. "And I missed him again?"

She had run out of ways to tell him about it without sounding as if she had become totally unglued mentally. Didn't Jesmet realize it would be like this? Maybe he did, and he just didn't care. After all, what had he said about things getting worse before they got better? She just wished he'd told her exactly *how* worse, and for how long. It would have been nice to know.

"It wasn't a dream, Margus." She held out the Stone, daring it to burn through the palm of her hand. "This isn't a dream."

He gingerly touched it again with one finger, then backed off and shook his head.

"I believe you. But how come it's just *you* who can see him every time? You know how weird that seems?"

She nodded and placed the Stone back in her pocket. They sat in silence for a long moment. If it had been the other way around, she probably would have wondered about Margus too.

"I know," she finally admitted. "It seems weird to me too, but I know what I saw."

"So what did he say?"

"That you snore."

"No, really."

"I'm serious." But she recalled for Margus the basics of what Jesmet had told her, not word-for-word the way she could have, but idea-for-idea.

"Worse before it gets better, huh?" He didn't look as if he was too thrilled about that part either.

"Yeah, that's what I thought too."

But what else could she tell him? That everything was going to be okay? Well, Jesmet had sort of said that. But getting there was going to be the hard part.

"Sorry," she told him, "but that's what he said."

"Hmm. So did he say anything about how we can fix the shuttle?"

Finally they heard a soft groan from Wist's direction.

"What's going on?" asked Wist, the way someone would ask if they had been disturbed in the middle of a sleep cycle. "What are you guys doing?"

Oriannon instantly lowered her voice even more.

"Nothing, Wist," she whispered. "Go back to sleep."

"I will be sleeping if you two will please be quiet."

Oriannon apologized, but the sound of slow, steady breathing told her Wist had already fallen back asleep. Meanwhile, Margus motioned for her to follow him toward the door.

"What now?" she whispered as softly as she could. "Where are you going?"

"Same place I was going before you woke up. To check on the shuttle."

She grabbed his arm to stop him, but when he doused the glowstick, her eyes could barely make out his shadow in the near darkness. Only a tiny red light from one of the filtering machines now lit their room.

"What are you, crazy? You're not going anywhere. Didn't you hear what Alymas told us?"

"I heard." He slipped out of her grip. "But listen, it's been hours since we got here, and we haven't been able to check back on the ship. You've seen all the crazy characters around here. Who knows whether they've already hacked it up for spare parts? I have to go see. Come with me or not."

"But the crowds." She tried one more time. "You saw how mean they were. They're convinced we're stirring up trouble. If you get stopped— "

"If I get stopped, I'll just tell them we are leaving, and that will be the end of it."

Oriannon shook her head.

"None of us expected this, Margus. I'm sorry. But don't go out there—not yet."

"I have to, Oriannon. Come with me, and we'll see about getting the shuttle patched up so we can go home."

"You're going to do it?"

"I can do some. Maybe we can get someone to help us. Either way, I have to go see."

Oriannon wasn't so sure about that, but she wasn't going to argue any more with him. After checking again on her father and Wist, she unlocked the door and slipped out into the dark, narrow hallway with Margus. She would be back, she told herself, before either of them awoke. And though she couldn't quite see, she assumed Sola was asleep in the corner.

"One good thing." Margus still kept his voice down, even after they had left their hiding place behind and retraced their steps through the maze of narrow lower-level hallways. "I think people do sleep around here."

True enough. The way station's overhead lighting had been dimmed to a barely-visible copper glow, perhaps to give the sensation of a sleep cycle or to mimic a planet's conditions. And the best part about that was that they might make their way across the station undetected.

Did anyone see them? Oriannon held her breath several minutes later as they tiptoed through the commons under the shadow of the tall towers and the Trion star sculpture. If only she could keep her footsteps from echoing on the polished steel floors! She paused to step gingerly over a little Translucent girl curled up against her mother, snuggled under a shredded foil blanket and using a frayed, dirty backpack for a pillow.

How far did they come to find safety here? she wondered, and the weight of what she knew about the approaching Troikans made her want to shake these families awake, to warn them of the danger. How could she make them listen? As she stood wondering, the little girl rolled over, opened her little pink eyes, and gasped at what she saw.

Their eyes met and locked for a moment as Oriannon froze in fear. All she could think to do was raise a finger to her lips and back slowly away. The little girl blinked her eyes, whimpered quietly, and rolled over once again.

"Come on!" whispered Margus. "You're going to wake the whole way station!"

As they hurried away Oriannon fought the urge to sprint all the way to the landing hangars, never mind that she would surely disturb all these sleeping people. Silently she and Margus approached the large glassteel double doors, pausing a moment as they swept aside with a hiss of air to open the way into the wider and brighter hallway leading to the hangars. A woman's voice stopped them as they stepped through.

"Caution," said the flat, digitized voice. "Access to this section is restricted."

"It'll let us through," Margus told her, but she wasn't entirely sure. The recording sounded pretty sure of itself. Even so, no one challenged them, not even the scribe who walked by from the other direction. He kept his head down and muttered to himself all the way down the hall, and they did nothing to attract his attention. Three minutes later they emerged from the hallway into the high-ceilinged landing bay, topped by massive titanium beams and glassteel skylights that opened to black space far above their heads. When they approached the spot where they had parked the ship, Margus ran his hands through his hair and circled around.

"This is exactly what I was afraid of!" He parked his hands on his hips and looked around several times. He kicked at an imaginary target by his feet. "They've already carved it up."

"How do you know?" she asked, afraid that he might be right.

"Come on, Oriannon." He no longer whispered. "The shuttle is gone, can't you see?"

"I can see, Margus, but I don't think we need to panic yet. Maybe they just moved it."

"Moved it to take it apart. This is serious!"

"Okay, then. What if it is? Who would do something like that?"

"You know, the pirates and con men camping out on this way station. People like Malek Fram. He probably thinks we owe him, after what you did for Alymas."

She poked her head into a couple of maintenance bays—smaller garages off the main hangar area, walls lined with pneumatic tools and testing equipment tethered to the wall with hoses and wires.

A shuttle or two might be stored in such a place. In fact, one of the bays housed an old and very much disassembled three-seater, charred from re-entry heat and with gaping holes where viewports used to be. The other housed a stripped-down space bus, dusty and scarred, the kind mining operations used to ferry workers to and from their worksites on distant asteroids. From farther away, Oriannon thought she heard voices and the popping sound of a hammer on metal, and she turned her head to hear better.

Margus was already hurrying toward the noises, perhaps coming from another set of maintenance bays opening off the far side of the main hangar. When he reached the large garage door, he paused with a finger to his lips.

"Follow me."

"And do what?" she asked. Oriannon didn't have time to argue with him as he burst through a side door into the maintenance bay. She stepped on his heels, nearly tripping over him in the confusion.

"Hey!" yelled Margus, and Oriannon stood next to him, wavering and wondering what they were seeing. At the same time, Margus must have realized he didn't have a plan either.

At first, the figure in dirty green coveralls didn't look up from his work on their shuttle. Yes, it was their shuttle, looking just as battered and charred as it had when they had landed. Now the whine of the welding machine and a shower of orange and gold sparks flew as the man worked around two gaping holes in the belly of the ship where the explosion had ripped through the shuttle skin.

"I said, hey!" Margus tried again, but Oriannon held him back. The movement caught the worker's eye. He looked up at them as if he'd been caught, his mouth open in a silent gasp.

"Alymas?" Oriannon couldn't be sure, but it certainly looked like him.

"You didn't do as I asked," he said, cutting the power of his welding torch and stripping off his protective goggles. "You could have been attacked."

All of which was true, but Oriannon couldn't think of a good way to apologize as they came closer. Maybe Margus couldn't either, as he pointed at the shuttle.

"But what are you doing here?" he asked.

Alymas frowned. "What does it look like I'm doing? You had quite a hole in your craft, so my friend and I are welding it shut again. Unless you plan on staying here for a long time, that is."

"Alymas?" came a muffled voice from inside the shuttle. "Who are you talking to?"

"It's the Coristan elder's daughter," Alymas yelled back.

"Who?"

"The elder's daughter!" He raised his voice even more. "The owner of the ship, fool!"

By then Alymas had already covered at least half of the jagged holes with a sheet of titanium plate cut to size. Although the repair might not have looked pretty, it appeared stout enough, perhaps even more so than the hull itself. Alymas picked up his welding torch once again, just as the other Translucent poked his head out of the hatch above.

"I resent the tone of your comments, Alymas," said the friend, "in Coristan, no less, and I still didn't understand what you're trying to tell ... oh!"

Finally the Translucent caught sight of Oriannon and Margus, and he nearly dropped his armload of circuit boards and electronic etcetera.

"Pardon me," he nodded. "But I thought you were still in hiding."

"I tried." Alymas threw up his hands. "But apparently they didn't care to stay hidden."

"Isn't it typical? They're Coristans."

"It's my fault." Margus tried to take the blame. "Oriannon would have stayed put, but I thought we should check on the ship. I thought maybe ..."

"You thought maybe it would be stripped to the bones." Alymas finished the sentence. "And I have to say that normally, that would have been the case. Our people are rather … resourceful."

"But Alymas had other ideas," added the other, a touch of pride showing through his voice. "And since I know a bit of electronics, well, we already have most of your systems back on line."

Oriannon touched the Translucent's arm as he replaced his goggles and picked up his torch again.

"You didn't have to do this," she said.

"Perhaps not." His torch popped to life with an intense blue flame. "But lately I've been, well, shall we say … unemployed. For perhaps the first time in my life, I haven't had anything else to do, and now I can't even tell you what's going to happen an hour from now, much less a day or a week. Although …"

He lowered his torch again, extinguished the flame, and pushed his safety goggles back up on his forehead.

"I can predict we'll have a visit from an angry group of scribes very shortly."

"Alymas!" Oriannon wasn't sure what to make of his words. "You've given up telling futures."

But now he seemed to stare past her shoulder, and she couldn't help turning around to see an angry-looking group of scribes marching across the hangar floor, coming straight at them. And Stratus Main led the charge.

9

"We opened our doors to you," huffed Stratus Main, his face red and puffy, "and look what happens!"

As the scribes fanned out in a half-circle around them, Alymas held his welding torch at the ready, as if it might help defend them.

"What happened?" asked Oriannon "I don't know— "

"Then let me enlighten you," interrupted the scribe, "We've been overwhelmed. We have no security, and no ability to enforce order. And now it's become abundantly clear you've come here with the sole purpose of disrupting and causing division among the residents and guests of Asylum 2."

"That's not true!" Alymas tried to defend them. "They set me free."

"And that's another thing!" The scribe glared at him. "Do you have any idea in what kind of awkward position your little ... confrontation has placed us?"

"You're not serious," Margus blurted out. "You're saying gangsters like Malek run this way station?"

Status Main dodged the question.

"He has nothing to do with it. The only issue now is that you've frightened children with your baseless stories of a fairy-tale threat. In fact, during the past several hours, we have been inundated with complaints from ordinary people who are suddenly worried that we're going to be attacked. This we simply cannot tolerate."

"Oh, come on," argued Margus. "Oriannon was only trying to tell you what she believes."

Oriannon wasn't sure she needed that kind of defense, but at least Margus was being honest.

"What she believes?" Stratus Main narrowed his eyes as he looked from Margus to Oriannon. "Well then. Perhaps you can clarify for us, Miss Hightower, exactly what you do believe. If nothing else, that could assist us to bring a semblance of order to this difficulty."

Oriannon swallowed hard and took a deep breath.

"All right ..." she began. "Since you asked. I believe we're all in very great danger, more than you imagine. Asylum 1 has been destroyed by the Troikans; it no longer exists."

"You can substantiate this accusation?"

"Well, you haven't heard from Asylum 1, have you?"

"An absence of communication proves nothing. Solar activity frequently interferes with com channels. It's not the first time."

"But we saw!" Oriannon tried another way. "We were right there where it should have been, and— "

"And your instruments could have been malfunctioning." Stratus waved at the shuttle. "You've been damaged. And besides, even if it were somehow true that Asylum 1 was not where you thought it should have been, there's no evidence linking the Troikans to that which you think has happened."

The other scribes around him murmured their approval.

"You can believe me or not." She straightened her back as she told him. "I'm telling you that you're in danger, and so are the other way stations. I don't understand why you won't at least listen to what I'm telling you. The Troikans want to take them all."

"Take them?" He laughed. "Where would they take them? I'm afraid you've been seeing too many science fiction stories. We're not a threat to anyone, and we never have been."

"It's not because you're a threat," she answered. "It's because you have something they want. This place. That's what I've been sent to tell you."

This time Stratus Main crossed his arms and turned to the others with a knowing smirk, as if they'd just come to the "I told you so" moment. Slowly he held up his finger to make his point.

"And that's the heart of the matter," he said, turning slowly so that his friends could hear him. "You've insulted one of the most influential leaders in the Translucent community, and you've been responsible for destroying a stable economic relationship between him and his … er, colleague, all in the space of … how long have you been here? I shudder to think how much more damage you could do if you were allowed to stay any longer."

"You can't— " Margus tried to break in, but he was silenced by Stratus Main's accusing finger.

"I have the floor, young man. And it all comes down to this, this so-called mentor you say has sent you here. We've done a bit of research. Isn't it true that this Jesmet was executed back on Corista for being a faithbreaker?"

The anger sparkled in his eyes as he accused her of being a friend of evil, and the accusation chilled her to the core. Even though she knew how wrong he was, she couldn't help gasping in shock.

"He was," she said, "but— "

"And isn't it true that he conspired with the Owlings on your planet to overthrow the legitimate government of Corista?"

Oriannon shook her head at how twisted this inquisition had become.

"No! That's not true. Jesmet isn't interested in overthrowing anything. He's— "

"Don't you mean, he *was*?"

By now Stratus Main grinned in a way that told everyone he'd won, that he'd made his case against the intruders. The rest of the scribes cheered him on, though he raised his hands for silence.

"I'll tell you what, Miss Hightower." He looked down his nose at her, while his voice dripped with condescension. "Your father held an honored position on Corista and would be respected even here among the most remote of way stations. For his sake I'm going to allow you, him, and your friends to leave — without punishment or delay — despite the obvious trouble you've caused us. Others may not be so lenient, which may prove to be an issue if you linger."

He paused and pointed at Alymas. "As for you, I'll give you four hours to complete whatever work you were doing. I can't guarantee their safety any longer than that — or even that long. In fact, even walking across the station, I overheard opinions much more extreme and less reasoned than mine."

"What are you talking about?" asked Margus. "All this, just because of what happened with Alymas?"

"They're frightened of what they do not understand." The scribe shrugged. "However, I would suggest you not wait, because if you run into the wrong factions ... well, there's little I can do, you see."

Alymas looked the scribe straight in the eye and didn't back down. Instead he popped the flame of his welding torch once more, nearly setting Stratus Main's robe on fire.

"I won't need four hours," said Alymas, yanking his safety goggles back over his eyes.

"I'm glad to hear that, for your sake." Stratus Main retreated to a safe distance. "In the meantime, none of you will speak any more about Troikans, or invasions, or your dead mentor. Have I made myself clear?"

He stood for a moment with his eyebrows raised, his point made. Alymas only grunted as he returned to his welding, while Oriannon barely nodded as the scribe led his followers away.

"Nice guy," whispered Margus.

Oriannon didn't reply. She stood quietly for several minutes as the scribes cleared the area—except for one who hung back. The young man bent over as if adjusting his leather sandal, looked around to see that no one else was near, and finally faced them.

"I'm very sorry they treated you like that," he said in a soft voice that thankfully did not carry far. He stood no taller than Margus and hadn't shaved many times, but his bald head left no doubt that he followed the practice of the scribes. "I would have liked to have heard more about your mentor."

"Too bad your friends can't say the same thing," answered Margus.

The scribe shook his head.

"Please take no offense. Stratus Main is a good man, and he knows the Codex well. Perhaps he feels the way station is threatened. I don't know."

"What?" Margus snorted. "I don't think we're a threat."

"No, please listen." The scribe interrupted. "Stratus Main spoke truth about the very real danger here. I have seen myself that many of the refugees, particularly the Translucents, are excitable. So the sooner you repair your ship, the better."

Alymas had already started back to work, immersed in a sea of sparks that didn't seem to bother him.

"Working on it!" he told them over the sizzle and pop of his welding. His friend had already disappeared back into the belly of the ship to continue his repairs. What could Oriannon tell this young scribe?

"You know our names," she ventured, "but yours?"

"Jorr." He bowed his head. "A student of Stratus Main."

"So anything we say to you," said Margus, "we say to your mentor. Isn't that how it works?"

Jorr looked around uncertainly. "Perhaps I should go."

"No, wait!" Ori stepped forward. "You said you wanted to hear more of our mentor. But look, do you know of the Maker's Song?"

He nodded without hesitating.

"Every scribe knows. Codex twelve, forty-seven." And he recited the reference from their holy book: " 'He is the Song that brings light to the heavens, the chorus of life that fills Corista, like the light from the Trion, and . . .' Shall I go on?"

Naturally, Oriannon knew the reference by heart.

"Yes, but who do your scribes say this Song is?" she asked. "It refers to a person, doesn't it? Not just an idea? Isn't that what you're taught?"

"We discuss that question often," he told her, his eyebrows curled in puzzlement. "It's a difficult problem. Different mentors have different opinions."

"Then, here. It's really not that difficult if you can actually hold it." She trembled just a little as she dug the Pilot Stone from the deep folds of her pocket and placed it in his hands. For a moment she worried that she should have kept it hidden after all. But no. She could feel its warmth and heard its Song—the same chorus found in the Codex, written eons ago. Would he hear it the same way? His jaw dropped as he stared at the glistening treasure in his hands.

"A Pilot Stone?" he whispered. "I've heard of them."

"There are only a few, I think. You've heard the Song lives in such a Stone?"

"Inscribed over the ages." He nodded. "But my mentor said Pilot Stones were just an ancient legend, without truth."

"Ancient, yes," she replied. "Legend, no."

"But how— " he began.

"It was given to me to share Jesmet's Song, but we found there was more than that. It guided our ship and brought us here."

"And from here?" he wondered.

"Now I know the way by heart. I don't even have to touch it anymore, and I can still hear the Song. I can feel the Song, like it's part of me. So I can't strap myself to this Stone anymore. I'm slowing it down for the purpose Jesmet intended. Maybe the best thing for me to do is to just pass it along to you … and get out of the way."

Oriannon hadn't practiced the little speech or even had the slightest clue that she would give away the precious Pilot Stone. In fact, the words coming out of her mouth startled her apparently as much as they did the young scribe, who stood there with his mouth agape, his fingers lightly cradling the gift.

"If this is what I think it is …" he didn't finish his sentence, but now shook his head. "I can't accept it. It's too much. Too precious."

But Oriannon held her hand up and backed away just as Alymas's friend poked his head out the main hatch.

"Nav systems back on line," he announced. "Almost there with the atmosphere generators."

Oriannon smiled her thanks and still held out the Stone for Jorr.

"Please take it," she told him, "and just listen to the Song. When you hear it, you'll understand."

"What if I don't hear it?" he asked.

"You will. My mentor says it's one thing to hear, but another thing to understand."

He looked at her as if he understood, finally accepting the gift.

"Just don't lose it, huh?" Margus put in.

Jorr clutched the Stone and shook his head. He would not lose it. Meanwhile, Margus nudged Oriannon toward the exit doors.

"I hate to say it, Ori, but we need to walk back through there to get your dad and Wist."

A gust of fresh air from the ship blew her hair to the side.

"Got it!" yelled the Translucent from inside. "We've got air!"

Oriannon closed her hands around Jorr's—her way of saying good-bye.

"Consider it a loan," she added. "When you know the way, you pass it along to someone else. It's that kind of thing."

"I understand," he replied, smiling broadly.

Now she knew in her heart what she had not understood before, and before she could change her mind and grab the Stone back she turned and joined Margus as they hurried for the exit.

"Twenty minutes, Oriannon," shouted Alymas. "We'll have the rest of it patched up. You just be back here with your father and the Owling friend. Twenty minutes!"

"We'll be back," Oriannon promised him, and without another word she and Margus retraced their steps through the exit and down the long entryway to where it opened into the great hall. Only this time, the way station beyond their shuttle hangar had come to life, and the lights had been turned up to day-bright. Several Translucent women sat tending small cooking fires in simple domed stainless steel braziers, and a sickening smoke made Oriannon's eyes water.

Surely the scribes don't like this! she thought. As she wiped away the tears, the smell reminded her of burnt plastic, and her stomach turned when she looked down to see several charred . . . she couldn't decide. The six legs and singed hair told her they were probably preparing a vile rodent of some kind, or maybe a huge insect, but twisted beyond recognition. This was breakfast?

Waving off nausea, Oriannon paused in the midst of the crowds as hundreds of refugees pressed in around her, much like the day they had arrived. The only difference this time was that instead of offering a show for Oriannon and Margus, now Oriannon herself felt watched.

"Stay by me," Margus took her arm. He hadn't done that before, but this time she knew why, and she shivered all over again as she felt the malevolent stares and heard the whispered comments brimming with sharp, venomous barbs.

"That's her," said someone off to the side. "Someone tell Malek."

"The elder's daughter and her friend," whispered someone else, in a tone no less sinister.

Margus guided her around a frowning Translucent man, his arms crossed in an unspoken challenge and the corners of his lips curled down in a simmering snarl. The man barely gave way, forcing them to weave around him and step over a stack of large water jugs.

Just ahead, a huddle of four ragged-looking young Coristan men gathered around a dim 3-D projection of a talking head, shaved in the manner of a scribe and quite worked up. But like boys on the playground who had been caught looking at something naughty, they snapped off the projection and just stared at her and Margus as they passed by.

"Hey," said Margus, his voice sounding weak and hoarse. "How's it going?"

Oriannon wished he had kept his mouth shut, but the young men didn't answer, only stared. Overnight, she and Margus had turned into the worst kind of pariahs, and now she knew all too well that every eye in the huge open mall had fixed on them. Even from the balconies overhead she could make out the shadowy figures of scribes, sometimes pulling discreetly back behind shades, but other times leaning boldly forward, watching.

Margus fumed and mumbled something about being sorry for not having taken a sonic shower the past couple of days. But they could only hurry on, zig-zagging through the waking crowd as quickly as they could, avoiding bedrolls, babies, and backpacks. A young Translucent boy came running through the chaos, sliding to a stop when he nearly ran into them, then backing away as if they carried a plague.

Oriannon stumbled over another boy's foot, outstretched purposely or accidentally, she couldn't say. Margus did manage to grab her by the elbow before she sprawled on her face. He shook his head then, dug his heels in, and lifted his chin to the crowds.

"That's it," he mumbled. Oriannon wasn't quite sure what he meant, but she was quite sure it could not be good.

"No, Margus," she whispered, then yanked on his hand. This time he would not move. "Forget about it. Let's just keep going."

Margus would not listen.

"What do you want with us?" he yelled at the top of his lungs, and instantly all the murmuring and the whispering around them stopped. If people had been staring before, now Oriannon and Margus had become the undisputed main attraction. A baby fussed from somewhere in the far corner, and someone coughed. Ori remembered the same kind of quiet back home in the temple courts of Seramine, the kind of quiet you could almost reach out and touch, when hushed whispers could barely be heard above the cooing of moordoves.

This time, however, she would rather have disappeared into the cracks between the glazed floor tiles then stand there and let everyone stare at her. Margus, however, had a different idea.

"That's right." Now he raised his hands and twirled. "Since everybody's staring, maybe you can just take a really good look and get it over with, huh?"

"Margus, stop. Please stop." Oriannon whispered in desperation as she tugged at his sleeve. No one said a word in reply; they just stared at the strange and disruptive visitors.

"Margus," she tried again. "If we don't get out of here right now, that fellow Malek is going to show up. Didn't you hear what they were saying?"

Fortunately and finally that seemed to make sense to Margus, and with some effort she was able to drag him along. He frowned, and they made their way through the crowd once again, and the people parted to either side.

"Seen enough?" asked Margus, but no one answered. Oriannon wondered if anyone might think to follow them into the maze of tunnels, where she prayed Wist and her father still waited.

"This way," she guided Margus right, then left, ducking her head to avoid a low-hanging pipe. She looked back frequently to see if anyone trailed them, while keeping one hand on Margus's shoulder.

"Glad you remember," Margus told her. "I'd be totally lost in here."

Oriannon didn't answer. Part of her wished she could strangle him for what he'd just done to call so much attention to themselves. But another part knew that he had probably not changed anything. They rounded a corner and stopped, both of them breathing heavily, and they listened.

"What's that?" Margus cocked his head to the side, but Oriannon shook her head and pushed on through a quieter stretch of tunnel. A red light mounted on the wall seemed to blink a warning.

The echoes of distant footsteps made her press on faster, and they continued deeper into the maze toward the hiding place where her father and Wist waited with Sola Minnik. A minute later, Margus stopped again.

"This way, right?" He pointed down any empty hall that looked unfamiliar to Oriannon. Large ventilation pipes lined the low ceiling, shaking in a sort of harmonic tremor.

"No." She turned the opposite direction, but now that choice looked just as unfamiliar. Truth was, in the panic of the moment she couldn't be sure. Margus looked at her with wide eyes.

"Ori! Can't you remember the way back?"

"Sure I can." She looked left, then right, then left again. "This just doesn't look like anything I remember."

Finally they started down the hallway Margus suggested. They had only taken a few steps when they heard voices almost right behind them.

"In here!" whispered Margus, motioning to an open access hatch. They dove through the round opening and pressed in as closely as they could, but Oriannon knew they would not be completely hidden if anyone chose to look carefully. Still, it was the best they could do as their pursuers came closer.

"They're in here somewhere, Malek," said one of the voices just outside the hatch door. "I know I saw the elder's daughter go this direction. They couldn't have disappeared."

"Well, when we find them," answered Malek, "they truly will."

Oriannon hugged the shadows and tried to ignore a scorching geyser of steam only centimeters from her face. Margus closed his eyes and didn't move as the voices moved past and faded.

"Are they gone?" whispered Margus. Oriannon didn't answer as she unfolded from their hiding place and started down the hallway in the opposite direction. Three steps later, she broke into a run, racing Margus in a mad dash as she let her memories take over, leading them down one long passage to the next. Finally they stood gasping outside the door to the storage room.

"I told you ..." Margus gasped for breath. "You would know the way."

Maybe so. But with Malek and his friends now searching the hallways for them, they had run out of time to talk about it. Oriannon pushed at the door carefully, and wasn't surprised that it would not open.

"Wist!" she leaned closer and called, rapping her knuckles on the heavy metal door. "Wist, it's me!"

Without hesitation the door swung open, and Wist pulled her by the arm into the darkened room. Margus tumbled after them.

"Where in the world have you been disappearing to?" Wist sounded more desperate than Oriannon had expected. "It's not making me confident when I woke up and you are gone."

"I'm sorry, Wist." Oriannon gripped her Owling friend's shoulders and wished she could explain. "I thought we would get back sooner, but Malek Fram — "

"We barely made it through the great hall," interrupted Margus. Wist's eyes grew even larger, if that was possible.

"We'll explain later," said Oriannon, "but right now we have to get out of here!"

Oriannon followed Wist's look to where Tavlin Hightower stood shivering against the wall, a blanket around his shoulders. At least he was standing; perhaps that was a sign of improvement.

"He says he is feeling better," whispered Wist. "But ever since he's been waking up he's been shivering, and I don't think he's all the time knowing where he is. He's not knowing who I am."

Oriannon stepped over to face her father.

"Daddy?" she searched his eyes for a clue, but they looked far away and distracted, and he struggled to keep his balance. This was not the father she had once known. But at the sound of her voice he seemed to snap to attention, and he looked down at her with a hint of his old self, the Assembly elder and strong father she had always respected. A twinkle of hope glittered briefly in his eyes, only to disappear as quickly as it appeared. Even so, he remained on his feet, drew the blanket around his shoulders a little more tightly, and managed a weak smile.

"We'll get you out of here soon, honey." Now his voice sounded barely above a hoarse whisper, and as she leaned forward, she did her best not to let him see her trembling. He pushed away from her shoulder, then wobbled a bit before leaning up against the wall. "I'll take care of you, so don't you worry a bit."

"I'm not worried about that." If she could just get him past Malek Fram and Stratus Main, away from this insane place … "We'll find you a proper healer at the next way station."

She turned away in time to see a movement in the shadows and realized with a sinking feeling that Sola hadn't left them. Sola dared to show her face, and step out into the light.

"I knew we should never have come to this place," said Sola in her best I-told-you-so voice. Oriannon couldn't believe Sola would still have the nerve.

"You don't know anything!" Margus shot back, and Oriannon didn't blame him. Without warning and without knowing what had suddenly bubbled up inside her, Oriannon brushed by Margus and stepped over to confront the woman herself.

"You did this to him!" Oriannon told her. She didn't care about being nice. So what if anyone else heard? She clenched a fist in front of Sola's unseeing eyes, wishing she could use it. "You did this to us! And you know what? I hate you. I hate you!"

Once again her own words startled her, only this time in a very different way. Who was this angry person about to attack a blind woman? Sola wrinkled her face and squinted, as if she was trying desperately to see what was happening. As Oriannon opened her trembling fist, Sola cringed and turned away.

"You hate me, Oriannon?" she finally whispered. "You and me both."

"Oriannon." She felt her father's hand on her shoulder, but she shrugged it off and escaped to the front of the room, near the door. This time she wanted no comfort, she only wanted to hold on to what was left of the boiling hate. Margus said nothing, but Wist looked at Oriannon with horror.

"That wasn't you, Ori," she said. "You're not meaning that."

"I do too. You know it's true." The acid words now burned her tongue. "You of all people."

Wist tried to turn away, but Oriannon wouldn't let her.

"She's the one who turned your people into slaves," said Oriannon. "Or have you forgotten already?"

"I'm not forgetting. It's just that— "

"She's the one who nearly killed Father and who totally destroyed the Corista we once knew. It's too late to defend her."

"You know I wouldn't be defending her for any of that. But, Ori ..." Wist fumbled for words.

She can't say anything because she knows I'm right. Doesn't she?

"Ori," put in Margus, motioning toward the door. "We need to cut this short."

"Fine. But you know what else?" Oriannon did her best to add another layer of right to her argument, which felt like it was slipping fast and was in need of shoring up. "This gives us a chance to leave the wicked witch of Corista behind in a place where she's sure to be more at home. Right, Sola? Why don't you just leave us alone?"

"I wish I could," whispered Sola. She stood in the middle of the room by herself, and she fumbled as if she didn't know what to do with her hands. Oriannon looked at Margus, who stood watch by the door. He nodded at them and motioned for them to get ready.

"As soon as it's clear," he told them, "let's get out of here while we still can."

10

By the time they gathered at the door, the twenty minutes Alymas gave them had long since passed. Still, the only thing for them to do was to follow the lead of Margus, and make a run for the shuttle. Oriannon quickly filled Wist in on the details of what Alymas had done for them.

"This reminds me too much of the last place we had to escape," Margus told them as they slipped through the door and out into the corridor. He was just about to secure the door behind them when they noticed Sola Minnik still standing in the middle of the room, her shoulders shaking. Strange how one minute she could be so defiant and thumbing her nose at the world, and the next minute ...

Pitiful.

"Don't leave me here," said Sola. She must have known they hadn't left yet. "Please. I know you hate me, but they'll kill me here. I know they will. Please help me."

Where had they heard that line before? Please help me. Hanging off the landing ladder of the shuttle, just about to slip to her death?

Oriannon and Margus looked at each other, and this time Ori couldn't make herself respond. Surely it would have been so much easier to close the door behind them. Surely it would have lightened their load.

As it turned out, Wist was the first to move. Without a word or a complaint she backtracked and took Sola by the arm. Sola didn't even ask who it was but accepted the helping hand.

"They don't know me here," mumbled Sola. "I've tried to tell them, don't you know? But no one will believe me. No one listens."

"Wist!" Oriannon blocked the way. "She's our enemy. Don't you get it? She's using you again. Playing the sympathy card, like, poor-blind-woman me. Don't you see?"

But Wist wasn't backing down, and it must have surprised Margus as much as it did Oriannon.

"Maybe she is. But she's going to be dying here as sure as your father would—unless we take her with us. Are you wanting that on your conscience?"

"It's not like that, Wist."

"No? You helped me pull her into the shuttle, even when you knew who she was. And didn't you say Jesmet said to be keeping her with you?"

"But that was different. That was before ..."

Oriannon's voice trailed off as she searched her memory for a loophole, some kind of way to change the truth that had come crashing down on her head. But no matter how hard she tried, she could not find one.

"Listen, guys," said Margus. "One way or the other, we've got to get out of here. With Sola or not, but we're going. It may already be too late."

Finally she sighed and stepped aside, ignoring Margus but holding fast to her father. Did Jesmet really want them to drag this woman along, no matter what she had done to the Owlings and to her father? No matter what she had said? It made no sense. Perhaps she really had misunderstood him, or his intent.

"I think we need to go, Ori." Her father's thin voice broke the silence. And while she could not be sure how much he understood, she could not argue. They had to hurry back to the ship now, before the angry Translucents caught up to them. Alymas was probably wondering what had happened to them.

And now he would have all the more reason to worry. As they came around the last corner before the ceiling opened up into the grand hall, they faced Malek Fram and his mob of fifteen or twenty Translucents. Several held hefty titanium prybars, crudely sharpened into brutal weapons. Perhaps they couldn't match a security's high-tech stun baton or the devastating effectiveness of a particle weapon, but the effect would be the same. And Oriannon didn't want to imagine what that might be.

Before anyone could say a word, however, her father broke free of her grip and walked uncertainly toward Malek. Margus jumped to hold him back, but they ended up standing nose-to-nose with Malek and his taller friends.

"Father!" cried Oriannon, but it was too late. Though her father could hardly speak, he still apparently knew enough to recognize a threat when he saw one. And for just a moment Malek drew back, apparently confused.

"Do you know who this is?" asked Margus. He glanced at Oriannon as if to tell her to play along.

Malek found his voice.

"Don't know and don't—"

"He's Tavlin Hightower of Nyssa, elder of the Coristan Ruling Assembly. I believe you've met his daughter?"

"Daughter?" Now Malek looked really confused. His bodyguards still hefted their prybars and seemed as if they very much wanted to try them out.

"That's right. As a matter of fact, we were in contact with Coristan Security not too long ago. Maybe you didn't know, but several Coristan Security cruisers followed us. So if anything happened to Elder Hightower and his daughter, well, you wouldn't want to have to explain that now, would you?"

Oriannon held her breath as the Translucent considered Margus's threat. Well, it had been true that Security had been following them. At this point, however, it was probably better not to explain the circumstances in too much detail.

"I don't explain anything to Coristans." Malek sneered, but held his gang back on either side. Any one could have flattened her father with a single blow. But Oriannon knew that at least one of them would regret it. Though she had no idea what she would do or how to do it, she flexed her hands and got ready to spring at them.

Malek narrowed his eyes in unmasked hatred and slowly stepped aside, nodding with his head for his bodyguards to do the same. Oriannon lost no time as she and Margus guided her father away without another word. Hopefully Wist would follow right behind them.

"We'll see you again," said Malek, making no attempt to disguise his contempt. "You owe me for what you did to my business, you know. My property."

Oriannon didn't try to defend herself, but hurried away as fast as she dared push her father. She wondered how long he could keep this up. Once more the semiconscious fog had draped him in its arms, while she strained to keep him from stumbling.

"You with us, Wist?" She looked over her shoulder to see the Owling girl, and her heart fell when she realized Sola still gripped Wist's arm. Thankfully, Sola had not challenged Malek, which would have made things worse.

However, by the time they stepped into the crowded grand hall, Oriannon guessed that things had indeed grown worse—dangerously worse.

"Why are we stopping?" asked Sola, still gasping for breath after the hurry-up run through the corridors. "What's going on?"

She was right to be worried, as crowds around them darkened and filled in like thunderclouds before a downpour. Only in this case, the downpour came in the form of rotten aplon peels and pungent wey curds — the worst garbage these people could find.

Angry voices pressed in on them from both sides. "You're not welcome here," said an older man.

"Kill the Coristans!" screamed another. "Malek says they bring evil!"

A shiver shot up Oriannon's spine when a surge of the crowd seemed to agree with that statement. Whatever other lies Malek must have told them, these people had found a convenient scapegoat for their troubles.

Once again, the entire refugee population gathered in the open mall. This time, they weren't content just to stare and whisper. They pressed in around Oriannon, her father, Margus, Wist, and Sola.

"You think you're holier than us?" A red-faced Coristan man leaned in to taunt them as he spat out the words.

"Nobody wants to hear about your dead mentor!" yelled another woman, anger bulging her eyes. "Malek says my daughter is sick because of you. You did this to us!"

The words jolted Oriannon as if someone had slapped her across the face and the awful sting knocked her backward, reeling under the weight of truth. For a moment she wondered if her own anger at Sola looked or sounded anything like this.

She knew it did. But still she crouched between knowing and admitting, and in this insane cauldron of yelling and shouting people, she could not be sure of anything beyond the venom of the crowd.

This riot, however, did not allow Oriannon the luxury of contemplation, and she backed away from the woman who had confronted her. Right now she knew well how close they skated to disaster, or to someone getting really hurt. A chunk of something heavy — perhaps a piece of furniture — crashed at her feet, barely missing Margus.

Still they pushed on through the grand hall, bumping against the mob and wading through the angry odors of sweat and fiery breath. A solid wall of nasty, threatening refugees stood between them and their shuttle, jostling and threatening anyone who dared to pass. Did the angry crush spill over into the hangar area as well? Just over their shoulders the wonderful Trion sculpture stood watch. If they could only find a way out!

Even if they did manage to slip away from this nightmare, though, how could she escape herself? Her own hatred? She had no answer.

"How are we getting out of here?" asked Wist, whose viewpoint in the packed crowd would have been even more limited than Oriannon's. At least Oriannon could see a few layers of people ahead of her — not that it looked any better. She winced as another piece of well-aimed rotten simquat hit her square on the shoulder and splattered. It had either been lobbed over everyone's heads or — more likely — dropped from a balcony above.

"How dare you!" Sola screeched as someone pushed her from behind and she stumbled to her knees. Even the blind woman couldn't miss the hostile wave that had washed over them. However, her father showed no sign that he knew what was going on. In this case, thought Oriannon, that would be just as well. She reached out to help Sola to her feet, but then changed her mind and pulled back her hand. Oriannon avoided the Owling girl's quick look.

I don't need that, Wist, she thought, unable to voice her excuse. Right now she couldn't handle any more judgment — from the crowd, from Wist, or even from herself.

Maybe later. Not now.

Either way, they had to find a way through this horror show before someone was hurt, or worse. Before one of these hurled pieces of scrap metal met its mark and dropped them where they stood.

11

Long minutes later, Oriannon and the others still struggled through the nasty mob, ducking what was thrown at them from above and dodging insults and curses hurled at them from below. Margus held up his hand in front of Oriannon's face when a particularly angry young man spit at them.

"We've got to get out of here!" she told Margus.

Now more and more people began shouting and chanting in the peculiar Translucent language—harsh, insistent, and louder by the minute.

"Agez! Agez!" they shouted, shaking their fists in the air over and over.

A moment later it became clear that the Translucents weren't focused only on Oriannon and her friends, but they were also battling each other, as well as a few Coristans.

Two or three meters away, several tall young men scuffled with a small company of scribes, ripping at their robes and tearing at their faces. Oriannon took advantage of this disturbance and pressed ahead. As Oriannon pushed past, she heard one of the scribes grunting "Let them go!" and "They have a right to be heard!"

"Are they talking about us?" Margus shouted in her ear, for by this time the noise level had ratcheted up to the point where screams and shouts blended into an unbearable stew of noise, over-seasoned with a barrage of the most horrendous insults Oriannon had ever heard — and hoped she never would again.

It didn't matter who the scribes were talking about. The good news was that their line of unexpected defenders had opened up a narrow walkway for them, and now they were able to slip through under a new hail of pungent refuse. Oriannon slipped on aplon rinds while a small piece of jagged metal glanced off Sola's forehead, drawing blood before she clapped a hand on the wound with a cry of pain.

Still they pushed on through the riot, dodging curses and projectiles that grew thicker with every step they took into enemy territory. A Translucent's sharp elbow caught Oriannon in the chin, knocking her sideways and sending a lightning shaft of pain through her jaw so intense she gasped. She clutched her jaw with her free hand, held her father's arm with the other, and kept going.

How can these people be so angry? she wondered. *And who taught them to hate us so much?*

Next to that, her father's wide-eyed confusion told her all she needed to know for the moment. Since he had slipped back into his fog and didn't see the raging storm around them, she focused on getting across the great hall and escaping through the double doors to the hangar deck. From there, well, they would take that as it came.

If she couldn't get through this crowd, they would surely be trampled. In the fury of the moment Oriannon almost didn't see the face of the young scribe who had stayed behind at the shuttle — Jorr. He looked up at her and reached out just as he fell underneath the feet of that awful tide.

"Miss Hightower!" he cried. She reached for him and managed to grab his outstretched hand — and she was wrenched away from her father.

"No!" she screamed. Though she yelled for Margus to hold on, the crowd had already jostled her away and she was now next to Jorr, shoulder-to-shoulder. Somehow she escaped being trampled herself, though for the moment she couldn't move and could hardly breathe.

The poor wispy-haired scribe right next to her gasped in pain. "I am sorry we couldn't hold them back." Jorr's voice came in shallow gulps, barely audible above the screams and shouts of the crowd. Remarkably, he smiled as he spoke. "I wasn't able to pass it along yet. I would have. But here."

He held the Pilot Stone for her to take. When she hesitated, he slipped it into her hand and closed her fingers around it just to be sure.

"But ..." She wasn't sure how to say no to him. "No, wait. It's too soon. You have plenty of time to pass it along. I meant for you to have it. That's what Jesmet wanted me to do."

"Yes, you did." He nodded and smiled again but he didn't—or wouldn't—take it back. "And I'm sure he did too. But it's not too soon. You saved my life."

His words were strange, considering where he found himself. She looked around again at the crowd and smelled the death that pressed in around them, but she felt a strange calm and could not argue.

"I heard his Song, Oriannon Hightower," he explained above the din, and his words rang both clear and true as he quoted again the words of the Codex, now so much alive for him: "'He is the Song that brings light to the heavens, the chorus of life that fills Corista, like the light from the Trion.' Miss Hightower, I heard it for the first time!"

"But ... so soon? It took me a lot longer. Days. Weeks, even. How did you—?"

He shrugged as well as he could, though the effort made him grimace with pain when two more Translucents pushed in from the side.

"I've been looking," he whispered, his voice growing weaker. The light in his eyes dimmed. "As it turns out, so has he."

"No, please. Jorr! Don't let go."

He smiled again, weaker still.

"Will you give it to someone else now? I know where you're going; they'll want to hear the Song as well."

"But—"

"No, it's right. I know this is right."

Still he smiled, and as the crowd surged once more she lost sight of his face.

He should have kept it, she told herself. *I should not have taken it back!*

She clutched the Pilot Stone, once again feeling the comfort of its warmth. She did everything in her power not to fall beneath the crush of bodies. Suddenly, she felt a hand on her shoulder, a tug ... and a moment later she fell into the clear with Margus. She rolled once and rose to her knees before Alymas pulled her up and away from the chanting, angry mob.

"What about Father?" she asked, waving back at the crowd. Several scribes with worried expressions stood aside as Margus nearly pushed her through the double doors leading to the hangar deck.

"He's already on board!" shouted Alymas. "Now go!"

By this time their shuttle was already taxiing out of its place in the hangar, pushed by a little bug-like vehicle running on a track in the floor. The shuttle's hatch flipped wide open, while its engines whined, so there was nothing to do but run with Margus to the door, grab Wist's hand, and flop inside as the door slammed shut behind them.

"Alymas!" Oriannon looked back through the small viewport in the hatch and caught their friend's eye. He smiled and nodded, holding up his hand. She did the same.

Margus panted, catching his breath. "Did anyone else get the impression they wanted us to leave?"

Oriannon looked around just to be sure her father really was aboard, but felt her heart sink when she realized Sola had made it too.

"They didn't want us to leave," growled Sola, wiping the blood off her face as she made her way to her cabin. "They wanted to kill us."

The door closed with a swoosh behind the blind woman as she disappeared without another word. Oriannon wished she wasn't right.

Meanwhile, Tavlin Hightower rested quietly in one of the main cabin's reclining chairs. Once again Oriannon could not tell if he was awake or asleep, or just how alive he was. Wist sat crumpled on the floor in the forward control room, trying to catch her breath. And so they were off again. Only, to where? Oriannon thought she knew the only option as she followed Margus to a place in one of the three forward swivel seats.

"Asylum 3?" she asked. Margus sat and made a few adjustments to his controls. At least they seemed to light up this time. Alymas and his friend had come through for them in a big way.

"Wist and I were talking," he finally answered, and the words jolted her. "And, uh, we're both wondering if it's not time to get back to Corista."

"What?" She sat down. "Talking? When did you do that?"

He shrugged. "I don't know. While you were resting. Just, you know . . . talking."

"Talking behind my back!"

"Ori, wait." He held up his hands. "Don't take it the wrong way."

"How am I supposed to take it?" She pressed her lips together as they rolled through the hangar deck. Would her friends really betray her like this?

"Look," she told him, not waiting for an answer, "we still don't know what Corista is like, or how dangerous it is for people like my dad. It hasn't been that long, you know."

"I know." He frowned. "But it's our home, Ori."

"*Was*. Your parents are— " She bit her tongue before she could say "both gone," and tried to change the subject. "I mean, what about Sola?"

At least Margus could admit she was right on that point, and he thankfully ignored her slip of tongue.

"I suppose that might be a problem."

They both held on as the shuttle jolted, and the nav systems came on line with a hum. Through the forward observation ports, she could see massive doors opening out into the blackness of space. Distant white-blue pinpoints of light told her the way was clear.

"Okay," she told him, "so two things. First, the healer on Asylum 3 is way closer than Corista would be, and we need to get my dad some help as soon as we can. I can't tell if he's getting worse or better."

Margus sighed as if he knew she was right. "The other thing?"

"The other thing is that Jesmet told us ... *me* to keep going."

At that, Margus looked up from his controls and faced her.

"Keep going, Ori? For how long?"

"Look, Margus. I want to go home as much as anybody. You have no idea. But we need to keep going for ... I don't know for sure."

"You don't? Well that's just fine, because if we're going to go rocketing off to another asylum station, I thought it might be good if at least one of us was sure. You know what I mean?" He waved his hand wildly. "Because we sure had a great time at Asylum 2, didn't we! Is that what you think Jesmet wanted us to do in your dream ... I mean, your vision?"

Oriannon shivered at the thought that her best friend doubted. Still he looked at her, searching for answers that she couldn't yet give him, and she wanted to apologize for dragging them halfway across their solar system, for risking all their lives. But it wasn't her fault! And what else could she do but listen to the vision Jesmet had given her?

"I'm sorry," she began, struggling to find an explanation that didn't sound stupid or naïve, the way she felt. "I was just trying to—"

"Forget it, okay? Just forget it. I just thought you were more ... I don't know ... more of a Coristan."

"What? Where did that come from?"

"I don't know. I was just wondering if you thought you would ever go back home, or if you even think it's home any more."

His words dug to the heart of something she had not understood until now. What was she first? A Coristan? The daughter of her father? Or now something else entirely? The ship jolted once again, the engines whining louder and louder.

"What did you want to do?" she finally responded, raising her voice to make herself heard. "Stay there in the Owling prison camp? I can't believe you're saying this."

"Me neither." He frowned as he worked on the ship's nav and thrust controls. "But this really isn't the time, is it?"

Several loud alarms sounded, and a launch screen descended to eye-level, demanding their attention. But she couldn't let the matter just drop, not like this.

Wist didn't join in the argument; she remained on the floor and never looked up. By this time most of the fire had drained from Oriannon as well. Maybe, just maybe, Margus was right. Maybe it was safe to return to Corista, and maybe they wouldn't be arrested for a hundred different offenses, not the least of which were stealing a government shuttle and kidnapping the planet's dictator. Nothing they couldn't explain though.

From somewhere behind them, even over the noise of the engine, she heard her father cough. If it weren't for her father ...

"Margus," she tried once again from a different direction. "Please. I've never begged you to do something for me before. But this time I'm begging you not to steer this ship back to Corista. Please. After we get to Asylum 3 we can talk about it again."

"Why would things be any different there? How do we know they won't try to kill us there too?"

"I don't know, Margus. All I know is what Jesmet told me to do. I just need to warn them, and then if they don't believe me, well, I can't do anything about it."

"That's encouraging."

"That's all I have. I'll tell you this: Once we get there, I promise I'll listen to you. But my father ..."

Margus looked back at her father, then at Wist and her. He shook his head.

"All right," he finally answered. "For your dad's sake ... and for as long as this ship holds together. But I'm not going to all twelve asylum stations. And I'm going to have to do a lot of the navigating myself this time, since you got rid of that Pilot Stone."

The Pilot Stone! Oriannon reached into her pocket to feel its heat, as warm as ever, and she wondered what had happened to the scribe who had returned it to her.

"Actually, Margus." She held it up to show him.

The floor shifted beneath her feet as they catapulted away from the way station, out into empty space and on their own again. The ship groaned at the strain, and she winced at the sound of a crack somewhere below. Maybe the shuttle's skin could not bear the strain after all.

If that's what you have for us, Jesmet. Then that's what he had for them. No matter her doubts or anyone else's, Oriannon knew in her heart they had to go on.

12

Oriannon pretended to sleep as the ship continued on its new course to Asylum 3. The floor definitely vibrated a bit more than it had before, but the patch Alymas welded in place seemed to be holding—for now. So far, so good.

The good news was that Asylum 3 was much closer than Corista—only another five hours ahead if they continued on their present course and speed. She lifted her feet off the floor to keep from feeling the worrisome rumble, which felt something like harmonic feedback from a microphone placed too close to a loudspeaker. She curled up and snuggled deeper under the folds of a foil blanket that kept her more or less warm, since the environmental heating unit still wasn't working properly. Their ship's systems obviously weren't one hundred percent.

She could also tell something was not one hundred percent with *her.* No, not in the way her father battled his infections and internal injuries. But as sleep refused to come, she wished more and more for another vision from Jesmet—another sign that perhaps she wasn't going crazy after all.

She thrashed about in her chair, unable to get comfortable as her arms and legs twitched and her mind raced. If she understood what she was supposed to do — travel to the next way station and warn the people there of the Troikan threat — why did it still seem so complicated? Wasn't there a better way?

And if she was supposed to tell the scribes about Jesmet, why did that seem so hard as well? She could think of one reason.And though she tried to steer her thoughts away from Sola, she still could not help seething with anger at the thought of what the woman had done to her and to her family. To all of Corista!

She still thinks she can act all weak and helpless now, thought Ori, *and Wist will feel sorry for her and forget what she did to the Owlings.*

Somehow, Oriannon vowed, Sola's charade had to stop — and maybe she was the one to stop it.

She lay curled up, her mind spinning and fuming, when a familiar sound caught her attention and she cracked her eyes open to see Sola's door grind open. Sola's dim form stood in the doorway for a moment before she reached out her hands and felt her way into the main cabin. Still Oriannon watched, silently, waiting to see where Sola was going, watching as the woman approached the place where her father lay resting. Oriannon tensed up, ready to spring to her father's defense. Perhaps her blanket rustled; Sola paused and turned her head while Oriannon froze, still curious.

What is she up to?

Sola inched closer, pausing every few shuffle-steps to get her bearings. Oriannon watched and waited, wondering whether she could get help from Margus and Wist quickly enough.

Only not yet, not quite. Now Sola stood almost directly over Oriannon's father and turned her head again as if listening for the gentle rhythm of his breathing. It would not be hard; Oriannon could hear it from where she crouched several meters away. Still Sola hovered, as if deciding what to do. But when she turned her head just right, Oriannon saw what she expected least.

Sola's tears.

Oriannon could hardly believe Sola knew how to cry real tears. But here, Sola would not be aware of an audience — no one to put on a show for.

"I suppose you wouldn't believe me if I told you I was sorry for the way things turned out, would you?"

Sola's words nearly made Oriannon shout a reply. She'd heard more than enough lies from this woman. Who needed one more? But she held her tongue to see what would come next as Sola reached down to rest her hand on Tavlin Hightower's shoulder. And then Sola laughed, softly, and with a measure of sadness.

"We make quite the couple, I suppose." Her words held none of the usual swagger, which surprised Oriannon but made her no less suspicious. "I can't see you, and at the moment you can't hear me. I suppose that's justice. You always did say your Maker wanted justice above all else, didn't you?"

For once Sola had it right. Tavlin Hightower's Maker did in fact demand justice and obedience, as Oriannon had learned growing up in an elder's home. Oriannon had in fact been raised with that kind of Maker, cold and distant, the cruel judge of anyone who dared step beyond the narrow bounds of what was expected. Perhaps that had been why the Owlings had seemed so strange to her when they sang and danced and claimed to know the same Maker. Perhaps that was why Oriannon had taken so long to recognize Jesmet's Song. Perhaps that was why Oriannon couldn't help listening as Sola went on.

"Well, now that I'm on the receiving end of that justice, I can't say that I've enjoyed it. I'm much better at dishing it out."

Again she chuckled, yet even softer and with more sadness. Oriannon's father didn't move, and his eyes didn't even flutter.

What are you doing? Oriannon nearly shouted, but something held her back. Perhaps morbid curiosity, the way some people gathered around a terrible accident, unable to keep their eyes from a collision. Sola Minnik had more to confess.

"But let me tell you something, Tavlin," she went on, almost as if speaking to a friend—which she most certainly was not. "I want you to know that I only acted to save Corista. I only wanted what was best for the planet, if you can believe that. Maybe you can't. But it's the truth. My mistake was believing the Troikans when they first came to me. My mistake was actually believing all they wanted was the Owling workers. Wouldn't it have been nice if that's all they wanted?"

Slowly it began to make sense. But now Sola turned away to wipe another tear from her glistening cheeks, even as she waggled a finger of warning at Oriannon's father. As if he could see her pitiful warning, and as if she could see his lifeless reaction.

"I'll tell you what, though. You elders could have made it easier for me. So much easier. Didn't you realize? You could have backed me up, shown a united front, and things might have been different. We could have stood up to the Troikans right from the start. But, no! You forced me into the corner. And when they started making more demands on us, I needed to show them I was strong! We had no choice if Corista was going to survive. Don't you understand?"

Oriannon's reasons for hating Sola grew. But the clearest emotion she could conjure up felt like a feeble blend of pity and contempt, a low-grade loathing that made her want to take a sonic shower to rid herself of the greasy feeling.

Meanwhile, Sola dissolved into more tears, taking several moments to compose herself again. It was a good thing she didn't know Oriannon was listening to every word of this confession.

"So now perhaps we've lost the planet," said Sola, "not just the miserable little Owlings. Oh, and all the asylum way stations as well. I fail to see how that's a major loss, however, given the kind of lowlife those stations have attracted over the years."

Oriannon might have mentioned some of the scribes who risked their lives to help them escape, but she once again bit her tongue. Besides, Sola wasn't finished yet.

"I'll tell you one thing, though, Elder Hightower: I may be blind and slipping off the emotional edge, but I am still not as helpless as you might think. If there's a way to strike back at these Troikan pigs, I'm going to find it!" She leaned toward Tavlin's face. "I am not going to be just *your* worst nightmare, Tavlin Hightower, but *theirs*! I'm not finished yet. I'm going to destroy them or die trying!"

Her rising voice finally woke Oriannon's father. He stirred and twisted his head slightly, blinking his eyes as he emerged from a deep sleep. He didn't seem to recognize the woman standing in front of him, a fact which she seemed to understand even if she could not see his face. In an insane display of emotion, she turned from rage to contrite sorrow, almost from one breath to the next.

"I regret hurting you, Tavlin." The tears returned now, streaming down from her unseeing eyes, and she reached for his hand. Oriannon almost couldn't watch; her stomach turned at the sight. "I—I'm sorry. Do you hear me? I'm apologizing once, and it's not going to happen again, so you'd better listen. I should have trusted you more. Of all the elders, you were the one who stood up to me. Now look what's happened to us. But I'll make it right. Ask your Maker if I won't!"

She turned away, her words finally spent. She let Tavlin's hand drop just as Oriannon's blanket slipped off her shoulders. Sola stiffened as she wiped the tears from her cheeks with a sleeve of her frayed tunic.

"Who's there?" she asked, and the hard edge returned instantly to her voice. "I heard you!"

Oriannon could have hidden in plain sight if she had enough patience. Come to think of it, maybe she should, because right now she had no stomach for Sola Minnik, no desire to say one word to her, no matter how many apologies she had just heard from the woman's lips. Perhaps Jesmet would not act this way, but for the moment she could do nothing else.

So she simply said nothing, while Sola's face turned red. Sola sniffled and swiped a stray tear, steaming with obvious anger or embarrassment, or both. Seconds ticked by.

"Fine," Sola finally muttered after the long face-off. Hands outstretched to make sure she didn't trip, she hurried back to the shelter of her cabin without another word.

For her part, Oriannon settled back into her chair, wishing again for a vision to keep her resolve from slipping. She couldn't help feeling more and more alone as the ship rumbled on. The only thing she knew for sure was that she would not find sleep before they got to where they were going.

13

Five hours later they put down in the smallish landing bay at Asylum 3, just as they'd hoped. Margus looked out the viewport as their craft shuddered and the engines started to wind down.

"Hey, now that's what I'm taking about!" He smiled at the others as he folded away a landing nav screen and punched up the overhead lighting. "Right on time, right on course, right on the money. The Stone was sure doing its thing. And look out there. Looks like we even have a welcoming committee."

He pointed out the nearest viewport at a line of scribes in festive white robes with pleasant smiles on their faces. Most appeared fairly young, and none shaved their heads as she had seen scribes do on other stations. Maybe this would be a welcome change after all.

"Do you think the people here will be anything like they were at the last way station?" asked Wist, twirling a strand of hair around her finger.

Oriannon wished she knew. At first glance this way station seemed smaller than the last one, since the asteroid itself appeared less imposing. As far as she could tell, Asylum 3 had been built beneath a single large plexi-bubble stretched across the top of a single deep crater. Once inside, they found that the hangar deck barely accommodated their shuttle.

On the other hand, the builders of this place had clearly placed a higher value on aesthetics. It looked a lot prettier. Off to the sides, she could make out brilliant white stone columns and a marble façade covering the sheer inside crater walls. Rushing water coursed down an artificial stone waterfall, framed on each side with lush green ferns and rambling lonicera vines. Cerise blossoms added a riot of color to the well-tended display, and it looked to Oriannon more like the inside of a Coristan resort or a temple than the landing area for a working way station.

"I guess we'll find out," Oriannon finally answered.

By that time, the shuttle's pressure had finished equalizing inside and out, and their hatch popped open with a subtle hiss. Different? Instead of the dank, recycled odors they'd gotten used to on Asylum 2, this time . . .

"What's that smell?" Margus pointed his nose and breathed deeply, smiling as he did. "Is that really orsianthius?"

"I think so." Oriannon nodded and scrambled for the doorway. The three of them poked their heads out at once, smiling and giggling at the heady scents of flowers and green living things. After so many days in the shuttle and on the rather stark Asylum 2, this seemed like a vacation resort.

"Welcome to Asylum 3!" The first scribe in line beamed up at them as they climbed down to the tiled landing. "I'm Cirrus Main."

"Cirrus?" cried Oriannon. He seemed taken aback that she recognized him, and whispered nervously to the scribe standing next to him. She couldn't bring herself to mention his cousin. Finally he nodded and turned back to her.

"Yes, good to see you again. I trust your father is well? You're all welcome here, naturally."

As Oriannon introduced Margus and Wist, the older scribe presented them with garlands of bright yellow orsianthius flowers on a string, which he gently wrapped around their necks in a sort of impromptu welcoming gesture. When Oriannon sniffed one of hers, though, it seemed to have no scent.

Odd. Where did the flower scents come from? Perhaps plants here were different than at home.

"You do remember me, don't you?" Oriannon wanted to be sure. "You showed us around Asylum 1, before it was ... you know."

Yes, he knew. Before it was blown up by Coristan Security. Cirrus Main responded with another stiff nod. "Of course."

Still he didn't loosen up, and he didn't seem to want to volunteer any information about how he got to an entirely different way station, millions of klicks away from the first.

But she didn't have time to wonder, as each scribe in turn brought them a welcome—some a smile and a warm handshake, others a gift of flowers, until all three were loaded down with blooms.

"You'll be staying awhile, I trust?" asked Cirrus. "Our crew will be happy to service your vessel."

He reminded Oriannon more of a courtly maitre d' at an expensive restaurant back home in Seramine, rather than a humble scribe whose job it was to study the Codex. Behind them, a team of technicians began to examine their ship, attaching feeder cables and charging devices. But Cirrus Main had asked them a question, and suddenly Oriannon felt ill for having forgotten the real reason for their journey, if only for a moment.

"We're not sure how long we'll be here," Margus finally spoke for them. "But we do have ... Oriannon's father. He needs medical attention."

"We were told your healer is well equipped," said Oriannon. Cirrus sprang into action, gesturing to two of the other scribes.

"Naturally. But why didn't you say so? We'll have your father taken to the dispensary and treated immediately."

Oriannon would have helped, but by that time Sola blocked the entry, her arms outstretched. Cirrus paused and looked to Oriannon.

"How long has your friend been blind?" he asked in a low voice.

Oriannon did not want to explain how much Sola was definitely *not* her friend. He might find out in time.

"Only a few days actually." She would leave it at that for now. "There was an accident back on Corista."

He nodded as if that was all he needed to know, offering to have a healer look at her injuries as well. He directed two other scribes to look after Sola. By this time at least a dozen workers swarmed around their ship, and scribes were guiding a lev-sled up the narrow stairway. Apparently these scribes were much better equipped than their brothers on Asylum 2.

"I think maybe we came to the right place after all," said Margus, stepping over to a small pool at the base of the waterfall. A stone bench provided a place to sit next to the profusion of Coristan garden plants, carefully planted in the nooks of black volcanic stone. "I haven't been in such a pretty place for ages."

"Of course you haven't." Cirrus Main smiled and nodded as Margus reached out to dip his hand in the water.

"What's up with that?" cried Margus, pulling back. "It stings!"

"Oh, yes." Cirrus dismissed the problem with a wave. "I'm sorry. The water takes a little getting used to. I assure you, however, it's perfectly pure. In time you'll get used to it."

Margus massaged his hand. It looked a little red.

"Let me show you where you'll be staying," Cirrus told them, waving several more workers past. "Once you're fresh and rested, I'm sure we'd all love to hear more from you."

Strange. In all her reading, Oriannon had never heard of an asylum way station where ordinary people could not touch the water. She told herself she would have to find out more as they followed their new hosts away from the hangar deck to the main assembly area. The layout reminded her a little of the last way station, only on a much smaller scale. A moment later she blinked her eyes at the brightness as they emerged from the hangar deck's access tunnel.

"Our gathering place." Cirrus waved his hand at an expansive tiled courtyard, where formal gardens filled with ponds, plants, and gazebos offered plenty of areas to eat and gather. The air seemed thick with the wonderful living scent of green growing things. In fact, a thick carpet of flowering lonicera vines covered the steep crater walls, giving the impression that their lush little world had been carved into a giant living salad bowl, rather than solid rock. Several stories above their heads, the steep edges of their asteroid's crater rose to meet the domed roof.

Here on the main level, scribes—both men and women this time—sat under flowering orange flamboyan trees, chatting and sipping cups of what looked to be vupp, the strong Coristan blend of coffee. They seemed to take no notice of the newcomers, as the sound of laughter blended with the ripple of falling waters.

"Amazing." Margus seemed impressed as he looked up and around. "I could stay here awhile."

Cirrus smiled and nodded as if he expected the comment. But Oriannon had other things on her mind.

"Excuse me," she asked. "My father?"

"I understand you're concerned," he answered. "But naturally it would be too upsetting for you to accompany him. You've already seen more than enough. We'll take care of it."

"No, really. I'd like to see him."

"All in good time. Please be patient, and know that he's receiving the best of care. Your blind traveling companion as well."

"But—" Oriannon wanted to protest, wanted to be with her father, but their host had already taken them through an archway built into a gently flowing wall of water, leading to a comfortable lobby ringing the central gardens. Here more scribes sat in overstuffed dark leather chairs, many of them eating or huddled in conversation. Here and there she heard a soft laugh, as if someone was enjoying a private joke.

They walked across a lush carpet to the far outer rim, where numbered metal doors swept aside as Cirrus pointed a small remote. He directed Wist to the first room and Margus to the second. When the third door opened, he motioned for Oriannon to enter.

"Your room," he told her. "Please let us know if there's anything else you need."

She paused to thank him before entering, but by the time she turned around, he had disappeared. In his place, the air glowed just slightly, almost like flying fire-misix bugs on a warm evening. She could feel a shimmering burst of heat and smelled a faint burnt odor, as if someone had just snuffed a candle.

"Pardon me? Cirrus?" Oriannon glanced around the corner of a nearby stone wall to see where he went. In her exhaustion she might have zoned out for a moment, long enough for him to step away. Yes, that could have happened, and such a thing had happened before. But she saw no one around the corner. The scribes in the lobby didn't look her way either. Perhaps she'd been standing there for longer than she realized.

"I must be more tired than I thought," she told herself.

Oriannon knew she could not stay awake much longer, so without trying to figure it out anymore, she stepped inside, and the door closed silently behind her. Once inside, she ran a hand across the smoothness of dark pluqwood furniture and wondered if they imported these beautiful carved things all the way from Corista. She padded across a plush woven carpet to a wall-to-wall waterfall, illuminated by dappled golden light, which cooled the room and added a strangely soothing effect. She could get used to this, though she stopped herself from reaching out to touch the water, remembering what happed to Margus. Better to be careful.

Now that she was alone in this wonderful room, she could barely keep her eyes open. Her head in a fog, she stumbled over to the large bed and fell into its soothing, pillow-soft embrace. She fell asleep before she could remove her shoes.

● ● ●

"Father!" Oriannon woke up with a start and tried to shake off the heavy, groggy feeling that gripped her head. She couldn't tell if she had been dreaming, or how long she had been asleep.

The waterfall in her room gave her no clue; it only reminded her that she could use a good, long drink. Gathering her courage, she poked her finger into the glassy sheet of water — and yelped at the shock.

"Ow!" She shook her finger as Margus had done earlier, wondering how plain, clear water could carry such an electric shock. Still thirsty, she decided to explore her room a little more.

A quick look around told her there were no chronos in the room, so no way to tell time. In fact, she could find nothing electronic — no coms, no climate control, nothing. Only black basalt walls on three sides and the waterfall on the fourth. The ceiling seemed to glow a little brighter at the sound of her voice. Or maybe it had another way of detecting that she was now awake and moving in the room.

The wreath of flowers she'd received from the welcoming committee still had no smell when she lowered her nose to the blooms. Even worse, her neck burned and itched.

"What am I, allergic?" She tore off the wreath and ran her fingers across an angry red rash where the flowers had been, feeling nasty raised welts around her neck. This was not turning out so well after all.

But really, none of that mattered. She felt a guilty pang for falling asleep without knowing how her father was doing. Without worrying how she looked, and trying to ignore the pain around her neck, she headed outside to look for answers.

Everything looked the same. The curved lobby area seemed to glow with the same kind of golden light she'd encountered in her room, while scribes still relaxed around tables in comfortable chairs. She turned aside to the room next to hers, hoping Wist or Margus were inside. She looked for a buzzer of some kind—a doorbell or a way to let them know she was there. Nothing. She tried knocking on the door, but the titanium seemed to swallow the effort, and no one appeared.

"Oh, come on." She sighed and parked her hands on her hips, wondering what to do next.

"Is there some way I can help?" came a voice behind her.

"Oh!" Oriannon held a hand to her throat and turned to see who had surprised her. She hadn't recognized Cirrus Main's voice.

"I'm so sorry," he told her. His fine white linen robe billowed as he bowed slightly. "I didn't mean to startle you."

"Not a problem," she answered once she'd caught her breath. "I just wanted to see my friends."

"Oh, you wouldn't want to do that. We don't want to upset them if they're resting."

"No, really. They won't mind. I just want to see how they're doing."

"Quite well, I assure you. Margus is now sleeping at level five, which is encouraging, and I'm assuming neither Wist nor Sola will be awake for several hours. In any case ..."

She tried to keep from frowning as she wondered how he knew all this.

" ... I'd suggest you come with me." He motioned for her to follow. "I'll get you something for that rash."

That would be good, she thought, *except—*

"My father," she told him, stopping short. "I really need to find out how he's doing."

"He's resting comfortably as well." This scribe seemed to have an answer for everything. "And I'm sure you'll be able to visit him in time. In the meantime, perhaps you'd like something to eat? Some vupp, or perhaps some fresh doan biscuits? I can show you the way station if you like. Then, when you're ready, you can tell us why you're here."

"Actually, Cirrus, you're very kind." She crossed her arms and stayed where she was, wondering why he made her feel this uncomfortable. "But I'm not really hungry, and I can tell you right now why we came."

"Oh?" He lifted one eyebrow, as if mildly interested. At the same time, he took her arm and guided her away from the rooms and through the lobby. "You'll find we're a little more laid back here than you may be used to. It was an adjustment for me as well when I was transferred from the other way station. All that to say, you really shouldn't feel compelled to share your personal journey just yet, if it upsets you. You look upset. All in good time."

Well, she wasn't upset before, but right now his smug tone made her want to shout at him.

"What are you talking about? Listen to me. I'm here to tell you that this station is in danger. We saw Asylum 1 destroyed, just like *that*. We're pretty sure it's the Troikans, but we don't know exactly how they're doing it, only that it's going to happen again."

"Please." The thought seemed to pain him. "I've found that speculation and living in the past is stressful and not conducive to spiritual health."

"What? I just told you what we've seen. Asylum 2 is full of refugees from Asylum 1 and who knows where else. Your cousin is there. And the Troikans haven't made it here yet, but you'll be in huge danger when they do. Jesmet said to expect them very soon."

This time Cirrus looked at her as if she had just told him she'd had a very good night's sleep indeed.

"Jesmet?" he raised an eyebrow.

"My mentor," she told him. "He's the Maker's Song."

"Perhaps one of many. How does that particular Song make you feel?"

"How does it make me feel?" She shook off the impression that she was dreaming this conversation and that this Cirrus Main was just a figment of her imagination. "Wait a minute. Didn't you hear what I just said? There really are Troikans, and they're . . ."

Again he smiled and nodded at a passing friend as they strolled through the lobby, following the rounded waterfall. Oriannon tried to stop but he kept walking, so she hurried again to keep up with him.

"You'll find the aploncake here is quite good," he told her. "Are you sure you won't have a piece? We have servers who can provide you with— "

"You haven't heard a word I've said!" She raised her voice, but he only held up a finger to quiet her. Even so, the contented smile never left his face. Certainly there was some mistake here. This could not be the same Cirrus Main who had been forced from his way station home only a short time ago.

"Yes I have, Oriannon. I just don't like to see you or your friends upset, and I know how exhausting long-distance space travel can be. I'm pleased you met my cousin. And since you do appear sincere about your experiences, perhaps they're true for you."

"You've got to be kidding." Oriannon shook her head and looked around. "What did they do to you? Is everybody else like this around here?"

"Well, I'm not certain what you're implying, but that's an interesting question. And you know, just to reassure you that I value your perspective, I'd like you to share your views with the others sometime. We do have enlightening discussions."

"Discussions? I thought scribes were all about studying the Codex."

"Actually ... we take a slightly different approach here, one more conducive to fostering relationships. While we are inspired by the general purpose of the Codex, we are free to take its mandates more as fine literature or poetry. You understand. Not everything is meant to be taken literally. But as I said, you're welcome to join in, as long as you observe our three core values."

"Which are?"

"On Asylum 3 we respect diverse truths as different paths to the same goal. We seek each other's comfort as if it were our own.

And we never upset the brethren, since discord breeds divisiveness, and divisiveness is to be avoided at all cost. Everything is for harmony."

"For harmony. Oh." Oriannon wasn't quite sure she liked this kind of harmony, as she thought about how the news of the Troikans might upset these brethren, or how they might think she was not seeking their comfort by telling them such bad news. She knew then that convincing the scribes in this station might be just as difficult as it was in the last—only in quite a different way. Everything she said was met by a tolerant smile and a closed mind.

"You really don't believe me," she asked, "do you?"

"Oh, yes, I believe you are sincere and that you believe what you say. That's valuable to a point. But you're new here, as I was just a few weeks ago. I came here with only a few outdated books and the clothes on my back, and look! They have welcomed me with open arms, with no reservations. I've found a place here as a respected senior scribe. You'll learn. You do seem very bright."

Maybe that was as far as she could take her warning for now. Still she risked breaking Cirrus Main's pleasant expression and pressed the issue.

"You said you'd allow me to speak?" she asked. "How soon?"

"You know, first-time visitors like you often seem to have similar issues, always wanting to speak in absolutes. I confess I was of that mind. Many seem obsessed with a time schedule. We've found those attitudes are easily modified after you've been here for just a short while. In fact, people very much come to appreciate our perspectives."

"In other words, you don't want to set up a time for me to talk to your friends?"

"Time?" He shivered as if she'd just used an awful word. "Oh, dear. That's not the kind of terminology we use here. I'd prefer to keep our options open, if you don't object?"

Oriannon sighed at the way he ended all his sentences up, like questions, as if he wasn't sure about anything. He hadn't talked like that before. She rubbed her neck and wondered if she could do anything differently, or say anything that would change his mind. Maybe not.

But no matter what this scribe thought, she knew that didn't change the truth. What Jesmet told her and the plans the Troikans had for this way station were true. Faced with Cirrus Main's waffling, her own resolve to tell them about Jesmet and the Troikans grew more firm.

The only questions she had were how soon would the Troikans arrive, and when could she see her father.

14

"Am I feeling better?" An hour later Oriannon's father looked up at her from his bed with eyes half open. "Yes, I think so. I feel as if I've been in a fog. How long have I been out? Where are we?"

So Oriannon explained, and as she crouched next to his cot in the well-equipped medical center, she told him everything, from Cirrus Main's strange behavior to the fact that flowers here gave her a rash and that they couldn't drink the water.

"Really?" he looked at her. "I've had some. It tastes normal."

Oriannon glanced at the half-empty glass of water at his bedside, next to a shapely, clear pitcher and a monitor with a soothing green light that seemed to track her father's breathing and heartbeat.

"It didn't sting you? When I touched it, I got an electric shock."

Her father shrugged and shook his head.

"Maybe I didn't notice it the first time. Actually, I'll have some more, if you don't mind."

Oriannon was about to help him, but he reached over and took the glass.

"Well, if you're improving," she said, "maybe that's all that counts."

A young scribe entered their dimly lit room and stood off to the side, causing Oriannon to glance over at him. He wore his light chocolate hair a little longer than most, and something looked a bit crooked about his face, but otherwise he resembled any other young scribe in his white linen robe.

"Pardon?" The scribe cleared his throat and shifted from foot to foot. "My name is Iakk, and I'm here to see that your needs are met. Is there anything I can do for you?"

"Very kind of you, Iakk." Tavlin Hightower's voice could barely be heard, and his face still looked pale and weak. The fact that he spoke at all gave Oriannon hope. "But I think I'll just rest a bit more."

With that he set the glass aside and closed his eyes again. His bedside monitor showed slower breathing and heartbeat. Oriannon looked from her father to the scribe and knew that she had to find out more. Too many things didn't make sense here at Asylum 3.

"What did you give him?" she asked, stepping back from the bed. "What did you do for him?"

But the young scribe simply nodded his head and backed away with a half smile on his lips.

"If there's nothing else ..." he began.

But Oriannon didn't let him get away. She caught him by the arm before he could leave the room.

"Actually," she began, "there is something else."

He looked around with a terrified expression and led her out of the room.

"Please," he told her, his voice lower. "Let me show you something."

Oriannon had no idea what Iakk was up to, but she followed him out of the dispensary and out through the bright, pleasant commons area with its ornate central fountain. Here, large mushroom-shaped black rocks draped in cascading water filled the air with a soothing, pleasant splash—a soothing backdrop to soft conversation and laughter. As before, scribes had settled casually in neutral-toned comfortable chairs arranged around the commons. These people liked to talk—all except her new guide.

"I'm not just going to follow you anywhere," she finally told him. "Not unless you clue me in."

The scribe wiped the sweat from his forehead—it wasn't that warm—and continued on past a row of beautiful black stone columns set into the asteroid walls. Along the top someone had carved an intricate frieze, or raised carving, of Coristan animals: yagwars chasing borinds, viria songbirds flitting along the upper edge, and treb bears wrestling. Finally he paused in front of an unmarked entry door at the far side of the commons, a good distance away from the main meeting area of the other scribes.

"What's this?" asked Oriannon.

He placed a thumb on a readerpad next to the door and spoke his name, Iakk Rorsiba, before the door quietly slipped aside and he motioned her inside. When she hesitated, he turned to her once more.

"Please," he said. "This is the best way to answer your questions. The only way."

Against her better judgment she followed him inside, wondering what kind of tour he was leading. Once inside the room, she began to understand. She breathed deeply the musty, ancient smell of books—so rare in her digital world. Only scribes and museums had books, and usually behind plexi displays.

The ambient lights didn't come on by themselves, so Iakk Rorsiba lit a candle with a tiny torch he pulled from his pocket. The candle threw a golden halo of flickering light all around them. She could make out disorderly stacks of dusty, ancient leather-bound books piled all around them.

"This can't be your way station library?" she asked, knowing the answer. He nodded.

"It was. Well, I suppose it still is. It's just that, well, as you can tell, no one has used this place for quite some time. Years."

"What happened? I thought scribes were all about, you know, studying. Reading. I saw it on Asylum 4, where I met Cirrus Main. They studied there."

"Well, Cirrus Main came here a few months ago as a senior scribe, and he brought some of his books with him." He pointed to a dusty table piled high with thick volumes. "He left them over there."

"You're saying he doesn't read them now?"

Iakk shook his head no. "Not anymore."

"I don't get it. I don't get any of this."

He picked up a book and blew the dust off its cover.

"The water," he said. "You haven't tried it yet, have you?"

"What does that have to do with anything?"

"Or the vupp?" he added.

"No, not yet. Every time I touch it, it gives me a shock. But—"

"That's just the first time. You get used to it. And then it changes you. It changes the way you think."

She thought back to the strange way Cirrus Main acted, and the even stranger things he told her about harmony and divisiveness, about not speaking in absolutes. Iakk's words started to make sense.

"Changes the way you think ... forever?" she asked. "What about my father?"

"I gave him water from your ship." He sighed. "But I'm afraid it's not going to last long."

"Wait a minute." She looked him in the eye, but he turned away. "So you're saying if any of us drink this water, or anything made from water, like vupp, we're going to change too?"

"Happens to everybody. It's like a drug that changes your personality over time. People just smile and stop caring about anything except hanging out, drinking vupp, and talking about harmony."

"Cirrus Main did mention that."

"Sure he did!" Iakk waved at the dusty books, and the pain showed on his face. "What they used to think was important isn't important anymore. Look at this! When I first came here, people used to read. People used to *think!*"

"So what happened to you?" asked Oriannon. "What makes you different?"

"About a year ago I twisted my ankle and had to stay in my room for a day, so I didn't drink any vupp for a few hours. And, it was weird, I could feel my mind coming back. And I don't know why, but I wanted to see what would happen. After a few more hours the effect wore off, and I was almost back to normal."

"And then?"

"I can't go very long. Once in a while I try to go without water, but it's not easy. So this time when your ship came in, I tapped into the water supply. Nobody saw me."

"Okay, but ... I would think the others would want to know what was going on. Haven't you told them?"

"I tried." Iakk shook his head. "But they don't care. Nobody cares."

"I don't believe it." Oriannon walked around the shadowy room past beautiful carved ironwood tables and matching chairs set nicely between tall shelves. She could pick out wonderful ancient commentaries on the Codex, histories of Corista, philosophy—most of which she knew by heart—all sitting in crooked piles on the tables and floor. She carefully picked up a volume dating from thousands of years ago, and the yellowed pages crackled as she opened it. Her finger skimmed a familiar passage.

"'Because you are the last asylum,'" she read in a quiet voice, "'spread the light so they will hear beyond Corista—even where the Trion is but a faint glimmer in the night sky.' Codex one hundred one, verse—"

"You can read the old Coristan!" Iakk interrupted her.

"You mean you can't?" She looked up in confusion. "I thought all scribes knew how to read the old language."

"My father could. He was a scribe too. And his father. We've been scribes for generations."

"And he didn't teach you?" Oriannon wondered aloud.

"My father died when I was young, and they took me here. I've tried to teach myself, and I can make out a few words, but that's it."

"I'm sorry. I shouldn't have asked."

"That's okay. I was actually excited when Cirrus Main arrived. I thought maybe he would teach me." Iakk's voice trailed off. "But then ..."

But then it had never happened. They stood in the dim library for a moment, neither speaking. Iakk's candle flickered, casting its eerie glow on the nearest table.

"So why did you bring me here?" she finally broke the silence. "What do you want me to do about ... all this?"

"I don't know. Maybe I just wanted you to understand. This is one of the only rooms where we won't be monitored. I'm sorry."

That explained how Cirrus Main knew so much. Hidden monitors. She supposed she and the others had been watched ever since they stepped off the shuttle—though the scribes never seemed to care about anything. Iakk turned to go, but she held him back.

"Wait," she told him. "There's something else I need to tell you."

He waited, looking at her with a curious stare as she went on.

"I actually tried to tell Cirrus Main, but it didn't turn out too well."

"Now you know why I can't get people to listen to me. You can tell people here whatever you want, and they're just going to smile and say that it's great for you, but their truth is different."

"Exactly. But listen. I don't know how else to tell you, except to just tell you. See, my mentor, Jesmet, sent me to this place to warn you about the Troikans."

"Troikans?" He closed his eyes and nodded, as if her words held no surprise. "You're sure about that?"

"Do you know about them? Cirrus Main acted like they were a figment of my imagination."

Now Oriannon could tell she'd struck a nerve, as Iakk began pacing. Finally he stopped and faced her.

"He's lying," said Iakk. "He knows. Everybody here knows about the Troikans."

"That they're coming for this station?"

"Not that part. But that doesn't surprise me. Nothing surprises me."

Iakk's attitude surprised Oriannon, but she didn't interrupt him again. He sighed and put down his sputtering candle on a nearby table, being careful not to set it too close to a stack of books.

"All right," he told her. "Six months ago, a team of Troikans came to visit Asylum 3, and it was ... you know, very pleasant. Everything's always pleasant here on Asylum 3. That's what we are. You know, harmony."

"We seek each other's comfort as if it were our own." She recited one of the core values Cirrus Main had mentioned to her.

"So you've heard about that. Well, at first the Troikans seemed like they just wanted to know more about the way station and what we believed here. The scribes welcomed them, the same way they welcomed you. That's how they always do things. But then ..."

"Then the Troikans drank the water?"

"No, they stayed on their own ship and used their own supplies. Then they started asking about the Breach, and after a week they left with eleven scribes. They said they needed consultants for a special project of theirs and that our people would be back in just a few weeks."

"Okay, okay." Oriannon held up her hand for him to slow down. "You lost me. Am I supposed to know what the Breach is?"

Iakk brought his hand to his mouth, as if he had just said something he should not have. He shook his head and apologized.

"Sometimes we assume everyone knows. I'm very poor at the technique."

What technique? Oriannon was confused, and her face must have shown it. Iakk sighed and his shoulders slumped.

"Okay. Stand where you are."

He drew himself up with a deep breath and closed his eyes. As Oriannon watched, his body seemed to blur a little, as if she were looking at him underwater, before he came back into focus and opened his eyes again.

"See?" He frowned. "I can't do it very well. The only thing that happens is— "

In a blink he completely faded from view. He was replaced by a light glow, a burst of heat, and a distinct burnt odor. This she had seen before. The only difference was that Iakk reappeared less than a meter away, still trying to finish his sentence.

" —happens is I get hot and I sweat a lot. See?"

He must not have realized what happened, except that now he looked at her with a quizzical expression.

"Wait a minute." He looked at where he'd been standing, then held his hands up to be sure. "Did I just—?"

She looked from the old spot to the new spot, back and forth, while Iakk smiled for the first time since she'd met him.

"You have no idea how long I've been waiting for that to happen," he told her. "I can't believe it!"

"This is the first time?"

"That's right." He stepped out the distance between where he was and where he had been. "Looks like about a meter and a half."

"Well, congratulations. I think." Oriannon didn't know whether to shake his hand or run. "Although ... I'm not sure what this all has to do with the Troikans."

"I'm not sure either. All I know is they wanted to tap into the Breach technique."

She thought of what they had seen when passing the place where Asylum 1 was supposed to be, and a thought occurred to her.

"So," she asked, "is it possible that much larger objects can be ... breached? Not just scribes?"

He thought for a moment, scratching his head.

"It's a breach in the fabric of space; I don't know its limits. Some of the older scribes have ridden the Breach really far. It takes a lot of concentration, and it's more dangerous the farther you go. It's also very hard to control, and it takes years of practice."

Oriannon wanted to ask how the scribes had discovered the Breach, or why the secret had never been mentioned in Corista. But first she needed to know something else.

"What about the scribes who went with the Troikans?" she asked. "What happened to them?"

His expression turned deadly serious once more.

"We don't know, and we haven't heard from them for more than four months. Not a word from the Troikans either."

"Well, I can tell you that's about to change."

"Pardon?" He looked at her carefully, as if trying to decide if he should trust her, or if she was crazy after all.

"You have to believe me, Iakk! The Troikans are coming back, and soon. My mentor Jesmet told me they're going from way station to way station, taking every one. Maybe that's where the Breach thing fits in. Isn't there some way you can get your friends to listen?"

"If I did, and people actually believed such a thing, then what?"

"I—" Oriannon's voice caught. "I'm not sure. Jesmet didn't tell me that part. But if you open your arms and try to talk to them the way you did before ... If not, you're going to lose the way station and maybe everyone on it. I know it's hard to believe, but ..."

He turned away, and when he faced her again he wiped away tears.

"I believe you, Oriannon Hightower."

"You do?" She choked in surprise as he nodded.

"I come to this library and try to read what I can. I've read about the Maker's Song in a couple of books that I *can* read." He picked up the dusty Codex again. "I don't always understand, but I know it's not what my mentors have told me."

"Jesmet sometimes is a little hard to understand," she admitted.

"But I want to know what you know. So I'm wondering ... if you leave here, would you have room for one more?"

The question caught her completely off guard, and she stuttered even more as she tried to figure out how to answer.

"Why would you want to leave here?" she finally managed, though the answer seemed obvious.

"You ask me that after everything I've just told you? Oriannon, I can't defend this place alone against the Troikans, especially if they come as soon as you say they're going to. I hate this place. I hate the Core Values. I even hate vupp."

Before she could answer with anything that sounded intelligent, they heard a beep on the other side of the door, as someone checked in from the outside. They heard a muffled voice, and Iakk shoved Oriannon into hiding on the far side of a floor shelf—just as the door slipped open.

"Iakk?" The voice sounded surprised. "What are you doing here? I thought you said you were taking our guest on a little tour."

"Oh, ah, Mentor Cirrus." Iakk stumbled with his answer, and she heard a jumble of books falling on the table over her head. "Right. I was just, er, straightening up a few things."

"In the dark? In here?" Cirrus Main didn't sound convinced. "You were seen with Miss Hightower. Do you have any idea where she is?"

"Actually, yes, I did see her for a few minutes. She, ah ..."

Oriannon held her breath as Iakk paused. She was not quite sure why she was hiding, but she was sure she did not want to be discovered this way, and not by Cirrus Main.

"She was talking about her mentor's warning," Iakk went on. With these words, his voice seemed to change a little, as if he was telling a bad joke about a mindless fool, and someone would laugh at her expense.

"Oh yes, the warning." Finally Cirrus Main's voice relaxed, and he actually chuckled a bit. "If you see her, tell her some of the other scribes said they'd listen to her at the festival tonight. Don't mention this to her, but I think they're looking for a little amusement."

Oriannon drew back as far as she dared into the shadows under the table and bit her lip. She could see his sandaled feet; what if he could see hers as well?

"I'll tell her," said Iakk. "Let me just put this away and I'll be right out."

"Yes, well, don't hurry, but I thought you'd like to greet our new guests in the landing bay as well. They're back."

"I'll find Oriannon and be right there." Iakk sounded casual, and Oriannon tried not to gasp at the news.

The Troikans must have already arrived!

15

If the Troikans had really landed, Oriannon knew, this would be the end for Asylum 3. After Cirrus Main left the library, Oriannon scrambled out from her hiding place under the table and faced Iakk.

"It's them," she said, but for some reason she felt a strange calm. "Isn't it?"

"Maybe not. Mentor Cirrus would have said so."

He turned to go, and Oriannon had no choice but to follow. She would find Margus and Wist as soon as she could.

Outside the library, no one would have known anything was wrong. Groups of scribes still laughed at each other's jokes, and a lone musician played a fair erhu for a small but appreciative audience. They all clapped politely as he launched into another tune.

Any other time, Oriannon would have stopped to listen, to remember what it was like to make such a gentle, melodic sound with the stringed instrument. Even now, she paused, staring for a moment at the way the musician's hands stroked with his bow across the upright strings, and the way he cradled the delicately inlaid wood base. For just an instant she recalled how Mentor Jesmet smiled as he directed their school orchestra, and the intense way she focused on his hands as she followed tempo with her own long-necked erhu.

But there was no time for any of that now, and she hurried on. When she reached the hangar deck with Iakk, a new crowd of welcomers had already gathered, just as they had for Oriannon's shuttle. Oriannon had to admit that the ship looked nothing like she'd expected.

She stared as fumes and fog released and a rather loud landing thruster wound down. Although the ship itself seemed smaller than their shuttle, she could not make out any markings or clues as to its origins. The tail section, which appeared well-charred from re-entries into hot atmospheres, didn't seem to match the rest of the craft, and the underside of the ship was pockmarked and blackened from contact with space debris. On the side, several titanium panels didn't match the main body, as if they had been patched together as well. Observation windows looked totally scratched, hardly see-through any more. And one of the five landing legs gave way with a lurch as the hatch popped open.

"These aren't Troikans, Oriannon," whispered Iakk, his face turning pale. "Have you ever met a Makabi?"

"Looks like I'm about to," she whispered back.

That the Makabi had even made it here safely in such a craft was one thing. But the men who emerged through the hatch seemed to match their ship well: dirty and unshaven, wearing mismatched black and blue coveralls that probably should have been used for rags many light years ago.

Even so, Cirrus Main stood at the head of his welcoming committee and bravely put on a wide smile as he welcomed them to the way station.

"You've met them before?" Oriannon asked Iakk.

Iakk chose his words carefully.

"A few times. They stop here and want to trade for supplies. They're really prickly though. Loud and rude, and they're always looking for a fight. Usually they find something to argue about — politics mostly — and then they leave in a huff without paying."

Somehow that didn't surprise Oriannon. The lead Makabi squinted at them with a darkened eye and a scowl that sent a shiver up her back — despite the fact that he stood no taller than a young child. The Makabi, it seemed, looked as if they didn't believe in haircuts or sonic showers.

"We'll be needing supplies." The leader growled more than spoke, brushing past the outstretched flowers Cirrus held out to them. "And flowers aren't one of them."

"They're certainly not." Cirrus took a step back but never lost his smile. Oriannon had to give him credit. "But you do come at a wonderfully opportune time. The Apogee Festival is being prepared even now. If you'd like, you can rest for a short while in your guest quarters, and then you're welcome to join us."

"Food?" The Makabi looked at him sideways. "What kind of food?"

"Oh, I'm certain you'll enjoy it." Cirrus Main laughed. "This is Asylum 3, after all, so I'm certain we'll ..."

His voice trailed off when the lead Makabi paused and sniffed, his nose wrinkled as if something didn't smell good.

"What's that smell?" he demanded, and for the first time Cirrus Main looked a little flustered.

"Oh!" Cirrus cleared his throat. "I suppose it could be any number of things. We have an olfactory steering committee that makes those decisions, and our atmospheric scent generator is scheduled well in advance to provide a pleasant mix. Usually our people prefer the scents of flowering plants and such things as remind them of Corista's outdoor environment. However, if you have any special requests, we — "

"Yeah, as a matter of fact." The Makabi leaned a little closer to Cirrus, perhaps uncomfortably close, though he had to look up to meet the scribe's eye. "Turn it off."

Cirrus pressed his lips together, trying to decide how to react, but he finally nodded and squared his shoulders with an almost imperceptible shiver.

"Naturally we'd like to do everything we can to make you more comfortable, as always. I just want to assure you it's carefully formulated and non-allergenic, so you needn't worry about any allergic reactions."

"I'm not worried about sneezing." The Makabi's face hardened. "It just stinks, so turn it off."

Again Cirrus Main swallowed hard, but he bowed in submission with his hands folded in front, urging the Makabi to contact him should they have any needs or questions.

"My name is Cirrus Main, by the way. I don't believe we've met before, since I haven't been stationed here at Asylum 3 for a long time. And you are ...?"

For a moment Oriannon thought the Makabi wasn't even going to share his name, as if he couldn't be troubled with such a detail. He tugged at his wild beard and brushed the hair out of his dark eyes.

"Modiin," he finally grunted, and he pointed at a small team of way station workers who had approached with lev carts full of tools. "You deal with me and nobody else. And anybody touches this ship without my permission — I'll personally pull their thumbs out."

That seemed to put a quick but effective damper on the welcoming party. The committee took its cue and dispersed without delay. The maintenance man nodded as he backpedaled, pivoting his cart and disappearing back the way he'd come. Yet Cirrus Main seemed not at all fazed by their rude guests.

"We'll make certain your ship is not disturbed," Cirrus told him, his voice in his usual smooth monotone. "And I'll send someone to accompany you to the dinner when everything is ready. I think you'll enjoy the food — and the conversation."

It occurred to Oriannon that if she was invited to the same affair, this might be her only chance to share her warning about the approaching Troikans, as well as the truth about her mentor. She glanced at Iakk, who by this time seemed to have collected himself as well.

"Best to stay in your room with the Makabi here," he told her after ten of them marched off their ship and disappeared into the way station — probably in search of food. "They can be pretty excitable if you get in their way."

She raised her eyebrows. "I hadn't noticed."

"Yes, well, I'll come and get you and your friends when it's time." This time Iakk spoke loudly enough for his mentor and the rest of the welcoming committee to hear. "I'm sure we're all looking forward to hearing your stories."

Maybe Iakk was. But Oriannon wasn't sure about the rest of them.

What do I say to these people? she wondered as she retreated from the hangar deck, retracing her steps to her room.

Her mind spun as she slipped inside, and she imagined herself speaking to a gathering of scribes who would actually take her seriously. Perhaps they would let her explain how Jesmet, the Maker's Song, had returned to life. She imagined them listening and nodding, asking intelligent questions. And she imagined what might happen if they actually believed her words and decided to follow Jesmet as their mentor, as well.

"Did you see them, Ori?" asked Margus, launching out of a plushy chair as she entered. Wist had been pacing by the waterfall and turned to her as well.

"What?" Oriannon jumped and paused just inside the door, waiting for it to slip shut. "What are you two doing in here?"

"Waiting for you!" Margus parked his hands on his hips as if it were all her fault that she'd been scared out of her skin. "By the time I woke up, you were gone and nobody knew where you were. I was beginning to panic, and I went to see if you and Wist had gotten together, but she didn't know either."

"I'm sorry." Ori tried to explain. "I— "

"And then while we were standing outside our rooms ..." Wist continued the story. "These scary-looking men in dirty black coveralls be walking down the hall. Can you be guessing who they're talking with?"

Oriannon shook her head. "I have no idea."

"Your friend Sola!" said Margus. "This is the first I've seen her since we've landed, and she's in between these two guys with black beards, talking like they're old friends."

"Friendly?" Oriannon had a hard time picturing it.

"More like intense," Wist put in. "Like she's having something important to be telling them, and she's wanting to make sure they're listening."

"So ... did she see you?" Oriannon corrected herself. "I mean, did they see you?"

Margus shook his head. "If they did, they had no idea who was watching them. Are they the Troikans you keep trying to tell us about?"

Oriannon was about to explain, when she remembered what Iakk had told her about being watched. So instead of spilling everything inside her room, where curious scribes with monitoring equipment might listen in, she signaled them to follow her outside into the commons area. She wasn't sure how safe it was out there either, but guessed it was probably better.

"I was just checking on my dad, see," she began, "and there was a scribe there who was helping, and ..."

It took her the better part of an hour to tell them everything, from the dangers of drinking the local water to all that had happened with Iakk in the library, along with Cirrus Main's strange behavior and the arrival of the diminutive but pushy Makabi.

"I'm thinking this is serious." Wist suggested in her soft voice after Oriannon finished. "Aren't you thinking so? I've never heard of Makabi."

Margus kept looking around the large open area, as if on guard.

"I've heard of them," he told them, "just never seen one. I thought they were supposed to be, like, pirates or something."

"Not pirates," explained Oriannon. "Separatists. Rebels, maybe. They've been separate from Corista for generations. Some of them want to restore Corista, you know, back to the glory days ... something like that. I'm not so sure about that part. I do know they hold a different view of the Codex than the scribes."

"So why was Sola talking to them?" asked Wist. "Like she was knowing them. That's what I'm not understanding."

No one had an answer—not even a clue. Then they saw Iakk hurrying their way. He smiled as he approached.

"This is it!" he told her, excitement coloring his words. "Cirrus and his friends are ready for you now."

16

"You sure you're ready?" Iakk asked Oriannon.

"I have a choice?"

If this was why Jesmet had brought them here, perhaps she was ready. But suddenly Oriannon felt weak at the knees, and her stomach turned at the thought of explaining herself to a room full of scribes looking for their evening amusement. Even so, she nodded and followed Iakk across the commons, waving for Wist and Margus to keep up.

"I smell food." Margus sniffed as they approached a tall set of double doors. Oriannon smelled it too, and though she couldn't quite identify the scents, her stomach was growling. Yes, it smelled good. But as they began to follow other scribes through the slowly opening doors, a solemn young man stepped up with his hand raised.

"I'm sorry," he told them, blocking the way. "The invitation is only for Oriannon Hightower to address the gathering."

"What?" Oriannon protested. "You mean my friends can't come inside?"

"I regret any inconvenience."

At the moment Oriannon doubted his regrets very much, and she would have told him so if Margus hadn't spoken up.

"No big deal, Ori," he told her as he backed away. "We'll just take a walk. Wrap something up in a napkin for me, huh?"

"No!" Oriannon looked for a little help from Iakk, but he looked just as surprised. "I mean, if they can't go, I won't either. This is just ... rude!"

She turned to face her friends, but Wist shook her head, and Margus turned her right back toward the door.

"It's really not being a problem, Ori," Wist told her. "Go ahead. We'll be waiting outside. We're not wanting to be sitting through some stuffy banquet anyway."

Except perhaps for the food. Oriannon tried to protest one more time, but they would have none of it. So with a sigh, she nodded helplessly and then stepped with Iakk into the grandly furnished banquet hall where she was greeted by a hundred rich and wonderful scents.

Lush maroon and violet tapestries draped the walls behind tables decked with tureens of steaming soup, crafted titanium pots for vupp and clemsonroot tea, finely sculpted chocolate treb bears in various poses, and trays overflowing with three or four varieties of starfruit, sliced cheeses, sweet pastries, aploncakes, canapés, and open-faced sandwiches of every description.

The scribes sat behind long, decorated tables arranged in seven rows. They were dressed in their finest white and gold robes, and they leaned back in their carved ironwood chairs. Between conversations, they drank a deep amber liquid from crystal flutes, while several young scribes cruised around the gathering serving each guest from lev-trays laden with even more finger food.

"These are all scribes?" Oriannon wondered aloud, and Iakk nodded his head. In the far corner a four-piece band tuned up, preparing to play. Iakk pulled Oriannon past the buzzing crowd to a semi-circular head table where Cirrus Main and six others sat behind plates piled high with aromatic curried meya plant quiche ringed with slices of blue and orange starfruit. At length Cirrus looked up from his food and noticed Oriannon standing there, looking awkward. He broke into his customary wide smile.

"Oriannon Hightower of Nyssa," he held up a glass as if to salute her, and though Oriannon saw no microphone or other instrument, his voice reverberated throughout the room. "Daughter of the last surviving elder—who unfortunately could not attend this banquet due to health concerns—we are pleased you could join us."

She wasn't sure how pleased he actually was. But at the sound of his voice, the buzz of five hundred conversations dropped to a hushed whisper, joining the subdued background clinking of glasses and plates and the quiet hum of lev carts criss-crossing the room. Oriannon could now also hear the grunts and grumbling of several Makabi who had commandeered one of the food carts and helped themselves to a noisy meal.

She felt a breeze rustle her hair and looked up to see a small silver globe descend slowly from the high ceiling. It probably amplified voices.

"Your attention please," Cirrus Main announced as the floor beneath their table began to rise, and ceiling lights illuminated her spot. Even the Makabi momentarally stopped eating to see what was going on. She did her best not to tumble off the edge of the rising platform. By the time it stopped, she commanded a view three meters over the heads of the crowd, and everyone could see her clearly.

Well, this wasn't exactly what she had expected, but Cirrus and the others kept their polite masks on while Iakk nodded his encouragement from the crowd below.

"In keeping with the tradition of tolerance and open discussion here on Asylum 3," announced Cirrus, "we've agreed to have our guest share her story with us. Perhaps you'll find it entertaining or even enlightening in some way. In any event, please join me in welcoming Oriannon Hightower of Nyssa."

Oriannon felt her cheeks redden at the smattering of polite applause, but then the room went nearly silent, except for the Makabi. She cleared her throat, said a silent prayer, and faced the crowd.

"I know that news from Corista doesn't always reach Asylum 3," she began, "but you may have heard about Jesmet ben Saius."

At the mention of his name, the crowd instantly switched from the usual dinner-murmurs to deathly silence. Oh, they had surely heard the name. With a deep breath she went on.

"He was my music mentor at Ossek Academy, and they put him to death in the star chamber. You know why? After he had been banished to Shadowside, I was attacked by a yagwar and he crossed the border to save my life. So they killed him."

"For that and much more, my dear." Cirrus Main interrupted, as if he was narrating her presentation. "Our audience should be aware that he was banished for being a faithbreaker."

"If teaching about the Maker is being a faithbreaker, then maybe he was. If making an entire cafeteria full of food disappear, then maybe he was. If bringing my friend Brinnin Flyer back to life after she broke her neck and was killed falling from a ladder, then yes, maybe he was. You can call him whatever you like. I call him the Maker's Song. He is the one the Codex speaks of ... for those of you who still choose to read the Codex. I understand that many of you no longer do."

That brought murmurs and groans from the crowd, and Oriannon wondered if their brand of tolerance was now coming to the test. Tolerance lasts until the opinions expressed make them uncomfortable.

"This is all quite fascinating." Cirrus shook his head with a condescending smile, as if she was a little girl making up fairy stories. "But I believe your time is nearly up. Perhaps you can come to a conclusion for us."

"All respect, sir. I believe you told me quite recently that *time* was not the kind of terminology you use here, and you prefer to keep your options open. Do you object?"

Again the audience twittered with laughter, but this time at Cirrus Main's expense. He sat back with a red face, and the edges of his ever-present smile wilted as he waved obligingly for her to continue. Well, that was magnanimous of him.

"They killed my mentor, the Maker's Song. They didn't understand. But the best part of my story is that he's alive today."

At that, even the Makabi paused from their rowdy eating.

"If you're quite finished— " began Cirrus Main, but Ori shook her head and continued.

"No, actually, I have a message for you from my mentor. An open invitation, really. He doesn't teach at Ossek Academy anymore, but he will be your mentor. He is the Maker's only Song, and he wanted me to warn you that we must stand against the Troikans or— "

At that point the tickle of air from the ceiling globe microphone shut off abruptly, and Oriannon realized her message had been cut off. Since the people in the first few rows could still hear her above the growing shouts from the crowd, she raised her voice and went on.

"We must stand against the Troikans," she shouted, "or everyone on this station will be killed!"

Well, that was more than enough for Cirrus Main, who now struggled mightily to take control of the situation.

"We cannot allow such a blatant disregard for our core values." His voice now boomed above the agitated crowd as the platform quickly lowered back down to floor level and the crowd rose to their feet. "Please! We seek each other's comfort as if it was our own. We never upset the brethren, since discord breeds divisiveness, and divisiveness is to be avoided at all cost. Everything is done to maintain the harmony!"

Perhaps so, but right now the crowd wasn't listening, and they pushed in at the edges of the platform. Oriannon still had a pretty good view of the sea of faces, and the tide had turned decidedly ugly.

They must not be amused, she thought. Suddenly one of them grabbed her leg and pulled her into the boiling crowd.

"You dare speak against the Troikans?" The man spat in her face, and the veins on his forehead looked ready to pop with anger. "They were our guests!"

"You leave her alone!" Without warning Margus jumped to her defense, tackling the angry scribe to give Oriannon a second to slip away. Oriannon had no idea where her friend had come from.

"This way!" shouted Iakk. He and Wist formed a shield on two sides and ahead, while Margus took up the rear. One angry woman managed to grab Oriannon's hair for a moment.

Meanwhile, Cirrus Main continued to exhort the angry crowd from the platform, reminding them over and over about their core values, and of how tolerance guided their thinking. A table overturned, sending a river of soup cascading over the marble floor.

"Please!" Cirrus told them. "Please take your seats!"

He hastily summoned the musicians to play again while Oriannon stumbled into the clear and finally to safety outside. She paused outside the ballroom doors, catching her breath and listening to the chaos slowly settle.

"One thing's for sure." Margus brushed himself off as he popped an aplon puff pastry into his mouth. "You sure know how to bring it, Oriannon."

But it made no sense, and she turned to Iakk for answers.

"I wasn't surprised that Cirrus didn't want me talking about Jesmet," she told him. "But when I brought up the Troikans ... I thought, after what you told me about them, I thought for sure the scribes would hear me."

"It's a touchy subject." He shook his head sadly. "And you rubbed their noses in it. I think they still want to believe the Troikans are going to return our people the way they promised, as long as we don't challenge them."

"After all this time?" she asked.

He nodded. "What you were saying made the Troikans sound like the enemy, and the scribes look like fools for believing them."

"But it's not their fault."

"Maybe not. But you know that our core values say we have to welcome everybody, even ..."

His voiced dropped off and Oriannon turned to see. Even without seeing the problem, Margus and Wist moved together again, acting as bodyguards.

Yet they would not have been able to stand against the powerfully built Makabi who now strode up to them. The one named Modiin faced Oriannon directly, while four of his men stood ready behind him. He bit off a gnarled piece of lakris root and worked it around in his mouth before addressing her.

"Liked what you said in there, Hightower of Nyssa," he growled, looking her over. Oriannon did her best to pull in behind Margus and Iakk, but she could not escape his gaze.

"I only meant— " she began, but he cut her off with a raised hand. She could see his long, untended fingernails even from the front of his hairy palms.

"I don't care what you meant, and I don't care about your mentor, dead or alive. That's your business. But my people and I hate the Troikans ..." He took the opportunity to spit on the floor between them. "We hate the Troikans as much as you do. They took three of our stations. I know what they're about."

"I see," ventured Oriannon, but he was still steering this conversation.

"These sheep here don't know what they're up against, but I think you do. We'll work together, Hightower of Nyssa, daughter of the last elder."

With that, he spit on the hair of his palm and extended it toward her. Oriannon paused as she wondered how to respond without offending the man.

"Actually," Margus said as he stepped forward, "daughters of elders aren't allowed to shake hands with strangers. No offense."

He held his own hand out, too quickly for Oriannon to stop him, and shook the large man's hand.

"I'm her aide, Margus. Wist is our Owling friend, and Iakk—he's not so much of a sheep as all the others."

That brought a deep laugh from Modiin, who didn't let Margus go that easily but kept pumping his hand.

"Good," said Modiin, nodding and smiling. His entourage behind him smiled as well. "Very good. You and I know what's coming here very soon. They don't know, but you and I know. Even your blind friend knows. So when the time comes, we'll work together, eh?"

What did that mean, exactly? Margus didn't seem to know how to answer, but Modiin laughed it off and motioned for his men to follow him once more.

"We'll get a little more to eat," said Modiin in parting. "One thing about these sheep, they know how to eat."

Oriannon looked at her hand, grateful that Margus had run interference for her, and that Cirrus Main had not followed them out of the ballroom. She just hoped the handshake didn't get them into more trouble than before, in case it carried some deeper meaning to Modiin.

On the other hand, Iakk seemed frozen in fear, staring at the Makabi as they disappeared back into the crowded ballroom. Music and laughter filtered out to the hallway. Perhaps between abundant plates of refreshments and free-flowing glasses of spiced citron mead, they had already forgotten about the ugly face-off. Oriannon wasn't so sure.

"What did we just do?" she wondered aloud.

"And what was he meaning that our blind friend knows?" asked Wist. "I'm wondering what she's been telling them."

It was a good question, but no one knew the answer.

"I don't know what we did," said Margus, not slowing his pace. "But trust me, Oriannon, you are not getting into an alliance with these wild men, handshake or no handshake. We're getting out of here before the Troikans arrive."

Oriannon didn't argue. She'd made her grand speech, but she couldn't make them listen. Surely Jesmet couldn't ask for more.

And Iakk? Though he kept up with them, he said nothing as he looked over his shoulder—nervous and fidgeting, as if expecting someone to follow. Oriannon thought about asking him what he was expecting to see, but she really didn't want to know.

17

A few minutes later Oriannon paced around the dispensary, arms crossed and mind spinning. She kept an eye on her father, still sleeping soundly in a dark corner. Margus, standing by the door chewing his fingernails, wasn't helping matters.

"Look, Margus." She finally stopped and tried to explain. "First of all, you're driving me crazy with that nail-biting of yours. And secondly, you do know how much I appreciate what you've done, don't you?"

"All I was trying to do was make sure the Makabi left us alone until we could get out of here." He dropped his hands to his sides. "I don't trust them for a second."

"Me neither. Even though I think *they* think we made some kind of deal."

"Yeah, well, now that the ship is ready, it's time to get out of here. We should wake your dad."

Oriannon paused to see how serious he was.

"I know you think we should go back to Corista," she told him. "I do too. I'm just not sure I can go yet."

"What?" Margus held his hands out, as if he couldn't believe what she was telling him. "I don't get it. Jesmet told you to go to

Asylum 1 or 2, I suppose, so we went. We both know that was a disaster. So Jesmet told you to go to Asylum 3, and we agreed on account of your dad. Look how this is turning out. The Makabi get here and there's a riot. And when the Troikans arrive, it's going to go from a horrible situation to a meltdown. You really want to be here when that happens?"

"Margus!" She tried not to shout. "Don't you see that if we keep moving my dad around, he's never going to get better?"

"Maybe if we'd brought him back home in the first place, we wouldn't be having this conversation."

"Exactly. If we'd taken him back home in the first place, we wouldn't be having this conversation because my father would be dead. Sola's Security forces would have seen to that."

"Don't you think by now—"

"By now it could be worse. You really want to find out? I can't believe you're saying this."

Margus shook his head and turned away.

"I think you're overreacting, that's all. And you know what?"

He must have decided something just then, judging by the way he set his jaw and looked back at her with a steely look.

"I'm going back, Ori. I've decided."

"But ... back to what? You don't have any—"

She caught herself before finishing the word "family," but the fire in his eyes told her he knew what she nearly said.

"Go ahead!" He challenged her. "Say it! Margus doesn't have any reason to go back. Well, I still have family, even if Mom and Dad are ..."

His voice trailed off.

"Margus, I'm sorry. I didn't mean anything by it."

"Yeah, well ... I didn't think there was anything for me to go back to either, but I've been thinking. I can't keep chasing around out here in space, from way station to way station."

"But I thought you ..." She stumbled on the words, doing her best to fight off the wave of homesickness his words brought upon her. "I never thought you would be the one to say this."

"Well, we belong on Corista, and I want you to come back with me, Oriannon. Of course, if you're still set on this vision thing, then . . . I'm really sorry. I'm going anyway. I just have to."

"I can't believe what I'm hearing." Oriannon felt as if someone had just slammed her in the chest, ripping the air from her lungs. If Margus wouldn't stay with her, maybe Wist would. She turned to her quiet Owling friend, but Wist would not meet her gaze.

"Look, it doesn't have to be this way." Margus was putting on his take-charge-I-can-fix-this voice, but it wasn't working. "All you have to do it go home with us."

"Please. I don't even know where home is anymore." The emotion made everything blurry for a minute, and she had a hard time forcing out the words. If her friends wouldn't stick with her now, what then? "Jesmet asked me to go. He told me to do this, Margus, so I don't have a choice. I can't go back yet!"

"I know that's what *you* believe Jesmet said. I never understood why he didn't happen to say the same thing to me, you know?"

"You said you believed me." This was getting personal, and Oriannon could feel the heat rising on the back of her neck. He didn't have to say it that way. "Now you don't?"

Not saying anything and turning away was a clear answer.

"So after all this," she went on, "and after all we've been through?"

"Ori, don't do this. We don't have to— "

"Margus, have you been drinking the water here? Iakk says it does weird things to people, like it's some kind of drug. Because if you did, we can get you some help."

"This has nothing to do with drinking water!" Now he turned to her, red in the face. "It's just Oriannon dragging us around on a wild chase, Oriannon calling the shots, Oriannon getting us into more and more trouble. Well, I'm done with that. I really wish you'd open your eyes, Ori, and I really wish you'd come with us, but I'm done."

"Wait a minute." She held up her hand and turned to face Wist. "Did he say *us?* Wist, please tell me you're not going back with him."

Now it was Wist's turn to look embarrassed, and she would not look Oriannon in the eye, but bit her trembling lip.

"Wist?" Oriannon squeaked, fighting back the tears. Surely this could not be happening, not like this. Not both of them.

"I didn't know we'd be gone this many days." Wist barely whispered the words. "I'm missing my family, Ori. I have aunts and uncles ... cousins. My sister has four kids."

Oriannon knew the Owling people were close-knit, but she hadn't thought about it *this* way.

"And I'm not even knowing if they're still alive," Wist went on, "after everything that's happened. Please. I need to be going back home. I just have to."

"I guess I can see that," Oriannon whispered, though it hurt her to say so, and Wist's words made Oriannon wish again that she had a sister too. A sister with kids, or an aunt or uncle who might be wondering what had happened to her.

She couldn't think about that now, though, and so she retreated to her father's side, wondering how she could go on. Why didn't the others understand what she had to do? On the other hand, going to all the remaining way stations was going to be a challenge without a ship.

"So you're really going to take the shuttle?" she asked. Now Margus was tearing up as well. She couldn't remember when she'd seen him like that.

"I don't want to do this, Ori." His voice came out now barely louder than Wist's. "Please come with us before it gets really ugly here. I'm begging you."

"But my father." She still couldn't believe it, and when she rested her hand on her father's shoulder, his eyes fluttered open once again. She hoped he hadn't heard any of this.

"Ori." Her dad coughed and raised a hand to grab her by the hand. Perhaps whatever the healer had given him had run its course. Now his face burned once again with the fiercest of fevers, worse than ever. Under the covers she could see his shoulders shaking uncontrollably. She turned to the others.

"Go get Iakk," she asked them. "Please. Tell him to hurry."

Without question Margus and Wist hurried out. Even if Iakk hurried, Oriannon wasn't sure it would do any good. She peeked over at the vital signs meter, and while some of the readings had spiked, others dropped to near zero. It didn't take a healer to see her father was in distress.

"Ori," he whispered once more, and she kneeled beside her father, her own heart beating with a fear she had not known before. Always before she'd had a plan. Now what?

"No, Daddy." She rested a hand on his forehead, clammy and searing hot at the same time. He trembled beneath her touch. "Please don't say anything. You don't need to talk right now. Help is on the way."

He only shook his head and looked at her with the intense eyes she hadn't seen for such a long time—since before all the troubles in the Owling death camp. He squeezed her hand.

"Do you know I'm proud of you, Oriannon?" he told her, the words coming with obvious effort. She tried once again to quiet him.

"You shouldn't talk if it hurts. Why don't you get some more rest first, and then you can tell me all you want how proud you are."

He coughed again—a dry, hacking sound that brought Oriannon to tears once again. He glanced over at the stand next to her, and she took it as a request for water, so she helped him with a labored sip from his glass. She dabbed the spilled water from his chin with a clean cloth.

"I'm very proud," he told her with a labored voice. "You did the right thing, following your conscience."

"You mean, taking you here to this place?"

He nodded. Perhaps he knew more than she thought.

"We both know what would have happened if you hadn't rescued me, Ori. You saved my life, and besides that ..."

He couldn't finish the sentence this time on account of the deep, heaving coughs. His chest heaved as he fought for breath and came up short. With a terrifying jolt Oriannon realized that her father might not win this battle, and it made her tremble. So where was Iakk or the healer? Her father motioned for her to lean closer.

"I have to tell you something, Ori."

"Daddy, you—"

"Please just listen!" His eyes blazed though the rest of his body seemed to fail him. His eyes spoke more forcefully than his crippled voice could.

"I'm listening." She leaned in and held him close around the shoulder. "I'm listening."

"I am not going back to Corista," he finally told her, his voice sinking quickly.

"What do you mean?" She had to ask. "You're staying here or ..."

She could not make herself say the words.

"I'm never going back home. You know what that means, and you know what's written."

This time she wished more than anything that she did not. But he knew that his daughter could quote him the chapter and verse of the Codex. She nodded.

"I know."

"'And the son of the elder shall rise up in his stead, the daughter if there is no son, so that the lineage may not be broken.' I know you can quote all the verses. Sometimes I don't know if you understand what they really mean."

Now he closed his eyes to rest, so he could not see her nod. She knew. And once more she wished with all that was in her that she did not. Or better yet, she wished it meant something else, something entirely different. He gathered his strength once more and went on.

"It means that as the daughter of the last surviving elder, you're the only one who can return to Corista and re-establish the Ruling Assembly. You're the only one."

She squeezed her eyes tightly shut at his words, as if they hurt her as much as they hurt him. When she opened them again, Margus had stopped by the door, listening. In the quiet room he must have heard it all, but he left quickly while Oriannon turned back to her father.

"What if..." she whispered, "what if I didn't go back to Corista, or something happened to me too? What then?"

"It won't happen," he replied, sounding more sure of this than anything else he'd said. "The Maker won't allow it."

She thought about it for a while, wondering if it was so.

"I wish I wasn't ... you know," she finally admitted, and he nodded knowingly.

"I know. This wasn't the original plan, was it? But there's no one else. You're the only person who can do this, Oriannon. You are who you are."

She didn't answer. She could not answer.

"Just promise me just one thing," he whispered, "then I'll be done."

She could not refuse him. The problem was, she knew it was a promise she could not keep. Still she squeezed his hand as an answer.

"Promise me you'll..." He paused as if reconsidering. "Promise me you'll go back."

She paused, still afraid to answer, and afraid not to.

"I will," she finally blurted out, not knowing where the words came from. "I will, if Jesmet allows."

He looked at her, and she would not let go of his hand now. She couldn't be sure that he understood what she'd said, but a shadow of a smile came to his lips.

"Good. You ask him. I'm very ... sorry for the way things turned out."

"You're sorry? I'm the one who caused you so much trouble. If only I had—"

"No, no." He interrupted her with a weak shake of his head. "I never wanted to hurt you or your mentor. Forgive me."

"Oh, Daddy." She lowered her face now and buried it in his chest, sobbing quietly. "I love you so much. And I know you always loved me."

"Always will. Don't forget."

"You know I don't forget."

"Yes, then …" He struggled for breath, and she could tell he still had more on his mind. "Ori, the dream I told you about, the one so real?"

"I remember, Father. The one that was not a dream."

"Not?"

"It was really him, Daddy. He really was there. I know, because he talked to me that same night. Did he talk to you?"

Now she could feel the hot tears on his cheek, but she made no attempt to wipe them away. These would be her father's peace offering.

"You remember what he told you?" she asked, and she knew by her father's reaction that he did. Finally he took a deep breath and tried to explain, in the process probably spending what little strength he had left. He barely whispered the words.

"He told me … he wasn't dead any more. I told him I was sorry, as I just told you now. So sorry for getting it all wrong."

By that time her father seemed to be struggling with the heaviness of it all, and losing the battle.

"But Jesmet wasn't angry with you," she asked, "was he?"

Her father shook his head slowly.

"Not angry, the way I expected. I asked him to take care of you, and …"

"And what?"

"I woke before I heard his answer. But perhaps you know."

"I know. He said he would, Daddy. He said he would."

"Good. That's what I thought."

Now Tavlin rested his hand on her head for a while, his breath growing more and more shallow. Finally she began to hear his whispered words of the ancient blessing, the rare words of Old Coristan that she knew so well, but that were only spoken at funerals or special high holy days. She shifted on her knees to lean as close as she could.

"May the Maker bless thee and keep thee within the sound of His Song ... Jesmet." Tavlin Hightower's breath came in gasps now, and Oriannon held him gently, and her heart leaped as he added the name that had not been written in the original texts.

"May His light of favor shine brightly on you," he went on with much effort, still resting his hand on her head. "And may the melody of His peace fill you always and ..."

He paused to catch his breath and repeat the last words.

"Always and forever."

She rested in his blessing, rocking on her knees and unwilling to let go, praying to hear the beat of his heart. Without thinking she slipped the warm Pilot Stone out of her pocket and into his hands.

"Do you hear the Song?" she asked him. She thought she heard him sigh as a weak smile crossed his face. But he didn't answer, so she cradled her hands over his, helping him hold the Stone. His hands glowed bright gold now, as if the Stone could shine through his skin, and it looked to her as if the life of the Stone had filled his hands.

If only it would do more than that, or keep his heart beating just a little longer! But she could no longer feel the soft rise and fall of his breathing, and she knew what had finally overtaken her father.

"Oh, Daddy," she sobbed over and over as the light faded and her father's hands finally grew cold.

She heard an alarm sounding in the distance, like a bell tolling for her father's death, and she looked up to see Iakk had arrived.

Too late.

18

Though Oriannon thought she knew what to expect at a funeral for Corista's last elder, she was not prepared for the stiff, almost smothering formality of it all, the day after her father's death. After a somber procession from the ballroom, the scribes stood shoulder-to-shoulder in the hangar deck, shifting from foot to foot, whispering to each other and looking very much like they wanted to be somewhere else.

Oriannon watched from a small raised platform as the ceremony unfolded, feeling numb. She did not want to show her emotions now that every scribe in the way station could see her.

Her only consolations were Wist holding her hand and standing close by on her left side, and Margus standing close by on the right with his arm cradled protectively around her shoulder. Thanks to those two and their strong arms, she would not collapse into a new puddle of tears. Iakk looked up at her from the front row, sympathy and sadness etched on his face. Though several meters away, he seemed to hold her as tightly as her two friends.

Cirrus Main, on the other hand, stood stiffly as the main speaker. The scribes and their families listened politely, nearly a thousand strong, and packed into the landing area.

If nothing else, the scribes of Asylum 3 remained polite, and certainly adhered to the decorum of a funeral. It was, as Cirrus Main had said only a few hours earlier, the least they could do to honor her father's memory.

"We witness here the end of an era," he announced, his amplified voice reverberating over the heads of the scribes. "An era when the Elders of Corista brought the wisdom of the Codex to the people of the planet and stability to the scribes of asylum way stations. Now we continue to work for the harmony, even as Elder Hightower would have wanted."

How do you know what Father wanted? Oriannon nearly shouted, but held back with the most stoic expression she could manage.

She glanced over to see how Sola was taking all this as she stood quietly at the edge of the platform. How ironic, she thought, that the woman who had done so much to bring about the demise of the six elders now stood quietly at the last one's funeral. At least Sola's blindness prevented her from seeing all that was going on. Perhaps that was a small measure of justice, if there could be such a thing at a time like this. Unfortunately justice wasn't going to bring her father back.

Oriannon stood, not catching many of the words as Cirrus Main droned on, and trying her best not to look at Sola. The woman did have some nerve being there. At least she would have no chance to whip up the emotions of gathered crowds the way she had back on Corista when she used to address millions as the First Citizen.

No, here someone else addressed the crowd, and someone else from the back of the crowd shouted over Cirrus Main:

"Corista will be restored! Vengeance for the planet and her people!"

Judging by the silence, perhaps the gathered scribes were just as stunned as Oriannon. Cirrus Main choked on his final words. But in the distance Oriannon heard a muffled grunt of approval, then several, then a clapping of hands. The scribes turned in obvious surprise to stare at Modiin and his ragged group of unshaven Makabi gathered in the back row behind most of the crowds.

Modiin! Oriannon hadn't spotted him at first. She hadn't imagined they would tolerate such a ceremony. But even the stares didn't seem to dampen the enthusiasm of the Makabi, who continued their demonstration for several seconds before finally giving it up. Modiin stared back at the scribes around them as he clapped.

Cirrus Main took the lead once more, and he directed everyone's attention back to the object Oriannon least wanted to see — the floating, silver bullet-shaped space casket containing her father's body. With a scribe's light touch on each end to guide it, they floated the casket past the crowds and into the airlock where visiting shuttles would normally land.

Oriannon exchanged a long glance with Wist. She was sure the Owling girl was thinking the same thing though it seemed so long ago. They couldn't help remembering when Wist's grandfather, Suuli, had passed away and all of Lior had gathered for the procession. The Owling people had filled their cliffside city with song, celebrating a life well lived and reminding each other of the hope they shared for a life beyond. There, sad smiles blended with tears and voices singing Jesmet's Song to electrify the city. It jolted Oriannon with the hope of life.

Here Oriannon doubted the polite scribes even knew how to sing.

Everyone pressed safely away from the outer landing area. The pallbearers left the casket and stepped back as the clear force-field curtain descended and separated it from the crowd. They all stood and watched — except Oriannon.

No, she decided, she would not just stand there, acting as dead and lifeless as the body in the casket. She would not pretend to be calm and officious, qualities these scribes cultivated. Her father deserved better. She began humming the Song they had sung for Suuli's funeral in the Owling city, the Song that Mentor Jesmet taught them in orchestra class, the Song he had sung the first morning after he'd been executed.

Wist joined her immediately, and a moment later so did Margus. He harmonized with the Pilot Stone's deep melodies, learned from the mentor himself. Oriannon didn't care if anyone else understood, or if it sounded strange. They claimed this music — Jesmet's Song — for their own, and through tears, Oriannon claimed it for her father.

Perhaps no one else could hear it anyway, although Iakk leaned forward in concentration. Even Sola seemed to hear, but she snapped her head around in what looked like alarm, and the bitter knit of her brow furrowed even more deeply — as if the soft music of eternity hurt her ears. Oriannon almost expected her to scream at them to stop, though she would hardly have obeyed.

This music didn't need the words, though Jesmet had taught those too. It was enough for them to comfort themselves in the shared music. It reminded Oriannon of the times her father had calmed her when she was a little girl, crying and afraid of dark or scary things in her closet.

Cirrus Main paused a moment, then nodded and signaled for the massive outside triple doors to open. The casket seemed close enough to touch, but the clear force-field curtain shielded them. With a hiss the outer landing bay evacuated its atmosphere and the casket along with it. And so the casket began its long, symbolic journey to the Trion, which the Codex told them the Maker created first.

Abruptly, the strange, somber ceremony concluded. The hangar deck's tri-doors slowly closed, breathable air flooded the area with a renewed hiss, and the safety force field faded. Without another word Cirrus Main accompanied Sola from the platform. The scribes dispersed, and gentle conversation once again seasoned the air, as if they had been waiting for a signal to return to their pleasant routine once more.

"Ori." Wist finally spoke. "If there's anything we can do ..."

Oriannon shook her head and tried to smile. "Actually, I just need a little time to myself, you guys. Can I meet you back at the rooms in a few hours?"

Wist understood. She nodded and turned to leave, while Margus shrugged and turned the other direction, toward the small storage bay where their shuttle was parked.

"I've got to check a couple of things on the ship," he told them. "Some of the controls still need to be calibrated."

She understood the tone of his words. Right now, though, she could only think of her father, and she needed a few moments to pray and for everything to sink in. As everyone else dispersed, she walked quietly to where the tri-doors had released her father into the blackness of space beyond. A couple of viewports allowed her a peek out, while a glimmering yellow laser stripe hovering just above the floor told her not to approach too closely.

"Please take care of him, Jesmet," she whispered, and it didn't seem such an odd thing to ask. She stood with her arms crossed, peering out at uncountable points of light. She never tired of looking at the stars, since she'd so rarely been able to see them through the constant brightness of Corista when she was growing up. Here the Trion seemed so much more distant.

" . . . even where the Trion is but a faint glimmer in the night sky."

The verse from Codex seemed to fit now, more than ever. But deep in thought, she didn't even hear the footsteps coming up behind her—until a hand rested on her shoulder and it was too late.

With a cry of surprise Oriannon spun around to face Modiin and two of his well-muscled men. They had not cleaned up since they'd arrived at the way station.

"I didn't hear you coming." She gulped and backed into the tri-doors, breaking into the warning zone and setting off an alarm.

"Warning!" came a disembodied voice as the air flashed yellow all around them. "Please back away from the doors! Please— "

He pulled her roughly away from the warning zone, setting her down on the floor behind the laser lines. The noise stopped, and she backed away as far as she could, but the three Makabi surrounded her.

What if I screamed? she asked herself. Maybe Margus would hear her, maybe not. Or maybe he had heard the alarms. Either way, she didn't see anyone coming to investigate.

"This changes things, you know." Modiin looked around as if he thought someone might be listening, and perhaps they were. Oriannon nodded and wondered what he was getting at.

"Excuse me." She tried to find an opening between them and get past. "I was just leaving."

"Not yet." The Makabi didn't budge.

"What do you want?" she asked. She could always step into the warning zone again to set off the alarm. But even with his gruff exterior, Modiin didn't look as if he would hurt her. He made his point with a finger stabbing the air.

"There's no other elders left, eh? That's what the woman tells me. You know what that means?"

Now he was asking her questions? Oriannon had an idea what he was getting at, though she couldn't fathom why he would care about the successor to an elder. She cleared her throat.

"By 'the woman,' I assume you mean Sola Minnik."

"She don't give up, even if she can't see a hand in front of her face."

Oriannon stepped back to avoid Modiin's unpleasant breath.

"I noticed she was spending time with you guys," she blurted out, and instantly regretted it. Modiin spit on the floor as he'd done before, barely missing Oriannon's feet.

"That a problem?" he challenged her.

"We just noticed, that's all, and ..."

And Oriannon wished he would go away. Nothing these men could do would make things better, and this fellow Modiin made her nervous.

"All right, so notice this." Modiin sucked on his crooked teeth and lowered his voice. "Because you're going to be right there in the middle of it. You know what's going to happen as soon as the Troikans try to take Corista, don't you?"

He clearly wasn't looking for her answer as he went on.

"The Makabi will rise up to fight them, and when we all unite, we win." He raised his fist for emphasis. "But if we Makabi are to take our rightful place on Corista once again, we need a leader everyone can accept and recognize, someone who knows the Old Ways."

He made a dramatic pause before pointing directly at her, which hardly seemed necessary.

"That's you, Oriannon Hightower of Nyssa."

If her father's dying words hadn't sounded eerily similar she might have dismissed him or turned away with a laugh. As it was, she could not. But she also could not think of how to react as he continued.

"You know Codex can be taken to mean that you are the rightful leader of Corista. The *only* leader. Not a pretender like your friend Sola Minnik."

Oriannon wasn't sure whether to object to his use of the word *friend* in the same sentence as *Sola Minnik*, or if she should object to what he was saying about the rightful leader of Corista. Either way, she didn't want to hear it, but she had no choice but to keep listening.

"Your father would have wanted this, you know."

She shook her head to free herself of the tangled web this man had tried to throw over her.

"How do you know what he would have wanted?" she countered. "You have no right to say that, or to try to speak for him."

"Apologies ..." He bowed his head slightly. " ... that I'm the one to remind you of it, since the scribes here will not. But you know it's true. Being a Hightower, you know what duty to Corista means."

"That's where you're mistaken." She straightened up, finally more sure of herself. "If you think I'm going to go along with you and your ... rebellion, just because you think I'm loyal to Corista, well, that's where you're wrong."

"Oh?" He raised his eyebrows in surprise. "Then to whom would you be loyal, if not to your clan, your people, and your planet?"

He asked as if there was no other right answer than the one he offered, as if she could do nothing but submit to his preordained argument.

"I follow the Maker's Song now," she declared, and saying the words aloud helped fix her resolve. "Jesmet ben Saius."

The words took a moment to sink in, but then a smile crept onto Modiin's face. He quivered, then nearly doubled over in laughter, so his stiff bodyguards were obliged to chuckle along with him too, though they surely didn't understand why.

Oriannon just waited until he'd caught his breath again.

"You'll forgive me," he finally said. "I should have known."

"You know of him then?" She decided to press the point as he wiped the tears from his eyes with the back of his rough-looking hand.

"Yes, actually. Rumors. We heard them at Asylum 1, but didn't know what to make of them. He's the mentor who was executed, but now they say he's been sighted again? Pretty good trick; I wish he'd teach it to me. In my line of work it might come in handy someday."

"It's not a trick." She pressed her lips together firmly, wondering how much to tell him. "He *is* alive."

Modiin took this assertion with only the slightest of smiles. His voice, however, had taken on a condescending tone, as if he was now speaking to a younger girl with an imaginary playmate.

"Well then," he told her, crossing his arms. "What does your mentor say about joining in the struggle to free your own people? Certainly he's not against that kind of idea, eh?"

"Jesmet doesn't lead armies," she told him. At that his face turned red with rage. His hands clenched into fists.

"So does your Jesmet stand by while the Coristan empire is torn apart, one way station at a time? Does he wave his holy hand and give blessing while Troikans exterminate innocent people and drag away their homes to build their own world? Is that what he does?"

"No, he— " Oriannon was afraid Modiin no longer listened.

"Just wondering, Miss Hightower. You didn't happen to know anyone on Asylum 1? The one that was destroyed?"

Oriannon shook her head no, and by this time she definitely did not enjoy the tone of his questions.

"I'm sure you didn't," he went on. "You wouldn't know what happened to my sister Neera and her family."

Somehow Oriannon hadn't imagined a man like Modiin with a sister, much less a sister he seemed to care about. Still he wasn't done.

"She went there with a service team to upgrade their data processing systems," he told her, the sharp edge returning to his voice. "It was a two-month assignment, so her husband stayed home on Corista and she brought along her twelve-year-old daughter. The Troikans killed them both."

Oriannon stood awkwardly, not knowing what to do with her hands.

"I'm sorry," she whispered, and Modiin leaned closer.

"What did you say?"

"I said, I'm sorry about your sister and your niece. And I'm very sorry ... for you. What else do you want me to say?"

"Maybe you are." Modiin leaned back again. "So go ahead, get out of here. Get out of my sight."

Yet as much as she wanted to run from this strange man, now her legs would not obey her commands.

"I said go!" he shouted. Oriannon had no idea why they had not attracted anyone else's attention with all the noise and shouting.

"You don't understand," she finally told him.

"Is that what you think?" He patted himself on the chest. "I don't understand. Now the queen of Corista says I don't understand."

"I'm not the queen of Corista, no matter what you say. But Jesmet has sent me to warn the other way stations about the Troikans. That's why I won't go with you."

That, among a hundred other reasons.

"That's why you *won't*," he countered, "or why you *will*? Looks to me as if can we accomplish both your errand and mine, then your mentor would be more than pleased, eh? You'll come with us, along with the blind woman."

No, she would most definitely not go with him. Oriannon's stomach turned at the thought of leaving Asylum 3 with this man, with the Makabi, and most of all with Sola Minnik. She could think of nothing worse.

"We leave in ninety minutes," he told her, returning to the presumptuous air of someone used to getting his way. "So you'd best say your good-byes and gather anything you want to bring along."

Since he did not require an answer, she simply pushed past him to go.

"And you know the biggest irony of all this, Oriannon?" His question halted her, and so did the way he used her first name. "It's actually an interesting bit of trivia. My clan name is Nyssa. Do you know what that means?"

"It means you're lying. My father was an only child, and so am I. The other part of the clan is long gone."

"Long gone, you think, but we're still alive. You and I are distant cousins, Oriannon. So your relatives died on Asylum 1 too. The Troikans killed them. Does that make any difference to you?"

Oriannon bit her lip and hurried away without answering. It made no difference even if it happened to be true, which it most certainly was not. She would not travel with the Makabi. She would rather stay on the station and look for another way to go on.

"Margus!" she called out, still fuming that he had not come out to rescue her. "Where are you?"

19

Okay, but you need to explain that to me." It sounded as if Iakk had come back to debate with Margus. Oriannon heard the voices growing louder as she hurried back to their shuttle and stepped up the boarding ladder.

"I don't know what to tell you, Iakk," replied Margus. "You need to ask Oriannon. She always knows—"

When she stepped inside, Margus turned to her from where he sat on the floor, his arms buried inside an access hole beneath a control panel. So did Iakk, who stood over him with his hands full of spanners and magnetometers. Both fell silent the moment she walked in, but Margus gulped and reached for one of the tools.

"Here," he whispered, "I'll take that one."

Oriannon waited for a moment to see if they would ask first, but gave up.

"So what were you going to ask me?" she said.

Margus pretended not to know what she was talking about. "Ask you?"

"Oh, come on." She looked to Iakk instead, who dropped his tools on the floor and shook his head.

"It was nothing, really," he told her. "I don't want to disturb you ... not now."

Really, she didn't have time for this, so she shook her head and headed for the back of the ship, looking for Wist but hurting more with each step. She stopped for a moment to make sure both cabins were empty. Thankfully Sola was not on board. Oriannon stopped to look in her father's cabin and fought away the grief that threatened to wash over her again.

"I'm so sorry, Oriannon." Iakk followed her. "I don't know if I told you at the funeral, but I'm very sorry. About your father, I mean. All the scribes were sorry."

She dug her hands in her pockets, where she felt the comforting warmth of the Pilot Stone. Behind them, Wist breezed by with her arms full of supplies and deposited her load in the control room where Margus was working.

"Here's all the stuff you're needing from the lower deck," she told him. "But what about Oriannon?"

Ori poked her head out of the sleeping room just in time to see Margus hold a finger to his lips and point back her way.

"Like I didn't see that?" Oriannon stepped out, causing Wist to gasp when she turned and saw her. "Let's figure this out now, okay?"

The last thing Oriannon wanted was to drag this argument back out into the open, but she had no choice. Margus slammed the access hatch shut and kicked his tools to the side as he stood up to join them.

"Okay." He broke the heavy silence. "None of us wanted to put you in this position right now, Oriannon, with your dad ... you know."

"I don't blame you." Oriannon felt her shoulders slump. It wasn't their fault, she knew. "It's just the way it happened."

"We would have waited," Wist put in. "You are knowing that."

"I know. There's just no time. It just happened this way. I know."

"Okay." Margus nodded and looked up with a sigh. "So I'm hoping maybe you changed your mind, Ori, and you're going with us?"

Oriannon crossed her arms and shook her head.

"I wish," she told them. "I really do, and you must know that. But I have to keep going."

The words ripped at her heart. She tried to look at Wist, but the Owling girl had already turned away. Wist's shoulders jerked with emotion, and in a moment that would drag Oriannon's tears out as well. But she had already cried too much this day. She didn't know if she could handle any more.

"Okay, but ..." Margus seemed to take the high road, making his voice sound more gruff and official than he usually did. "If Wist and I take the shuttle back home, what are you going to do? You don't have any other way of getting to the next way station. I think you should stay here where it's safe."

"That's a lame idea," Oriannon argued. Of all people, Margus should know that what she said was true. "In fact, it's going to get really dangerous here really soon."

"You don't know that." Now Margus was getting stubborn again, and Oriannon felt her irritation rise. She couldn't help getting angry when he said dumb things like that, especially when he knew better.

"Margus, listen." She took a deep breath, trying not to snap at him. "We both know the safest place is where Jesmet wants us to be. Well, Jesmet wants me to go to the next asylum way station. He's told me that, or I wouldn't do it. Don't you think I'd rather go with you back to Corista?"

"If that's true," he replied, crossing his arms to match her challenge, "then you should. It was what you promised your dad you'd do, wasn't it?"

"Margus!" She threw up her hands in anger, and now she could have slapped him. "I'd go if I could, but you know I can't go yet. I am so tired of arguing with you."

Margus looked to Iakk, who stepped back a few paces to avoid the exchange.

"What about you?" he asked Iakk. "Why don't you leave with us? We can take a couple more people, anybody who's smart enough to leave before the Troikans get here—assuming they're coming."

Iakk looked from one to the other, as if trying to decide which side to believe, or what to do next.

"I—I don't know what to say," he finally mumbled.

"Well, don't worry about hurting anybody's feelings." Margus told him. "I think that's already been done all around."

He glanced at Wist, who leaned against the entry to the control room. Oriannon stepped up to her and rested a hand on her shoulder.

"It's not your fault, Wist."

"Don't be telling me it's not my fault!" Wist blurted out the words, and when she turned, her large eyes looked bloodshot. Oriannon had never seen her friend this upset. "It's all our faults, and we need to be stopping now and fixing this."

"We can't, Wist." Margus sounded deflated and defeated—not his usual way. But Oriannon was afraid he was right. "We need to go one way, and I guess Ori needs to go another. There's just no other way to work it this time. I wish ..."

He closed his eyes and sighed, and that said it for all of them.

I wish. Oriannon could think of lots of ways to finish the sentence for him.

I wish we were still all in this together instead of splitting apart.

I wish Father hadn't died and that he could help us figure this out.

I wish Jesmet hadn't asked me to go on this insane journey from way station to way station, and for what? That's when she came very close to throwing up her hands and giving up. She could give up and go home, and maybe no one would be disappointed with her any more.

No one except Jesmet, the one she'd promised. She closed her eyes and clenched her fists.

Okay, she told herself. *I keep going. And if I have to, I keep Sola Minnik with me, even if my best friends don't understand.*

She wrapped her arms around Wist's shoulders as they said good-bye. Margus waited a moment before he wrapped them both in a hug of his own.

"I'm so sorry it turned out this way," he whispered, but now Oriannon pulled back and held up her hand.

"No more apologies," she announced, wiping back the last tears with her sleeve, "and no more crying. I don't know about you, but I've done enough crying today to last me for the next ten years. I'll get back to Corista; just not now. You guys be careful, okay?"

She tried to smile, though the effort hurt her face. Margus pointed out the entry hatch.

"I'll offload some water bottles for you, enough to last for a while. Use them, okay?"

Oriannon nodded. No problem there. So Margus turned to their new scribe friend once more.

"And you never gave me your answer," he told Iakk. "I still think it would be a good idea if you came with me and Wist. What do you say?"

Iakk looked from one to the other, his mouth agape, until he finally whispered his reply.

"My life is not the same since you came," he finally told them, his voice breaking. "And I want you to know that I deeply appreciate your offer to me and your kindness. But when I came here, I made a vow to follow the Maker here in this place. Even if the others do not, I will. Thank you. But just as your place is back on Corista, mine is here."

They watched as he stepped away and down the ramp to the hangar deck below. Margus shook his head, but Oriannon understood why Iakk could not leave this place. She started to follow, but changed her mind as Iakk glanced over his shoulder and waved.

She would follow him just a few minutes later, but only after she had given Wist one more hug, and Margus had given her one more chance to change her mind.

"You know I'll come back," she asked, "don't you?"

Margus didn't answer right away, just raised his finger and pointed straight at her.

"You'd better," he told her. "That's all I can say."

●●●

An hour later Margus's words still echoed in her mind as she watched through a viewport from the level above the hangar deck. She pressed her hands against the cold glassteel and watched as the shuttle's blue running lights grew smaller and smaller, then disappeared entirely.

Funny how the scribes were so big on the welcome, but Cirrus Main hardly had a word for Margus and Wist as they left the station. Not that they needed a full going-away ceremony or anything. It just seemed weird to Oriannon as she thought about it, and even more weird to be watching them go. She gently thumped her forehead on the viewport and wondered what she had just done, or how stupid she had just been.

I let them go, she told herself, the pain welling inside. *I really let them go!*

It took a few minutes to convince herself that they were not going to turn right around and come back to her, no matter how hard she stared into the empty blackness beyond — only slightly more empty than what she felt inside.

And though she knew what Jesmet wanted her to do, that didn't mean she knew how to do it.

"What now?" she whispered into the darkness. "I did what you said, and now I'm stranded here."

But the darkness did not answer. She couldn't help wondering if she would ever get back home, or if she would ever see her friends again.

20

By now they're more than three hours into their flight, Oriannon told herself, trying to roughly calculate how far her friends had traveled. Three hours and forty-nine minutes times a maximum sustained speed of ...

Though as an eidich she remembered everything she ever heard or saw, those abilities never seemed to help her calculate navigational algorithms the way Margus could.

So she kept walking along the elevated walkway above the edge of the commons with Iakk as she imagined the empty reaches of space Margus and Wist were flying through. She forced herself to push away the heavy crush of loneliness and tried to think of something else.

Wist will be happy to see her family again, she thought.

If Wist could find them after they landed. If Securities didn't seize her and Margus the moment they returned. Right now those seemed like two very large ifs.

"Let me guess," Iakk said after another minute of walking. From here they could look down on the entire commons. "It's been four hours since your friends left, and you're already missing them. Am I right?"

Though he took a sip from a steaming cup of vupp, he didn't seem any different from the way he was before. Perhaps, she thought, he'd overestimated the whole vupp/water reaction. The thought surprised her but she let it stand.

"Three hours and fifty-two minutes." She nodded. "But it's not just that. Now I have to find a way to get to the next way station before it's too late."

"I admire that." He smiled and nodded as if he agreed with everything she said. "You care about what happens to other people, and not just yourself."

"Well ..." Now her words felt more like a duty than a desire.

"No, really. I understand your concerns, and I appreciate what you're trying to do. But please refresh my memory. What would happen if you stayed just a little longer, a few more days? You could tell me more about Jesmet, and about the Stone. Isn't that why you came — to tell others?"

Oriannon thought about it, and yes, that did sound very much like the reason she had come. Maybe Iakk was right. In fact, staying at this comfortable way station didn't sound bad at all, especially compared to the alternative. She looked around to see scribes sitting in comfortable, overstuffed chairs, huddled in their usual conversations or playing table games with pieces of red and green colored glass. Others reclined and watched stories on handheld screens.

"Besides," he went on, "you might not have a choice. I don't think any vessels are leaving here for at least another two weeks. Maybe longer."

She nodded in agreement, watching him as he took another sip from his mug. The sound of laughter and waterfalls drifted up from below, and she swallowed once again to fend off the growing lump in her throat.

"Sometimes I don't really know why I'm being so stubborn about this," she told him.

"You can always change your mind about anything. It's never too late."

The aroma from his steaming cup drifted her way, and it smelled even better than before, like some of the best vupp back home on Corista. If this brew was anything like that, she could use a good hot cup right now. Anything would taste better than the stale water supply they'd relied on for the past several days on the shuttle. It might help take her mind off the loss of Wist and Margus.

"All your friends are gone now," he said, "aren't they?"

She looked at his sad, tired eyes and felt sorry for this young scribe. "Maybe not all of them."

"Then it's good for you to stay." He held up his cup with a weak smile. "Good for harmony."

What did he say? *Harmony?* His words felt like cold water thrown in her face, and she knew in an instant it would be too easy to give up and stay on Asylum 3, forgetting what Jesmet had told her. What was she *thinking?* She gripped the railing and swallowed hard.

"Iakk, wait," she told him, shaking her head to clear her thoughts. "Didn't you say before that you wanted to leave? Didn't you say that sometimes—in between—you can really think? Don't you want to think again?"

He stopped, looking more weary now than he had before, and ran his fingers through his hair with a sigh.

"I *do* want to think, Oriannon. I just get tired sometimes. You can understand, can't you?"

Oriannon didn't answer right away, and as Iakk turned away, a sudden jolt—like an earthquake—nearly knocked them off their feet.

"What in the world?" The shockwave startled Iakk so much that his mug slipped out of his grasp, tumbling over the railing to shatter on the tile floor, fifteen stories below.

Oriannon prayed the falling mug wouldn't injure someone as the entire station reverberated. She grabbed for a railing to keep from falling to her knees. Overhead lights blinked twice, then went completely out before auxiliary power kicked in a moment later.

"Iakk! What's happening?" Alarms sounded all over the station.

"I don't know!" Iakk's eyes widened as he took her hand and they hurried for the stairs. "I've never felt anything like this before."

Scribes from all the top levels crowded behind them on the narrow concrete stairs, pushing and murmuring in panic as alarms shredded the once-calm air. One of them still carried his mug, but a dark splash of vupp stained his robe. Someone stepped on her heels from behind, threatening to push her over, but she held on to Iakk for balance.

"Don't push!" Iakk yelled over the sound of the alarms, but panic showed on his face too, like sweat trickling down their foreheads. They weaved down the stairs in tight circles, not knowing what to expect when they reached the main level. She could smell raw panic all around her.

Meanwhile alarms continued, forcing Oriannon to clamp her hands over her ears. Loud thuds from high overhead made it feel and sound as if a giant creature was clamped onto the way station's overhead plexi-bubble or that they were in the grip of something huge.

"This has never happened before!" Iakk shouted as they stepped over the debris of an access panel that had popped out of the wall. Bright blue sparks cascaded from one of them. A conduit popped loose from the ceiling, spraying green coolant over their heads, and several of the scribes behind and above them screamed in surprise.

Oriannon did her best not to trip on the heels of scribes just in front of them, but suddenly, at the sound of rough grunts and shouted commands, robes lunged to either side and the crowd opened to bring her and Iakk face-to-face with a handful of Modiin's Makabi.

"Move aside!" yelled the first one, fire blazing in his eyes, as he climbed ahead and pushed against the flow. Behind him his friends shoved everyone to the right and left, flattening startled scribes face-first against the walls. Several Makabi carried rigid black tote cases under their arms, as if they were busy moving their luggage from one place to the other. Oriannon steered clear as they continued up and shoved past without another word. She looked to Iakk for a clue, but he shrugged and shook his head as they helped a couple of scribes get back on their feet.

"They do what they do," he said, as if that explained everything. "Let's keep going."

By this time nothing should have surprised Oriannon about the Makabi.

The real surprise hit when they finally made it to the bottom of the stairwell and stepped through sliding doors out onto the commons. A wave of people swept by, taking nearly everyone in its path. Oriannon and Iakk stepped back into an alcove for safety.

"Wait!" Oriannon tried to stop one of the scribes as he ran by. She had never before seen scribes running this way, robes and arms flying. It was as if a deadly animal had been let loose somewhere behind them and everyone had to flee for their lives. "What's going on? What are you running from?" This one didn't even slow down.

They could see the mob was moving away from the general direction of the hangar deck. Several scribes tumbled in the panic but managed to pick themselves up and continue on. The way station shook again, and pieces of heavy ceiling tiles fell from above. Iakk tried to shield Oriannon from one of the pieces, but it hit him in the back and he crumpled to the floor.

"Iakk!" Oriannon screamed and fell to her knees. Iakk rolled over and groaned in pain.

"I'm all right," he told her, but from the strain in his voice and the gash on his back, she wasn't so sure. She helped him to his feet and dragged him back as far as she could into the alcove.

Now more scribes huddled there for safety. She wondered what could have caused this disaster. Then, almost as suddenly as it had begun, the noise and the bedlam stopped. Iakk pointed toward the hangar deck, then pulled his hand back suddenly and whispered into her ear.

"Say nothing," he told her, and Oriannon was glad to comply as she watched the strangers draw closer. They seemed to take no account of the crowds that drew away from them.

At first Oriannon thought she was looking at three Coristan men striding toward them, each one dressed in the loose-fitting tunic of an upper-class merchant or government worker. All wore the same style of straight, black, shoulder-length hair. Truthfully, Oriannon had a hard time deciding whether they were men or women. But a closer look at their chalky gray skin and heavily tattooed faces told Oriannon these were no ordinary Coristans. Certainly they looked nothing like the Makabi — no more than the highest Coristan elder looked like the lowest commoner.

All three held long-handled disruptor weapons of a kind she didn't recognize, but which clearly signaled this was no social call. Iakk knew what was happening. He pulled himself farther back into the shadows and leaned over once more to whisper in her ear.

"You were wondering what a Troikan looked like?" He nodded this time, rather than pointing at them. "There they are. They all look alike, don't they?"

The Troikan threesome came to a halt in front of the cowering scribes and waited until Cirrus Main came hurrying around a corner, skidding to a stop. Oriannon hadn't seen him move that quickly since she'd arrived, nor had she ever seen the look of terror that flashed across his face before he wrestled it away and replaced it with his usual composed smile.

"How good to see you again." Cirrus Main's voice shook nearly as much as his hands as he bowed before the new arrivals. "Please forgive me for not greeting you at the hangar deck. We weren't anticipating your arrival."

His words betrayed him, as Oriannon realized that Cirrus Main recognized the Troikans.

He knew them!

Finally the Troikan woman turned to Cirrus with a clear look of distaste.

"You will gather your people on the hangar deck immediately, where evacuation plans will be explained."

"Yes, I see. You must pardon our reaction, however. We weren't sure what was happening. I'm sure ..."

The Troikans didn't seem to notice his nervous prattling as they looked about the inside of the way station with detached interest. Oriannon couldn't help staring at their skin, every centimeter of which was covered in strange and awful designs — black, blue, and silver, mostly geometric, in a dark style that made her shiver. More amazing was the way the tattoos moved and glowed — from one small section on the neck, a pulse of energy slid like a serpent across the jaw and to the other side of the face.

Even more strangely, the dark glow of the tattoos seemed to flow freely from one Troikan to the next, roping them together in an unmistakable connection. The woman nodded slowly as the man closest to them glanced at her. Oriannon could tell these three people shared an odd link, as if all three spoke at once and the lips of only one moved.

"You're always very welcome here," Cirrus Main now babbled on. He was the spurned host who didn't know which foot to take out of his mouth first, while the strain of his monumental lies and desperate pleading creased his face and made him appear as if he would burst into tears at any moment. Poor Cirrus.

Although he kept up his brave face, Oriannon knew he would soon crumble under the weight. His lips shook as he pleaded. "We have never been your enemy. Please! You do know that, don't you?"

Beads of sweat now glistened on Cirrus Main's forehead, but he could not seem to unlock his hands from their pleading position.

"Please won't you come and rest? Perhaps you would like something to eat. A comfortable room. None of this violence is necessary. We can make your stay comfortable and profitable. We can provide you with everything you need, just as we agreed before."

There it was again—if Oriannon needed any more proof that Cirrus Main knew these new guests or that they'd had contact with the scribes before. Now Iakk's story about the scribes who had been taken away earlier by the Troikans was starting to make more sense.

And then without warning, Oriannon felt herself pushed from behind, hard, so that she tumbled to the feet of the Troikans.

She lay helpless as a sargeonfish out of water, gasping in shock and flat on her back, staring helplessly up at the angry faces of the three intruders, and the even more angry ends of their three weapons.

21

Oriannon instinctively covered her face as she lay on the floor in front of the three Troikan invaders. She knew death from a disruptor would be swift but painful when every cell in her body exploded.

"Jesmet," she whispered to her mentor. "I'm sorry I didn't finish what you sent me to do."

Instead of an answer, she heard one of the scribes announcing loudly that Oriannon had something the Troikans would enjoy. She chose not to believe that she recognized the voice, and she could not force herself to look.

"A stone that sings," announced the scribe, "and that possesses some kind of power. I've heard it brought her here to the way station, and she calls it a Pilot Stone. You'll be amused. She keeps it in her pocket."

Oriannon looked up to see Iakk bending over her, pulling her to her feet. She did not resist when he reached into her pocket for the Stone, but she grabbed his wrist long enough to look into his troubled eyes.

"Iakk!" she said quietly, shamed now for having trusted him so completely. "Why are you doing this?"

Iakk looked away just long enough to catch his mentor's eye, and Oriannon caught the slightest nod of approval from Cirrus Main before she released Iakk's wrist and he brought up the sacred Stone.

"For harmony, of course," he answered with a straight face. "You understand."

"I don't understand anything anymore. Did you really mean anything you said in the library? Or did you make it all up?"

"The library?" He looked at her with a genuinely puzzled expression. "I haven't been to the library in years."

In a way, she didn't blame him, and maybe this Iakk was telling her the truth. This Iakk was just doing what his mentor wanted him to do, and his mentor wanted to preserve the harmony on Asylum 3, no matter what.

Yet in another way she wanted to strangle him, as she'd wanted to do with Sola. And where was Sola, anyway? Never mind, Iakk was her problem now. Oriannon couldn't handle one more enemy—particularly not one who seemed sincere and seeking one moment and treacherous the next. The treacherous one held up the Stone and stepped over to the Troikans.

Oriannon knew they were sadly mistaken if they thought the Troikans could be distracted with something like the Pilot Stone. She was right; the Troikans were not interested in what the scribes had to offer. They ignored the Stone and scanned the area like wild animals catching the scent of danger. Another monumental thud sounded above their heads, the clear sound of something sinister happening outside the dome. Oriannon guessed the Troikans had arrived with some kind of grappling equipment—perhaps stage one of removing or destroying this way station. Was this the way they had eliminated Asylum 1?

The people around her drew back, anticipating an explosion. The Troikan woman stared at the promenade deck above them, where Oriannon and Iakk had been walking. As her brow furrowed, the tattoo on her forehead turned glowing amber, and then the sympathetic tattoos on the other two faces did the same.

"You didn't tell us of any other visitors." She directed her gaze at Cirrus Main, while Iakk held out the prize, his desperate attempt to appease this invader. Oriannon looked for a way to grab it back.

"Other guests?" Cirrus Main played dumb. "We're always happy to welcome anyone who arrives, like yourselves." If Cirrus had sounded nervous before, now his words ran together in a heart-attack slur.

The Troikans' tattoos suddenly turned flaming red, and the woman reached out and grabbed Cirrus by the throat. "Stop your babbling!" she hissed, pulling him face-to-face. "Who else is here at the station? Coristan Security?"

With a crash, several more ceiling tiles tumbled to the floor, causing everyone to cower.

"No, no!" Cirrus babbled on, having officially lost control of the situation. "No Security, I swear. We just weren't expecting you so soon."

If the Troikan woman took a tighter grip on his collar, she would surely choke him.

"Don't tell me who you were expecting. Tell me who is on this sorry little way station, or I promise you'll be first in line."

Which naturally led to the question, *the first in line for what?* But Cirrus Main and the Troikan apparently understood each other well. Iakk stood helplessly gripping his rejected bribe. He held it up one last time but was only threatened with the blunt handle of a Troikan disruptor. As he backpedaled to avoid the threat, Oriannon took her chance and grabbed the Stone out of his hand. Just then a high-pitched trilling made Iakk duck for cover, and a new barrage of debris rained on their heads. It appeared to come from the promenade deck above.

"What's going on?" demanded one of the Troikans, but he was too late.

"We are the uprising!" a chorus of shouts announced. Oriannon recognized the Makabi voices.

The Troikans aimed their weapons at the ceiling, but without warning a well-aimed chunk of metal the size of a chair dropped one of the Troikan men, pinning him to the floor. The remaining two fired their disruptors at the ceiling, which peeled off insulation and parts of walls. A walkway railing came apart in pieces above them, bringing an unfortunate Makabi attacker with it.

Oriannon understood whose battle this was, and she dove for cover once again, just as a small chunk of jagged metal sliced her forehead. The pain took her breath away. She reached up to cradle her wound, and her hand came back covered in blood.

"Oh no!" Gripping her wound and feeling faint, she buried her face in the shaking wall. Above them, the Makabi rained debris from every direction, throwing the heaviest and deadliest projectiles they could find. The Makabi must have had one or two smaller disruptors, because wave upon wave of searing green flame descended on the two surviving Troikans.

For their part, the Troikans laid down a wide swath of destruction with their own weapons while they huddled under what cover they could find in the rapidly growing piles of debris. Screams and explosions above their heads proved that the well-armed Troikan invaders could defend themselves handily.

In the space of seconds, the fighting escalated as disruptor fire filled the air with a ragged, back-and-forth buzz. Oriannon's eyes watered from the acrid smoke and the awful stench of ionized particles. She had lost considerable blood through the horrible gash in her face. A young scribe next to her hugged the wall too. He was sobbing in fear, so she kept an arm around his shoulder to comfort him. She had no idea whether Iakk or Cirrus Main still lived, but regretted wanting to hurt Iakk just moments ago.

Streams of foul-smelling green liquids pouring down from high above their heads told her that a series of pipes had ruptured. Wall material dangled from stringy metal reinforcements, and Oriannon was afraid to see who had been injured. She wasn't sure she could stand more grief. As the fighting paused, she knew she had to find out what was happening.

"Come on," she told the young scribe, speaking out of one side of her mouth, "let's find better shelter before the fighting starts again."

But when she stepped away from the wall, she realized the fighting was over. Three Troikans had been killed in the open of the commons—the first from falling debris and the other two by ... who knew? Oriannon's stomach turned at the carnage, and she tried not to look. From somewhere above she heard a whooping cheer, a yip, and the trilling sound of victory cries.

The Makabi.

They descended quickly, running downstairs to claim their prize. A short minute later, Modiin gathered with his handful of survivors, waving a small disruptor in his hand and whooping louder than anyone else. Judging by the burn marks on his clothes, his left shoulder had been hit by a disruptor's glancing blow. This arm hung weak and nearly useless. Still, he waved his disruptor with his free right hand in celebration.

"The rebellion started here!" he shouted, and his followers cheered even more loudly. "The rebellion against the Troikan invaders! Let everyone remember how the Makabi people were the first to shed their blood."

The rebellion. As horrible as this was, at least the Makabi seemed to understand the Troikan threat, which was more than Oriannon could say for Cirrus Main and the scribes. Again Modiin's small band whooped and cheered in spite of losing friends in the battle. The scribes gathered around them, staring in silence and disbelief. Finally Cirrus Main picked his way through the rubble, the welcome drained out of his face.

"You!" He pointed a shaking finger at the Makabi leader. "You have turned our station into a place of violence. You and the elder's daughter. She was there when my first station was destroyed. Now she's here when my new home is too. Look at this bloodshed! I blame you!"

Modiin didn't flinch, but he faced Cirrus with a scowl as he nursed his wounds.

"Someday you're going to thank me for what happened here, scribe. You didn't listen to us when we tried to warn you this was coming. You were this close to being killed."

"No!" Cirrus wouldn't believe it, and tears streamed down his dirty cheeks. His soiled robe, once resplendent, was torn in several places, and he dropped to his knees in the wreckage. "We would have stopped all this from happening if you'd given us a chance. We would have preserved the harmony, if you had given us time."

"No. Look around you." Modiin shoved his weapon under his belt and made no attempt to disguise his contempt. "My people are fighting and dying for you, and you think begging the Troikans not to hurt you would give you harmony? You sold out, fool! You had twenty minutes to live. Maybe less."

Now he mocked the scribe with a whining imitation of Cirrus Main's voice.

"'Oh, don't hurt us, please. We'll give you anything you want, anything!' You have no idea how disgusting you are, Cirrus Main."

Cirrus silently hung his head at the insult. Scribes began cleaning and repairing the terrible wreckage. Modiin and his band would take no part in that, so they gathered around their leader.

"We take back the planet now," he said, raising his fist. "We take back Corista and the entire system from the Troikan pigs. This is the uprising! Corista has her new leader!"

Oriannon's blood ran cold at the words, but she could not resist the determined little Makabi as they grabbed her from either side and escorted her through the rubble toward the hangar deck.

"You don't understand! I'm not your leader!" Oriannon's voice barely worked, but she did her best to put up a fight—which didn't amount to much with her head swimming from her wound. The two Makabi ignored her feeble struggles and kept her well in check. She'd never realized someone so small could be so powerful or their grips so firm. Though they stood no taller than her shoulders, they nearly lifted her off her feet. The disruptor at her back helped dissuade her from any thoughts of trying to escape.

"Oh, and I almost forgot to mention." Modiin halted for a moment, his hand raised, as his people halted along with him. "Thanks for the supplies, Cirrus. We'll put them to good use."

Oriannon glanced back at the ruined station, the scene of so much destruction. In the smoking rubble she saw Iakk leaning against a wall, his face covered in disruptor burns, his robe in shreds, and his shoulders heaving in sobs.

Poor Iakk, she thought as she was led away. He had seemed so close to the truth, and maybe he still was. Despite what he had done to her, she felt more sorry for him now than for anyone else on the way station—with the possible exception of Sola Minnik.

Right now, Oriannon had no idea what had happened to Sola. Perhaps she'd hidden in her room during the fighting. There was nothing she could do, so she kept a hand pressed against her wound until her head swam and her legs gave way beneath her.

"Jesmet!" she cried aloud.

22

Oriannon wasn't sure if it was the jolting and bumping that woke her — or the cold and the shouting in the midst of frenzied commotion. She shivered, and her breath turned to fog as she lifted her head from a greasy, cold metal floor that vibrated out of sync. She struggled to focus and figure out where she was.

Her head throbbed painfully.

"I *told* you to steer around those things!" Modiin's rough voice was the last thing Oriannon wanted to hear. "Is that so hard, idiot?"

They jolted again, as if something bounced off the side of the spacecraft. Oriannon held on to a frayed handle-strap attached to the wall to keep from sliding across the narrow room. When her eyes finally focused, she could see she was in a windowless compartment piled high with crates of supplies, like a cargo area. Ceiling insulation had been taped up but still hung from the ceiling, and spliced wiring had been randomly shoved into holes in the bulkhead. Here and there a circuit panel hung down, suspended only by a multicolored shock of wires. The inside of this so-called ship looked barely wide enough for a row of six worn seats on each side and a narrow walkway down the middle.

It was much smaller than the Coristan shuttle Oriannon had arrived in and hardly large enough for all the people now crammed inside. The air smelled of smoke and locker room. Foul, half-eaten travel rations littered the floor, along with dirty discarded shirts and several weapons — as if they had simply piled into the ship and left Asylum 3 in a very big hurry.

From where Oriannon sat against a bulkhead in the back, she could see the entire ship, all the way to the forward controls where Modiin and one of his men struggled to keep the ship under control. From the way he was sweating and cursing, Modiin must have been struggling even more, now that he had lost the use of his left arm in the firefight with the Troikan landing party.

Behind Modiin, four more Makabi sat in swivel stools along the outside bulkheads, each with their own flip-down monitor and a bank of switches and keyboards. Overhead, the low ceiling gave off a feeble glow, enough to light their little craft but not much more. Something hit the outside again, and Modiin cursed at his crew.

"Do I need to put you outside on a leash to see that mine?" he told them. "A few more hits like that, and we risk a hull breach."

"That would ruin your day, huh?" quipped the crew member sitting farthest back. He flipped his braids over his shoulder in defiance just as another impact sent the navigators flying out of their perches.

"Stay in your seats!" commanded Modiin.

"Doing the best I can!" The co-pilot slammed a fist on the bulkhead next to his head, setting off a warning buzzer. Modiin yanked the man's hand to the side to adjust a joystick.

"Not good enough," he told the co-pilot. "Didn't you see that one?"

"Novik didn't tell me the Troikans put so many mines out here. I can't be expected to — "

"Novik is dead," snapped Modiin, "just like we're going to be if you don't start steering better, Nesta."

Modiin kept his eyes forward, watching through a scarred viewport, while another Makabi growled and mumbled something Oriannon didn't catch, and probably did not want to. As they continued, a blue flash lit the empty space ahead, and they swerved hard to avoid another collision before Modiin threw up his hands.

"All stop!" Modiin pressed a series of buttons, and the craft jolted to a halt before he faced the other Makabi. "What are you, blind? Those things blow if we get too close! If you follow them with the scanner, we can steer around. But you're just staring like an idiot."

"All right, fine." The co-pilot ripped off a pair of ancient wired headphones and threw them to the floor. "If you think you can pilot this piece of trash through a minefield with your one arm better than me, go ahead."

"One arm is all I need to choke the life out of you," Modiin snarled, but that kind of threat wasn't stopping the other man from nosing up to the leader.

"Listen, Modiin. I didn't volunteer for this job. I just signed on as the ion drive engineer, remember?"

"You do what you're told." Modiin shoved back.

"Burn in Trion! You promised me I only had to stay back in the drive room and keep this old thing running. Who else knows about twenty-year-old ion drives, huh?"

"Plenty of people," snapped Modiin, drawing himself up a little taller.

"Name one other person."

Modiin could not, so his digruntled crew member went on.

"Did I complain when you handed me a disruptor pistol for the fight? No. But if they had killed me, you'd be in a whole lot more trouble than you are now."

"If you're so thin-skinned you can't take a little criticism, then—"

"Thin-skinned? You want me to keep this thing running, or not? Maybe you'd rather just drift through this part of space for the next fifty years, huh?"

With that he pushed away and stomped back through the craft, brushing rudely by Oriannon and leaving their commander red-faced. But the man paused by a rear hatch and groaned before he went on.

"And how am I supposed to work on the engines with *her* in there?" he asked, loudly enough for everyone to hear him. "You said we were going to leave her behind."

Oriannon craned her neck to see who he was talking about, but she was afraid she could guess.

"I don't need to explain everything to you, Nesta," replied Modiin. "Just do your job, keep your mouth shut, and we'll all be happier."

Nesta grunted and slammed the hatch behind him. The other eight Makabi ignored the argument. Maybe they were used to it.

Unfortunately, Oriannon could not ignore Modiin when he pointed straight at her with his good arm and grunted at her to come. She could flatly refuse and remain where she was. Given the unhappy look on his face, she decided to cooperate—for now.

She bumped her head on the low ceiling and had to stoop, which reminded her that she had a bloody head wound under the crude bandage wrapped around her forehead. No doubt it looked disgusting. Still, she imagined she probably looked no more disgusting than the ragged crew of Makabi manning the controls of this ancient, creaking vessel. She couldn't have dreamed, the first time she'd seen it pull into the hangar deck at Asylum 3, that she would be entrusting her life to its battered hulk only a few short days later.

But here she was.

"Sit down." Modiin motioned to the ripped cover of the stool next to him. "If we're going to get through this minefield, I'll need someone with two good arms to work the nav controls for me."

"You trust me?" she wondered aloud, looking over her shoulder at the crew. "What about one of your other men?"

"Good fighters," he mumbled, shaking his head. "True to the uprising. But they don't follow directions so good. Besides, they're busy."

"But I don't— " she started to protest.

"Doesn't matter." He would have none of it. "I'll tell you exactly what to do. You do it, and we live. Don't do it, and you die with a bunch of Makabi rebels."

Since he put it that way ... Oriannon gulped and wondered what she had gotten into. Maybe she should have pretended to be asleep or unwell on the floor. She might have gotten away with it, especially with her own battle wound. Before she could adjust her seat, the wrap on her head worked itself loose and fell to the floor beside her.

"Oh!" She reached down to retrieve it, but Modiin grabbed her shoulder first.

"That was a nasty gash," he told her, pulling her closer to see. She had no choice but to let him examine the wound. "I saw it before, back on the way station."

As he gripped her by the chin and ratcheted her head to the side, she wondered what could be so interesting about a horrible gash on the forehead. Maybe the Makabi had an even more morbid sense of curiosity than she'd feared. Finally he twirled her around on her chair to face the others and slapped the nearest crew member hard on the knee with the back of his hand.

"Kilo," he barked at the other man, "you wrap this girl's head the way I told you?"

Kilo looked up with alarm and irritation at the interruption. Startled, he looked closer, giving Oriannon the chills. One rough-shaven little man staring at her forehead was more than enough. Kilo blinked his eyes and shook his head in obvious puzzlement. She tried to back away from his horrible breath, but Modiin held the back of her neck so she couldn't move.

"So what do you see?" demanded Modiin, who obviously knew the answer. Kilo beckoned the others, and they all gathered closer. Oriannon wanted to close her eyes and disappear as Kilo poked a dirty finger at her forehead.

Strange. Oriannon couldn't feel the wound, and apparently Kilo couldn't see it either. He broke into a huge smile.

"Look at that!" he told the others. "I swear she was bleeding like a tremonian leech just a few hours ago when I wrapped her up. Thought she was going to die. Verex, you helped me. Tell them."

He stooped to pick up the awful bandage she'd been wearing, and sure enough it was soaked with blood, proof enough that she actually had been seriously wounded. The Makabi next to him nodded solemnly. What was there to disagree with?

"What do you see now?" asked Modiin.

"Looks like a baby's behind. Like nothing ever happened." Kilo told him what had now become obvious to the entire crew, and perhaps even to Sola Minnik who stood now at the rear of the compartment listening. Oriannon might have reacted to Sola's presence with more emotion if she hadn't already been so blown away by what was happening.

Oriannon ran her own hand across her forehead to convince herself the gash had healed. She felt smooth skin — no bump, no scar, no nothing, and she knew then that the Maker had touched her, as he had done once before when she'd been attacked by a yagwar.

"It was Jesmet," she whispered, almost to herself. Modiin must have heard her but didn't seem to catch on.

"No, really," she told them, raising her voice now. "Jesmet healed me."

They didn't understand, but the Makabi crew looked up at her with a new respect in their eyes.

"We don't know of this Jesmet." Modiin raised his voice as if he was giving a pep talk to his crew. "But we do know this doesn't happen to ordinary Coristans. Does anyone doubt we've got ourselves the next Makab — the next leader of the planet?"

Oriannon's mouth went dry as the men shouted their support with cheers and their peculiar trilling call — the one she'd heard just before the attack on the Troikans. Each one added more volume, until they all joined together in the call, louder and louder.

"We are the uprising!" they shouted over and over. "We are the uprising!"

Oriannon stood petrified, trying to decide how to react and avoid being drafted into the Makabi revolt. She was no "Makab." Or maybe it wouldn't matter, as another Troikan mine exploded outside and rocked the vessel. That one was close.

"We're drifting!" shouted Modiin. "Get back on course."

So Oriannon grabbed a handhold and found her seat again, ready to help get them out of the minefield. She wondered about using the Pilot Stone, but it felt cold to the touch in her pocket, and she sensed a clear "not yet" when her finger brushed its polished surface.

Had someone spoken to her? Uncertain, she pulled her hand back, but the words remained and echoed clearly.

Not yet.

Perhaps Jesmet had another plan. As the others returned to their stations, Modiin paused in front of his own controls.

"This doesn't change anything," he told her. "No matter who fixed your head or who you are—even if you *are* the next Makab of Corista—I'm still the master of this ship. And you're still going to do exactly what I say. Understand?"

She nodded her head and studied the screen in front of her, where a handful of green blips clustered around their position in the middle. They would have to wind their way through without hitting any more Troikan mines ... or die trying. She didn't like the second option.

"I understand," she gulped, gripping the guidance joystick with both hands. She hoped the one who healed her would keep her hand from shaking.

23

An hour later Modiin was still directing Oriannon at the controls, still staring at a flickering scanner screen for any signs of Troikan mines. The veins in the back of the man's neck stood out, and he chewed on an awful root of some kind, spitting black juice every few minutes into a corner of the floor. His eyes turned red, but he never seemed to tire or lose his focus.

Oriannon imagined she looked just as bad, but she didn't dare move from her post. And she didn't have a moment to think about it anyway.

"Down twelve," he told her, sighting another one, "right one-fifteen."

She did her best to comply, moving the controls first one way, then the other to dodge debris. She didn't want to imagine what would happen if she missed or overshot. But could they blame her? She barely knew what she was doing.

Margus should be doing this! she thought.

As the hours wore on, the excitable Makabi settled down to their navigation and began to treat her with a kind of deference reserved for one of their own. The Makabi leader slipped in the occasional question between commands and chews.

"I understand you two have a bit of a history." He jerked his head toward the back of the ship where Sola was standing, quietly listening. What had Sola told him?

Oriannon thought of not answering, but decided on a diplomatic answer.

"We worked together for a short time," she finally told him, "back on Corista. Is that where we're headed? It doesn't seem like the right direction."

"Our final destination is Corista," he told her. "But we have to make a stop first."

"A stop?"

"The planetoid is just ahead." He chewed on his root and grunted but did not offer any more explanation as he glanced back in Sola's direction. Sola retreated into the back room without a word, a habit she'd developed on the Coristan shuttle. Only this time, Sola seemed to have her own purpose. Two hours later Sola reappeared in the back of the main cabin, and one of the crew silently handed her a meal tray filled with stubs of reconstituted soy sausages. Oriannon wondered if Sola would even eat it.

Later she watched Sola conferring quietly with yet another crew member. He seemed to be explaining something in detail to her, sometimes taking her hands in his and shaking them. But no one smiled, and a heaviness hung over the rebels in their ship, much more palpable than the stench of rotted supplies or unwashed bodies. Even passing out of the minefield did not ease the tension.

"Why is she here?" asked Oriannon, finally standing up to stretch four hours later. "Does it have anything to do with the stop you mentioned?"

Modiin once again spit his foul black juice to the side but didn't move from his chair.

"You ask too many questions, leader of Corista. Better for someone in your position not to know."

"Why not? How can you overthrow the Troikans? There's only nine of you, and I'm sure many more of them."

"Only nine!" The strange but soulless sound of his laugh filled their ship. "You have no idea how many of us there are. But I'll tell you something, For what we're about to do, we don't need even nine—or five or three. We've got Sola Minnik, and that almost makes me believe in fate."

"What are you trying to do?" Oriannon stretched her mind to understand what he was getting at. "What's going to happen when we reach Corista again? And what makes you think I'm going to cooperate with you?"

"You'll cooperate. We're talking about the liberation of our planet. You don't have a choice."

"Well, I don't believe in fate."

He looked at her with a sneer, then shook his head slowly as he went on.

"Then believe in your blessed mentor, if you like. I heard what you said back on Asylum 3."

"And you think I'm crazy?"

"Naw." He frowned and shook his head. "You're the one who healed up without a trace. I guess that says something."

"It was Mentor Jesmet."

"Hmm. The one they executed."

"But he didn't stay that way."

And just like the scribes, he would not listen, but for different reasons—and surely not for the sake of politeness.

"I believe when men are put to death," he said with a frown, "they die. That's the only thing I've ever seen, and that's the only thing I've ever believed."

"So you've seen everything there is to see?"

"Enough." He shrugged. "Enough for me."

She sighed, wondering if she would ever convince anyone that Mentor Jesmet was actually alive. But she did have one more way to tell him. She reached into her pocket to be sure she still had the Pilot Stone, and this time it warmed to her touch. Now?

She thought for a moment before pulling it out and laying it on the control panel in front of Modiin. "Here." As she'd hoped, it instantly came to life, glowing deep with variegated color. The ship's controls clearly responded as well, lighting up in concert just as they had done on the Coristan shuttle. The Stone had no doubt taken control, and Modiin jumped to his feet in surprise.

"What are you doing?" he raised his voice, eying the Stone with suspicion. "What is that?"

Monitors showed them altering course slightly, making tiny turns and corrections. Jesmet would show the Makabi what he could do after all.

"It guides us where we need to go," she told him. "I know that sounds simple, but that's basically what happens. And at the same time, if you listen closely, you can hear Jesmet's Song."

"Your dead mentor's? I think not."

"Touch it," she urged him. "Unless you're afraid to."

"I go where I want to go," he replied, belligerence creeping into his voice. "Not where some singing rock tells me." Even so, he picked up the Stone and examined it.

"It took me and my friends to Asylums 2 and 3," she told him. "All the way from Corista."

"Any fool can do that with a star chart and a bit of luck. Doesn't take a rock." He tossed it back to Oriannon. "And we're almost there, see?"

Now they both peered out the viewport. A white crystal planetoid loomed ahead, growing larger and looking like a frozen piece of ice hanging in space. So this was the planetoid Modiin had been talking about. But something else glittered just ahead of them, and Modiin lunged for the controls ... too late.

"A stray Troikan mine!" he shouted as a flash of blue light illuminated their viewports like close-up fireworks, and a huge explosion rocked the ship more severely than any yet.

What? Oriannon fell to her knees as another Makabi flew out of his seat and crumpled into the wall next to her with a sickening thud. She hugged the nearest chair as their ship writhed in distress, and its engines whined.

"Your rock!" Modiin tumbled to the floor face-first, while sparks flew overhead. "What did it do to us?"

Now he believed?

"I don't know!" Oriannon didn't have an answer. It wasn't supposed to happen this way. Despite the chaos of the ship coming apart around her, she owned a strange, clear feeling, almost as if Jesmet himself had whispered in her ear. Now she heard the Song even as explosions rocked the control room and a bright cloud formed around the outside of the hull. An unmistakable roar outside told them they'd left the silence of space behind and entered some kind of atmosphere.

"We're being pulled into the planetoid!" yelled Modiin, doing his best to reach for a blinking red light on the nearest panel. "Everyone into the rescue pod!"

"No!" cried Oriannon. She held on to his wrist, strangely sure of what she told him. "We're all going to be okay. We just have to stay with the ship, and no one will be killed."

How did she know? He shoved her hand away with a puzzled look, but couldn't reach the release for the rescue pod anyway. And as the crippled ship continued to spin out of control, Oriannon held on, praying quietly, waiting for them to crash to the surface of the planetoid below.

24

Moments later Oriannon opened her eyes to the upside-down wreckage on the dark planetoid surface, wondering if she was alive or dead. Her head throbbed, which gave her a clue. But the floor was now the ceiling, the ceiling the floor, and everything inside had been shaken and twisted beyond recognition. Wires twisted everywhere, showering sparks in the dim light, and a strange silence inside contrasted with fierce whistling of wind outside. Her eyes watered, and she choked on bitter-cold smoke.

"Is anyone here?" She forced out the words and tried to push away from her wrecked seat, while soft groans told her at least one person was still alive. A dim pink light filtered in from a small gash in the ship's skin above her head, letting in a choking mixture of ice pellets, ash, and sulfur that made it nearly impossible to breathe.

"Modiin?" she called into the jumbled mess of seats, electronics and instruments. She tried not to shiver in the cold. Oriannon saw movement from behind a seat, while someone else started coughing. "Someone answer me!"

"Over here," replied a weak voice. An arm popped out of the rubble, while some of the wreckage cascaded away and Modiin rolled clear with a groan.

"Bit of a rough landing," said Modiin, dusting himself off and getting to his feet. Fortunately he still had the use of his right arm. "Looks like a chute saved us."

"Jesmet saved us," said Oriannon — of that much she was sure. And though she could not explain how, she was also sure they would pull out every Makabi alive. Modiin still gripped Oriannon's Pilot Stone, and he looked as if he knew where to place the blame for this disaster.

"Jesmet and his rock, eh?" In disgust Modiin tossed the Stone into the nearest pile of rubble. "He must really like me and my crew."

Oriannon wasn't sure how to answer as she retrieved the Stone, then helped him search for his crew under piles of supplies, crushed seats, and twisted pieces of metal.

"Nesta!" he roared, yanking a man by the arm from under a tangle of wires, like pulling a fish out of water. "You're the last one I thought would survive this crash."

"I never thought I'd be so glad to see your ugly face," replied Nesta, hiding a grin.

"Shut up and help me dig out the rest of the bodies."

Nesta coughed and complained but joined them in the search as they pulled out one, then several more of the crew to safety. Despite what Modiin had said, none turned out to be bodies, and everyone managed, with a little help, to crawl clear of the worst wreckage, though no one dared step outside into the howling wind. Finally Nesta held up a glowing green emergency lantern and peered at them from behind scratches and bruises.

"We're all here, Modiin." He faced their leader with a hand defiantly planted on his hip. His soiled coveralls looked even worse for wear, but so did everyone else's. "Your Makabi are tougher than you think."

"Yes, yes." Modiin didn't seem to share the other's amazement at still being alive. He just pointed at Oriannon with his bearded jaw. "She said you would all make it, but she didn't say anything about the blind woman. Has anyone seen Sola?"

The rest of the men looked around for a moment, poking half-heartedly at the wreckage with their toes. Oriannon wondered why Modiin seemed to care so much.

"Look for her!" roared Modiin, punching the nearest crew member in the arm and forcing them into action. When the crew member didn't jump quickly enough, Modiin grabbed him by the collar for a follow-up lecture — nose-to-nose.

"Listen to me, Birak," his expression darkened as he threatened the cowering man. "We're going to find that blind woman, and we're going to find her now."

"Sure." Birak tried to wriggle free, but Modiin only tightened his grip. "I don't know why you're so worked up about her. If you ask me — "

"I didn't ask you!" Now Modiin's face colored purple in his rage. "But just so you know, if we don't find her alive, our uprising is over. No blind woman, no uprising. Do you understand a little better now?"

Birak wrinkled his nose at his leader and shook his head in disgust.

"You just brought us here to die, Modiin, and now you're going crazy besides. What kind of place is this anyway? Looks like a blizzard and smells like a volcano, and — "

But Modiin had enough of that, and he shoved the crewman aside.

"Just find her. We'll see about dying later on."

As the men argued, Oriannon backed away to search on her own. A blast of cold sulfur made her shiver and cough at the same time, and she knew the crewman had been right. Outside, a white-out blizzard pelted what was left of their craft, and she could see no farther than a meter or two. No telling what this planetoid looked like, not that there appeared to be anything to see. Surely they would not survive here for long, and certainly not outside.

Over the sound of the wind she thought she heard a faint whimper toward the rear of the craft. She crawled over piles of wreckage, trying not to cut her legs on jagged, exposed edges of twisted metal. Back here, the entire tail section of the spacecraft had been twisted off, leaving a gaping hole exposed to the unfriendly elements. She looked up at what remained of the tail section. There, barely hanging on threads of metal, she could make out a melon-sized black wart—an unusual attachment that clearly did not belong.

At first she thought she was looking at one of the mines that had brought their craft down. But it didn't seem large enough for that, or if it was, it had not yet exploded. When she climbed a little closer, she saw a steady, blinking red light, and she heard tones—high and low, over and over.

A tracking device? Oriannon wondered. But she could do nothing about it now. Another blast of frosty, dirty ice pelted her in the face, and as she held out her arm for protection she heard a voice from below.

"I'm down here!"

Oriannon heard the faint words directly below her feet, and they grew louder and more insistent as she dug through piles of smashed plumbing. She called over her shoulder for help.

"Over here!" she yelled. "I found her!"

A gust of wind snatched her words out of her mouth, and though she tried to yell even louder, she could not get anyone's attention.

"A little help?" she yelled once more, with the same result. She kept digging, pulling aside chunks of ceiling and tossing conduit aside. She grunted as she pried away an extra-large piece of frame, forgetting about the ice and snow and wind swirling around her. Finally she was able to touch a hand, an arm ... and with it came the rest of a wet, infuriated Sola Minnik.

"What took you so long?" sputtered Sola, throwing off Oriannon's helping hand as soon as she could feel her way free of the wreckage that had buried her alive.

"Nice to see you too," said Oriannon. "You okay?"

"Okay?" Sola finally struggled to her feet, using Oriannon as a brace and frowning at the icy wind. "You call being buried alive and being left for dead okay? I hear laughing in the other end of this miserable wreck, and no one even gives a thought to looking for me. I don't call that okay."

"Modiin ordered his men to look for you. If you heard them laughing, didn't you hear that too?"

Sola paused, as if considering Oriannon's words. She grabbed Oriannon's sleeve and used it as a towel to wipe green sludge off her face — probably from a cooling system of some kind, but not as toxic as the freezing cloud of sulfur-sleet that now enveloped them.

"All right then," Sola finally decided, coughing as she spoke. "Let's get out of this weather."

By that time Modiin and his men arrived to help, and they managed to close off the aft part of the wreck, where a thick layer of frost had already formed on everything that was exposed to the constant onslaught of sulfur ice. That helped, but they needed heat.

"This generator." Modiin pointed at a small piece of machinery they had dragged from the wreckage. "We use it to start a fire."

So the Makabi men set about to start a small electrical fire in the center of their ruined craft, while others tore apart their landing parachute to patch the gash in the hull and keep out most of the ice and fumes. That done, they piled wall paneling and broken doors up around them in a sort of improvised tent.

Oriannon looked around at the survivors, keeping as much space between herself and the Makabi as she could. They held their hands out to the feeble electrical fire, though it seemed to give off more smoke than heat. She wasn't sure which was worse — the lung-searing smoke from the fire, or the nose-curling sulfur fumes that crept into their shelter and made each breath a challenge. And from every side the wind seemed to grip them like a giant, icy hand.

We can't last long here, she thought, and she wondered how long it would take for the Troikans to find them. Perhaps hours, or maybe even days. She wasn't sure if she should tell Modiin about the tracking device on their tail—if that's what it was. Perhaps it could be destroyed. Probably it was already too late. The Makabi hunkered down to wait.

The question was, did the Makabi know what they were waiting for?

"Does anyone know where we are?" asked Birak, and all faces turned to their leader.

"Could be any number of volcanic ice planetoids," he told them, putting up a brave face. "Most are uncharted. In fact, there are thousands of them on our course between Asylum 3 and the Gamma."

Oriannon had never heard of the Gamma before, and she wasn't sure if he intended to tell them, or if he just didn't care any more. Most of the men acted as if they'd heard nothing new, and Sola kept a straight face as well.

"Well," Sola finally spoke over the sizzle of the fire. "I want to know what you're doing to get us out of here and how soon we expect something to happen."

Again Oriannon thought of telling them about what she had seen on the ship's tail, but she kept still as Modiin pulled out one of their remaining disruptor pistols and stood. The sight of the weapon instantly dialed up the Makabi's morale as they cheered and clapped their hands. Maybe they expected him to dispatch the complaining guest right then and there. Oriannon assumed none of the men would have anything against that course of action.

"How about if we just concentrate on keeping you alive and warm for now, blind fool?" he asked, but that didn't explain the weapon.

Sola sat up stiffly, shifting her head from side to side but saying nothing.

The Makabi, on the other hand, were enjoying the show. They all cheered as Modiin flipped off the safety and charged up his weapon, then aimed the titanium muzzle at the pile of smoking rubble in the center of their circle. Perhaps he would heat up the fire in their midst, though Sola could not know this.

But when he pulled the trigger ... nothing happened. Modiin shook his weapon in the air before bringing it down hard on the floor. Perhaps he thought he could shake the weapon to life, but Oriannon ducked as he swung it around the group.

Still nothing happened. Birak grabbed it and did his best to make it work. He even pointed it directly at Sola and recklessly pulled the trigger, which made Modiin roar in anger.

"What are you doing, fool?" He swatted Birak on the side of the head so that the other man surrendered the weapon and shrank away.

"All right, all right, it doesn't work!" said Birak. "Must be all the sulfur in the atmosphere."

"Genius." Modiin sneered. "You figure that out all by yourself?"

Nesta, the engineer, pulled out another pistol and pointed it in the air, with the same result. Nothing. The rest of the men groaned.

"So here we are," complained Birak, "waiting for our people to rescue us, and we don't even have anything to defend ourselves with in the meantime."

"Doesn't matter, idiot." Modiin tossed his pistol into the smoldering pile and pulled up his useless left arm. "We're not waiting for our own people anyway. See that tracking device? It was on the tail."

He let his words sink in for a moment and turned away to point at the tracking device, smashed and tossed into the corner. So he'd found it! He kicked at it for good measure, though it no longer blinked. "They know where we are," he mumbled, and Oriannon wondered why he seemed resigned to his fate.

In any case, she wasn't going to fall asleep easily with a band of horrible Makabi men huddled around a makeshift campfire inside the remains of a shipwrecked space vessel on a sulfur planetoid in a perpetual ice storm. Not if she could help it. Oriannon couldn't tell the time of day, as ice flew around their ship and blinded them to whatever lay beyond. No one suggested going outside, for obvious reasons. So she wrapped a foil emergency blanket around her shoulders, shivering and trying not to bump against Sola—even if it meant they could have shared some of their body heat. Sola, it seemed, had the same idea, and shivered alone as well. The faint warmth of the Pilot Stone in Oriannon's pocket helped only a little.

The wind had picked up since they'd crashed, howling even more fiercely and shredding the fabric of the parachute patches they'd stretched around the outside of the ship. At least they had plenty of food, if one could call the awful Makabi rations food. Several of the men chewed dried meat from foil packets, spitting gristle to the side with no particular care. One of them offered Sola a bite, but she pushed it away when she smelled the rancid meat. Oriannon didn't blame her.

"You sure you don't want some?" Modiin extended a half-chewed piece of jerky in their direction, and Oriannon shook her head no.

"I'm not hungry," she answered. Actually, she didn't think her stomach would have held it down.

"Ah, yes," he said. "I keep forgetting the queen of Corista is a vegetarian. Well, you can vegetarian yourself to death here, if somebody doesn't show up pretty soon."

"That's enough, Modiin." Sola snapped at him. "I'm sick of hearing your complaints."

Oriannon wondered what made Sola say such a thing. Modiin narrowed his eyes but did not reply in kind, and the ends of her lips curled up in a twisted smile.

"That's right," Sola told him. "You're an intelligent man, as Makabi go. You need me to carry on your little uprising, don't you? Only—have you considered your chances of getting out of this alive?"

"We may all die, Sola." Modiin's tone turned serious and not nearly so sure of himself. Perhaps the thought of dying wasn't so glorious to this warrior after all. "In fact, we probably will."

"Actually, you have a chance, dear Modiin." She shook her head, and the smile on her face looked out of place. "Though I most certainly do not, not when they bring me before the Troikan Council, and you know I'll make sure that happens."

None of this made any sense to Oriannon, though she strained to understand the words as they grew rambling and incoherent. Sola Minnik, it seemed, was spiraling into insanity.

"You do know what they do to puppet regimes who fail them, don't you?" Now Sola threw her head back and laughed. "I didn't live up to their expectations. I didn't bring the proper amount of order to Corista. Almost, but Miss Hightower and her friends got in the way, didn't you, dear?"

Oriannon wasn't going to answer that question. She let her ramble.

"I would have had the Owlings prepared and delivered, as the Troikans wanted, and Corista would have been a better place for it. But no!"

"The Troikans?" Oriannon already knew the answer, but she wanted to hear it once more. "They were behind it all, weren't they?"

This time Sola took her time answering, slowing turning her head to face Oriannon.

"You know the Troikans are behind everything, dear. Did you really think poor Sola Minnik was the big, bad dictator who enslaved your Owling friends and brought evil to Corista?"

Oriannon stared at her enemy, knowing an answer was not required, as Sola went on.

"Yes, well, I was prepared to live with that, but it only shows how little you really know. By now they've put someone else in place. A new leader? It doesn't really matter to them, as long as they're still in charge, and as long as they're able to harvest all the resources they want. Or they may have tired of the whole puppet show and simply come in with their own people. After all, the Troikans were originally from Corista, you know, just like the Makabi. It would be a homecoming of sorts. However ..."

She held up her hand as if she wasn't finished.

"However, I wouldn't want you to get the wrong idea. We still have one more message to deliver to the Troikan Council, thanks to our friends the Makabi. Don't we, Modiin?"

Modiin only grunted.

"You should be nicer to me, Modiin." She still wasn't through. "Otherwise you might have to do my job."

"You talk too much," he finally told her, not disguising the disgust on his face. "You'd do better to keep your mouth shut and keep yourself alive for now."

Sola frowned at his insolence, while Oriannon decided to try one more time.

"That's all behind us, Sola," she said, forcing the words. Jesmet would have wanted her to say this, even if she did not. "You don't have to be this way anymore. I mean, it's not too late to change the way you think. Jesmet said— "

Sola cut her off with a vicious laugh.

"There you go with that Jesmet nonsense again. The dead man speaks!"

"But he's not— "

"I'll admit that whoever you found to impersonate your mentor did a rather convincing job. In fact, if we were still back on Corista we might derive some amusement from the act. Here, however, the issue is irrelevant."

"You don't know what you're saying."

"Don't I? I must say one thing for you, my dear. At least your nonsense is consistent. But look at what happened to Asylums 1, 2, and 3. All the miserable people living there have been evacuated or killed, and there's not a thing you or your precious Jesmet impersonator can do to stop what's going to happen to the rest of the stations, one by one, until the Troikans finally get to Corista itself."

"If there's nothing we can do about it—"

"I didn't say that. But now I'm the only one who can make a difference, the only one with a plan. Not you, and certainly not your dead mentor. Not even Modiin and his men can get close. I'm the only one who can poke a stick in the Troikan eye."

Oriannon had no idea what kind of stick Sola had in mind. But Sola just smiled and rocked quietly, offering no more explanations, while Modiin grumbled again about the blind woman talking too much. Just then, a sparkle of orange light from the fire caught Sola's unseeing eye, giving Oriannon the shivers. More than ever, the woman seemed possessed by something malevolent and wicked. Whatever Sola had planned, it could not be right. Either that, or the woman had finally slipped over the fuzzy line between evil and just plain crazy. Come to think of it, that seemed more likely than ever.

Oriannon heard a noise outside—a loud rumbling and the ping and groan of crushed metal, as if the hand of the storm had finally decided to crush them. Modiin dropped his meat and looked up—just in time to see the last of their tarps bulge under the weight of the ice.

"Modiin!" shouted Nesta, pointing above their heads. "There's something—"

No one else had a chance to shout as snow and ice ripped through the tarp, flooding the inside like a living thing. Oriannon took a quick gasp of sulfur-laced air before she ducked her head under her arms and surrendered to the crush of the avalanche's embrace.

25

Perhaps the Makabi crew had good reason to think themselves safe, considering their resurrection from the rubble of the crash landing. It seemed they had been rescued from one certain death only to be entombed in the foul, unrelenting ice of this lonely planetoid.

It reminded Oriannon of a time when she was very young and her father took her on a rare holiday to the seashore. He had buried her up to her neck in sand after she'd begged him to. Only then she had panicked when she found she couldn't move and imagined she could not breathe.

She remembered the feeling that swept aside all reason. Even her father's strong voice as he shoveled her free could not settle the sobs of fear. He repeatedly told her he was sorry, until she cried herself to sleep on his shoulder.

She would have given anything to have his shoulder to cry on once again, but all she could find was the heel of Sola Minnik's empty shoe, lost in the melee of the avalanche. As she grabbed it, she cried out, "Modiin!"

The ice shifted around her, and their ship groaned as if being picked up. She pushed through the ice, struggling for breath.

"Modiin!" she yelled again. "I'm here!"

Bright lights flickered through the ice, and she could hear voices shouting over the roar of engines. Once again the ice shifted around her, and she imagined her father pulling her from the sand. Suddenly, a powerful blue-white searchlight blinded her, and strong hands grabbed her by the arms.

"This one's different!" someone shouted. "Pull her out easy."

All around her, tall figures in blue flight suits picked through the wreckage. Only a meter away she thought she saw someone pull Sola out of the ice too. Above them she could make out the imposing overhang of a very large craft, hovering just above the ship. The flying ice, debris, and the hot backwash of ion engines prevented her from seeing how large the rescuing craft really was.

So the Troikans had arrived after all.

"Who are you?" she gasped, but in all the confusion she heard no answer. She did not resist when the man who had pulled her from the wreckage helped her toward a nearby boarding ramp.

"Watch your step," he told her. She managed not to stumble as he led her up a power-assisted walkway, and they ducked into the well-heated, brightly lit interior. Finally the chaos disappeared behind them, and she paused to catch her breath.

Should I celebrate being rescued, she wondered, *or scream and resist?*

Oriannon looked around with wide eyes. The Troikan man helping her paused obligingly. He looked like the three who invaded the way station. He wore his black hair braided and tied in back, like dreadlocks, and geometric red and blue tattoos swirled around his neck and under his chin.

"I'm Coristan," she finally whispered, hoping for some kind of answer but afraid to say more. He nodded.

"We know that much."

"Then where are you taking me?"

"Since you were with the Makabi rebels," he answered, straightening up and pointing her forward. "You'll be taken to the Gamma for questioning."

"The Gamma," she echoed. "What is that? And where are the others?"

He shook his head.

"You and the other Coristan will be treated well. That's all I can tell you right now."

So he was done answering questions. She had no choice but to follow him as he guided her by the arm through their ship's high-ceilinged loading area, where three small shuttle pods were strapped to a shiny stainless floor, and tools and strange-looking equipment lined the walls behind rows of sealed plexi cases. Everything looked spotless, shined, and in its place—quite a contrast from the Makabi ship. She imagined the entire Makabi ship could dock here, with plenty of room to spare.

"Looks big," she told the Troikan, but this time he didn't answer.

They continued to a small lift tube, and the Troikan motioned for her to step inside. A plexi door slipped shut behind them, and they were lifted to the next level, to a spotless inner control room run by a threesome of young Troikans in crisp tan coveralls, each hunched over their respective control monitors. One of the three obviously had fewer tattoos than other Troikans Oriannon had seen. Perhaps, she thought, the younger ones added more ornamentation over the years.

"This is the Coristan?" asked one, who looked up with mild interest. Without another word she was led into a small adjoining detention room just large enough to hold two cots.

"Wait a minute," she objected. "This is where you want me to stay?"

As if to answer, the Troikan stepped back and activated a translucent blue force field that sprang to life across the opening of her cell. Just in case she didn't understand, he raised his finger from where he stood on the other side and lightly tapped the field, raising a small shower of sparks.

"You can test it yourself if you like," he told her, his face expressionless. "But I wouldn't."

"Thank you," she whispered. "For pulling me out of the ice, I mean."

When he paused, his tattoos swirled in circles, looking almost like a computer-generated weather map. He said nothing, and left her alone with her unanswered questions.

Why did they rescue me? she wondered as she lay back on her cot—hard, but not entirely uncomfortable.

She wondered if the Troikans would hold her in the small room by herself, or if they would bring someone else to occupy the other cot. She wondered if they would bother to take Modiin and the other Makabi prisoner, or if they would leave them on the planetoid surface to die.

Oriannon didn't understand what was happening. Although her mind raced, she could hardly keep her eyes open. She couldn't tell how much time had gone by when she heard the hum of the force field snap off. She opened one eye to see Sola Minnik brought into her cell and directed to the other cot. But Sola wasn't going quietly, and she dug in her heels as they shoved her inside.

"How many times do I have to tell you?" Sola had taken on her most indignant tone, which was remarkable after everything she'd been through. There was no stopping this woman—not blindness or shipwrecks or avalanches. "I'm Sola Minnik, and I've been taken here against my will. I know Hanzib, on the Troikan Council."

"A friend of yours, you say?" Their guard looked interested as Sola nodded.

"Without a doubt. We've worked closely for the past several years."

"Well, that's unfortunate. Hanzib was deposed last week. So whatever friendship you may have had, if in fact you had one, will not count to your favor. I suggest you not mention him again, and you find another name to drop."

Sola's face fell for a moment, but she quickly regained her footing. "Well, Hanzib was a fool and I never trusted him anyway. But I insist on meeting with the Council. The others know who I am.

Ask them. We have much to discuss about the future of Corista, and it cannot be done from a holding cell."

"Perhaps. Meanwhile, you'll wait here, won't you?" He paused for a moment, closing his eyes while the tattoos on his face and neck seemed to come alive. He nodded as if someone close by had given him the answer to his question. "Yes, I believe you will. That is our consensus."

"But you don't understand! Listen to me! I'm Sola Minnik!"

"Noted. Please inform us if you require anything during your stay here. My name is Rovl."

Sola made it clear to Rovl that what she required was to be removed from this cell, and he could make her stay more comfortable by taking her to a proper guest room. But that didn't seem to change anything about her situation — at least not for the time being — and he quietly backed away from her tirade.

"You can't do this to me!" she announced.

"We can and we will. This is the detention center." He waved at their room, then back at the control room behind him. "And that is the security room, where we track many of the functions of the ship. I'll be there should you need anything."

Rovl returned to his station. Almost before the force field snapped back on, Sola was up and feeling the boundaries of their cell. Oriannon said nothing as the other woman moved around, tapping the wall and recoiling in fear when her hand brushed against the unpleasant snap of the security field. She cursed and shook her hand in the air as if she had burned it in a fire.

Undaunted, Sola explored with the toe of her shoe along the forward edge of the cell, then along the opposite wall until she arrived at Oriannon's bunk. She finally stopped, as if sensing her silent cellmate, and lowered her hands to her sides.

"It's you," she said quietly, "isn't it?"

Oriannon sighed and could no longer remain silent.

"I wish it wasn't, Sola."

As soon as she said that, she knew it had to be Jesmet's doing.

You put us back together again, didn't you?

That could be the only explanation. Sola continued her survey past the bunk to the back wall and the small toilet, then back around to her side of the cell. She paused to run her hand across a shiny dome mounted on the wall, which looked very much like a monitor to keep an eye on them.

"Three meters by two meters," Sola concluded, raising her hand and touching the low ceiling comprised entirely of luminescent panels. "By two meters. And fully monitored, in case you hadn't noticed."

That about said it. A warning buzzer and a voice over the loudspeakers warned the crew that they were taking off. Sola found a seat on her cot, and Oriannon gripped the edge of her bed while the floor and walls shook gently. Where were they going, now? And what about the Makabi?

Her mission had morphed into something different, though her fate seemed intertwined with Sola's. In that sense, at least, she supposed she was still doing what Jesmet had asked her to do. Because through no effort of her own, she'd kept the blind woman close by. Only now they were headed in a direction that only Sola seemed to know.

And she wasn't telling.

26

Oriannon felt like she'd slept ten minutes in the past twenty-four hours. Thoughts of where they were being taken and what the Troikans had in mind for them kept her awake.

What would Father have done? she asked herself, but she had no answers. So she worried about Modiin and his rebels, and she wondered what kind of scheme he and Sola had been talking about back on the ice planetoid. Whatever revenge they had been planning would be a moot point now. They would be moving to Plan B, if they had one. Anyone could tell these Troikans wouldn't be as simple to ambush as the unlucky trio had been back on the way station. Even now Oriannon's stomach turned at the memory, and she tried to block it out with something else.

So she hummed one of Jesmet's Songs and held onto the Pilot Stone, and that helped calm her mind a little, as her cellmate paced. First Sola took three steps one way, then paused just centimeters in front of the force field and pivoted. Three more steps would take her to the back wall, where her nose nearly brushed the wall. There she pivoted once more and started all over again. All the while she murmured something over and over, as if she was still complaining about the cell. Surely this woman was coming mentally unglued.

This went on for at least an hour or more, until Oriannon was ready to either scream or launch herself head-first into the force field. Anything but listen to the constant shuffling and whining. Finally Oriannon propped herself up on one elbow and faced her roommate.

"Maybe you'd like to sit down and rest a while," she suggested, trying to keep her voice from cracking. "You'd feel better if you did."

Sola didn't pause and didn't say anything back, just kept pacing like a caged yagwar. Her lips moved as if she was reciting her complaints, but no sound came out.

"I said, maybe you'd like to sit down?" Oriannon thought she'd try again, and she reached out to get Sola's attention. "You're driving me crazy."

Instead of stopping, Sola pulled back her hand with much more drama than the situation called for.

"Don't touch me!" Sola screamed, waving her hands wildly. Oriannon knew every move was being watched, and she wondered what had set the woman off.

"Look," Oriannon tried to keep a calm voice. "Settle down. I'm not trying to— "

"Settle down?" Now Sola bumped into the side of her cot as she backed away, and her voice upped several notches. *"Settle down?* I'm not settling down until I meet with the Troikan Council again. They're not going to appreciate hearing that I've been taken prisoner here. Are they, Rovl?"

Sola's hearing must have been sharp. When Oriannon glanced at the door, Rovl was stopping just outside their cell. He touched a wall panel to power down their force field but didn't answer Sola's inquiry. He simply motioned Oriannon to get up and ordered Sola to hold on to her cellmate's arm and follow him into the adjoining windowless security control room just a few meters away.

The two other young Troikan men ignored them, remaining seated in their padded chairs at matching U-shaped workstations. Each faced a dizzying array of readouts and glowing instruments.

"Are we on our way to the Gamma?" asked Sola, and Rovl's snaking tattoos paused at the question before twisting around his neck twice and then heading down his right arm.

"I'm not authorized to discuss our present course with you," Rovl answered, which at least told Oriannon that this Gamma was a destination somewhere outside, not a place *inside* the Troikan ship. "That would be up to the Council members."

"Well, then!" Sola brightened. "So the Council *has* been told how I've been treated, and that I must see them?"

Oriannon wondered at the desperation in her voice.

Why is she so set on seeing the Troikan Council? she wondered.

"They know," he replied. He pointed to a projected image in the middle of the room — three intertwined red and violet strands, very much in the style of Troikan tattoos. The two other techs didn't look up from their monitor arrays; each seemed busy studying images of other parts of the ship, from engine rooms to control centers. Occasionally they spoke quietly into small microphones curled around their ears.

"The Council also knows that your blindness prevents you from actually viewing their projected images here," Rovl pointed to the center of the room under the nozzle of a 3-D imager. "But you may speak to them as you would if they were standing here in this room. You can do that, can't you?"

"Certainly." Sola added a good measure of swagger to her voice, perhaps thinking she could make up for her handicap with attitude. But before Sola gripped her hands behind her back, Oriannon could see that they were trembling.

"Well?" Rovl looked to the techs. "What's the delay?"

The techs made several adjustments, and the intertwining strands disappeared and were replaced with a barely recognizable ghost of a highly tattooed face obscured by snow and fuzz.

"Sola Minnik!" a scratchy female voice called out. Oriannon thought the lips moved, but she couldn't be sure. A fuzzy image faded in and out, lighter and darker, while the voice eventually came through a little more clearly. "You look terrible!"

"Thank you, Councilor Ploril," Sola seemed to recognize the Troikan official's voice, and she rose to the occasion. "I wish I could say the same of you."

Rovl and the techs worked frantically on focusing the image, but it went from bad to worse, while the faraway woman's voice faded in and out.

"Enough pleasantries, Sola. We've been told you were blinded in some kind of incident on Corista, then rescued on a remote ice planetoid in the company of Makabi rebels, and ... they're being held in connection with the destruction of one of our advance parties."

"I can explain that," Sola began, but Councilor Ploril would not let her finish.

"After your disaster on Corista—and frankly, we hold you responsible for losing control of the entire Owling situation—you'll need to explain fully about this latest development."

"We were taken prisoners on their ship," answered Sola, her voice shaking. "I planned to escape at the first opportunity. Fortunately—"

"Fortunately you were not alone." The councilor broke in, sounding rather impatient even at this distance. "Who is the other Coristan?"

"We've not positively identified her yet, ma'am." Rovl broke in, looking at Oriannon. Oriannon was glad she had not yet revealed her name. But this would be the time for her to say something if she had any hope of staying with Sola from here on.

If this was what Jesmet really wanted?

"My name doesn't matter." Oriannon made up her mind and spoke up as loudly as she could, hoping the councilor could hear her. "I am Sola's servant, bound to her accommodation. I'm sure you'll agree that a blind woman should never travel alone."

"Is that right? And you put up with her? She's ..." Councilor Ploril's next words broke up in the subspace connection, coming in garbled and unintelligible while Sola sputtered her protest.

"No, wait!" Her jaw fell open as she looked around blindly in Oriannon's direction. "What are you saying?"

"The two of you will stand before the Council." Ploril's words rolled in and out while Sola still desperately tried to explain. "You'll explain everything to all three of us when you arrive."

"The girl misspeaks." Sola tried once more, and now she clenched and unclenched her fists while Oriannon stood by. "She is no servant of mine."

"Rovl, I can't hear what she's saying," Ploril came back. "But if you can hear me, you will ensure that Sola remains confined to her security quarters until she arrives here at the Gamma. Not to be trusted, this one, blind or not. Don't let her out of your sight, even if you're busy coordinating the asylum evacuations."

"Understood," said Rovl.

"No, wait!" Sola's face reddened, and she waved her hands. "This is a mistake!"

But had the faint image of Councilor Ploril disappeared entirely, replaced by the intertwining strands once again. Sola kept right on sputtering and waving her protests.

"Ploril," she yelled, "do you hear me?"

Ploril apparently did not, and Rovl took Sola and Oriannon by the arms.

"I must speak to the Council once more," insisted Sola, dragging her feet. "There's been a huge misunderstanding."

Rovl led them back toward their cell.

"I believe that's why we're taking you to them," he said, "so you can explain yourself more fully. We should be there in a matter of hours."

"But you're evacuating Asylum Way Station 3?" asked Oriannon. "Why? What about all the people there?"

He knew the answer, and he actually paused to open his mouth, but he changed his mind with a glance at the monitor and left them alone behind the force field. He must have known that even the watchers were watched.

Oriannon collapsed onto her cot with a sigh, while Sola returned to her agitated pacing. And though Sola seemed to know exactly where the curtain of high-density energy would stop her, she leaned over and slapped at the force field with her fists, bringing down an enormous fountain of multicolored sparks. Her hands shook violently, and she was thrown back, landing on her cot in a kind of seizure before Oriannon could reach her. When she did, Sola suddenly grabbed Ori by the neck to whisper in her ear.

"So this is how we're going to play the game from now on, is it?"

"It's not a game," Oriannon tried to pull away, but couldn't. Sola dug her long nails into Oriannon's neck and shoulders.

"No? Call it what you will, but if this is what you think you have to do to survive, you're going to play by *my* rules."

Finally spent, Sola shoved Oriannon away with a grunt of disgust and flopped back down on her cot. She pulled a thin blanket around her shoulders, though it was unnecessary aboard the warm Troikan vessel. Apparently she still wasn't satisfied; she curled up with her back to Oriannon, reached her right hand up and back, and raised her palm in the air. "I need another pillow, servant."

Oriannon looked at the lone pillow on her cot, hardly enough to cradle her own head. She looked at the black dome on the wall, wondering who watched them. So this is what Sola meant when she said they would play by her rules. She sighed and handed over her pillow.

At least she hadn't lied to the Troikan Council ... well, for the most part. She wondered how much trouble her rash statement would bring, even if it did guarantee they would stay together. Is this really what Jesmet wanted?

27

Sola Minnik's servant couldn't sleep although Sola had fallen into a fitful rest, rolling and groaning and thrashing. Whatever Sola was dreaming, it could not be pleasant. At one point she cried out, "Run!" and Rovl hurried over to check on them.

Oriannon kept completely still with her eyes almost shut as she watched him pause on the other side of the force field.

"Those two still okay?" asked one of the other techs in the room beyond. Oriannon could hear nearly everything from where she lay. "Couldn't see much on the monitor, but sounds like they were at each other before they fell asleep."

That sounded like good news to Oriannon. Even if the Troikans had been watching, maybe they couldn't hear everything.

"It's just the blind one having a bad dream," answered Rovl, finally satisfied.

"Quit worrying about them, will you?" said the other tech. "We still have a network issue on deck twenty-three. Have you checked that lately?"

"I thought I did." Rovl looked a little puzzled. "Maybe I should check again."

The others nodded innocently as he left the room. But as soon as the door slipped shut behind him they sprang to attention at their stations, as if they had been waiting for him to leave.

"Transmission from the Gamma's coming through in thirty seconds," said one. "Let's see if we can grab a better connection this time."

This seemed a little strange, so Oriannon craned her neck to see out through the force field. It couldn't hurt to know what was going on.

Out in the security control room she was able to make out another small screen on the wall that revealed two sleeping forms — their cell. But no one seemed interested at the moment. Instead, the two young Troikans gathered around their 3-D imager, just as they'd done when members of the Troikan Council had tried to speak with them earlier. Once again the red and violet logo flashed on, along with a label to indicate this transmission originated with Troikan System Operations. When the logo faded, a life-size image of a lanky man appeared in the middle of the room, nearly as clear as if he had actually stood there.

"That's much better," he told them in a gravelly voice, patting himself on the arms as if he actually had materialized, rather than just a 3-D image. "What was the problem getting through earlier — subspace interference?"

"We're still trying to determine the cause, sir," replied the taller of the Troikan techs. The man in the transmission wore trim-fitting navy blue coveralls with a stylized tri-serpent logo on his shoulder and deep green tattoos over much of his face and neck. He crossed his arms and frowned at them.

"Forget about it for now," he told them. "We have too much work to do. First, let me emphasize that we're not recording this conversation, correct?"

They both assured him they weren't, so he went on.

"Then tell me about the detainees. Have they both been positively identified, Vel?"

"There's Sola Minnik, of course," answered Vel, the tall one. "You know, our former covert representative on Corista."

The man frowned.

"A personal disappointment. I had great hopes she could have accomplished our purposes on that planet without us stepping in. But what can you tell me about what she's been up to? Trys, do you know?"

The other tech shifted and cleared his throat.

"Yes, sorry. Sola. Definitely. Sola Minnik. Er … We had lost contact with her for several weeks. There was an uprising in our detention facility on Corista. All the implants went offline, a total disaster. So after her failure on Corista, she's being transported to answer to the Council."

"You're telling me what I already know. What about the other one? The girl?"

"Claims to be Sola's servant. We're still checking it out, and we're questioning the Makabi rebels to find out what they can tell us. They've been placed in separate cells."

"You'll let me know what you learn, and very soon." By this time the man looked a little distracted as he peered into a handheld device. "In the meantime, you know the Council wants to be sure no one from the occupied entity is harmed, so for the record, I'm required to ask you if all the inhabitants of Asylum 5 have been evacuated to Corista … *safely.* If you know what I mean."

He rattled off the question as if it was a distasteful duty, but his tone did not match the words, and the green tattooed pattern on his cheeks swirled like a hurricane on a tracking screen. Oriannon didn't like the way he said "safely" either—as if it meant just the opposite.

"Uh, not exactly," Trys began. "We didn't have time to—"

Vel interrupted.

"Trys means we haven't had time to write a full report yet. But we share the Council's concerns, and …"

He paused, and Oriannon could see Vel, off camera for the moment, wrinkling his eyebrows in a very clear gesture for Trys to shut up. Trys swallowed and nodded as a wisp of fear crossed his face.

"Pardon?" The image of the man leaned in a little closer. "I didn't hear that last part. Are you having transmission problems again? And where's the third of your troika? What's his name, Rovl?"

"Right, sir. He's off checking a network problem, but we'll fill him in as soon as he returns." Vel gathered himself again. "But as I was saying, the Council can rest easy. Everything is under control here. All the inhabitants have been offloaded to Corista, where they belong, just as they will be for all twelve way stations. Well, eleven. But we can safely proceed with the last part of the Breach now, isn't that right, Trys?"

Vel and Trys exchanged a quick look, a wink of recognition between them. At the same time Oriannon did the math in her head, comparing how long it had taken them to get here to the "matter of hours" Rovl had told them it would take to reach their destination, to the number of hours it would take to travel to Corista and back to drop off prisoners. None of it seemed to add up — not even close. She could be wrong, but this man in the transmission had to know that as well.

"Very good. Then officially we're ahead of schedule, is that what you're telling me?" He paused to look up with a little smile. "If that's the case, the councilors will appreciate your good work, all three of you. You do so much more then just monitor your ship's systems, don't you?"

"Actually," Vel told him with a smile, "with the difficulties on Asylum 3, it has taken us a little longer than expected, so we're going to gain back some time by, er, streamlining the evacuation process on Asylum 5. It's all about efficiency, you know."

"I'm very happy to hear that, Vel. You and your team will be commended, and we'll proceed as soon as you have the transponders in place down on the surface ..."

They continued back and forth like that for a few more minutes, exchanging technical information, comparing readings on their instruments, and confirming checklists. Oriannon listened intently, wondering what kind of people used to live on Asylum 5, and feeling the failure for not making it that far before the Troikans did.

I didn't warn them soon enough, Jesmet! Maybe they would have listened. Maybe they could have put up a fight!

But she couldn't do anything about it now, not from a hard cot without a pillow in a cell on the Troikan ship, looking through a blurry blue force field. After a few more minutes, the two techs settled back into their workstations.

"Diverting power to transponders," Trys reported several minutes later. The power on the ship blinked as if surging. "Eighty-seven ... ninety ... percent."

Their lights blinked again, and a few moments passed before the smiling Troikan man returned to their view, still studying his handheld intently.

"The Breach appears successful." He turned aside to mumble instructions to someone else, then nodded and looked up. "Yes. Asylum 5 has arrived here at Gamma in reasonable condition. We'll get complete damage reports soon, but on a cellular level, it looks like it's reconstructed well. You've done your job. Now let's bring in Asylum 3."

On this side of the conversation, the two Troikans smiled and clapped each other on the back, but the man held up a finger of warning.

"Don't get too excited, however," he told them. "That's only three of them. We have eight more to go, and then the planet itself. Just keep doing your jobs, report back to me, and we'll see you all soon."

His image flickered out, replaced by the now-familiar serpent logo and the words "Transmission Complete." Vel immediately turned to Trys, his smile frozen.

"What was that all about, Trys?" Vel's voice turned hard. "You're as bad as Rovl!"

"What do you mean? I did everything you told me to! We breached the way station, no problem."

"Yeah, but for a minute I thought you were going to tell him we're dumping everyone from Asylum 3 to save time. Were you?"

"Come on, Vel! That's crazy. I would never say anything like that."

"Wouldn't you?" Vel gave him a long, threatening look. "You know if we actually took the time to transport all those people back to Corista, the way the rest of the Council wanted, we'd still be working on Asylum 1!"

"I know that." Trys pressed his lips together, looking quite nervous.

"This way the Gamma gets the stations they need on time, and we get all the credit. Sounds like a good plan to me, doesn't it to you?"

Oriannon recoiled in horror at what she was hearing.

"I know it's a good plan," answered Trys, but his voice seemed to tremble a bit too. "I've always said it's a good plan."

Vel waved in the direction of the cell, and Oriannon clamped her eyes shut.

"And we do have that crazy lady to thank for something. We'd have nine way stations to Breach-transport through twenty light years if she hadn't destroyed one of them by herself. It's a lot of work to set up a Breach, you know."

"You don't have to tell me that," replied Trys. "It's just that all those people—"

"Would you stop the whining!" Vel raised his voice. "I told you—"

He cut his sentence short as Rovl finally returned.

"Hey, Rovl!" Trys sounded far too casual all of a sudden. "We finished bringing in Asylum 5, no problem."

"Without me?" Rovl sounded like he couldn't believe it, but the conversation spun away into very intense tech-talk. Meanwhile, Sola thrashed about even more under the influence of a new dream, apparently a more terrifying one. She threw off her cover and moaned, rolling over on her back and holding out her hands in self-defense.

●●●

"No!" cried Sola, terror in her voice and sweat on her face. "Please don't hurt me. I thought—"

Whatever she thought, this had to be one scary dream. And on the one hand, Oriannon didn't mind letting her stew in her own torment for a little while.

She gets what she deserves.

At the same time, Oriannon felt chills run down her own neck as Sola thrashed again and again. For a moment she even felt a stab of regret for not waking the blind woman out of her obvious torture.

Besides, she thought, *I'm not going to get any sleep with all this racket.*

So with a sigh she hoisted herself out of her own bed, ignoring the overhead eye of the monitor and hoping the three Troikans weren't watching her very carefully. She slipped over to Sola's cot like a dutiful servant.

"Sola." She poked Sola in the shoulder and tried to keep her distance, as if she was poking a dead body. "Sola, wake up."

"What?" Sola snorted and shook her head. But before Oriannon could escape, Sola grabbed her around the neck as if she was still drowning in her own nightmares. Oriannon tried to stand, but the terrified woman would not let go.

"I was at the Gamma!" Sola hissed in Oriannon's ear.

"Is that good or bad? Now let me go."

But Sola would not, and only held Oriannon that much tighter. Oriannon could smell the bitterness of Sola's fear, could almost taste the tangled web of her fright.

"But I was there, I tell you! I know what the Troikans are trying to do."

"Wonderful. But I'm not the one you should tell your dreams to. Maybe your Makabi buddies, or—"

"I understand you hate me, Oriannon," she interrupted. "I don't blame you. I hate me. But this has nothing to do with my dream."

"All right, all right. How about letting go of my neck and explaining what it *does* have to do with then?"

Still Sola kept her voice down and intense.

"Listen, girl. I don't know what you're doing by telling the Troikans you're my servant, but you need to hear this."

Oriannon thought Sola would have relaxed her grip by then, but she only clamped on tighter than ever.

"All right, fine. I'm listening. But how about just letting me breathe while I do?"

"You don't need to breathe. Just listen. Landing on the ice planetoid was part of our plan; being captured was part of our plan."

"Nice of you to tell me. But whose plan?"

"It's probably too late."

"Well, I think it was too late a long time ago. But I seem to be along for the ride."

Sola sighed. "You don't get it. I brought the trouble down on Corista. Now it's my fate to bring down the Troikan Council. The Makabi and I worked this out."

"So that's what you were talking about before, when you said you were the only one who could poke a stick in the Troikan eye? Blind woman goes to meet the bad guys who are taking over our planet and all of our way stations, and then what are you going to do? Because, excuse me, but I don't think your martial arts skills are up to it."

"It has nothing to do with martial arts." Sola laughed. "It has everything to do with a biobomb."

28

A biobomb? Oriannon paused now, trying to take in what Sola just told her in this odd confrontation. Sola still would not let go of her stranglehold on Oriannon's neck, and Oriannon could not move from her cot. If Sola had secrets to spill, this was certainly one way to do it without the Troikans overhearing.

Oriannon wished Sola could find another way of spilling her plans. And with a sinking feeling, she imagined the organic components scattered throughout Sola's body, nearly impossible to detect until they all came back together again in an orchestrated horror. She'd heard that some biobombs brought together enough explosive energy to destroy a small city.

"You know what that is," whispered Sola. "Don't you?"

"Sure I do, Sola. I wish I didn't. But you can't be serious."

Oriannon still felt distinctly uncomfortable with her face so close to Sola's.

"I'm completely serious. The Makabi implanted it in my body, and the trigger is in one of my back teeth. Once it's triggered, there's a five-minute fuse, and— "

"Sola, no. This is too creepy. I can't let you do this."

Her stomach turned at the thought, and for a moment she really thought she was going to be sick in the face of such evil. Because it was one thing to hear about biobombs on the media, and quite another to be trapped literally a few centimeters from one.

"You think you have a choice? There's no way to stop me, Oriannon."

"The Makabi put you up to this then?"

"No, of course not. We came to a mutual understanding, based on common goals."

"Such as?"

"We both hate the Troikans and want to bring them down. They've hated the Troikans for generations, ever since losing much of their home world to them. My mistake back on Corista was thinking I could deal with them. Now I know better. Our Makabi friends never made that mistake, but they've never been able to pose a real threat until now."

"They made you do this." Oriannon still thought that's what Sola was saying.

"I told you they didn't! Modiin was going to do it himself, but he had no way of getting close enough to the Council. I do. And what is my blind life worth? I'm certain they intend to put me to death anyway."

"No, Sola. This is not the way."

Oriannon wasn't sure why she argued — only that the entire idea repulsed her and she knew it could not be what Jesmet had in mind when he'd told her to stay close by Sola.

"Then what is the way?" asked Sola. "You can't stop them, even if you wanted to, and I should think you would want to, as a Coristan. But you can't. I can."

"Okay, but even if you can, then what? You slow them down for a few months, but they'll just put in a new Council. The Maker has to change them from the inside-out."

"Spare me from another sermon." When Sola laughed it sounded like a sob, and Oriannon couldn't quite tell the difference. "Next you're going to tell me that your dead mentor can help."

"If he was dead, he couldn't," Ori snapped back, feeling a hot sting of irritation. "But he's not, and he can."

"Like all the scribes who welcomed your ideas with open arms? I didn't see too much enthusiasm there."

"Pardon me for saying it, Sola, but you don't see too much of anything lately."

Sola didn't have a quick comeback for that, but she still didn't sound convinced.

"I may no longer see, but that's why they won't be expecting what will happen to them. And if you have any inclination to warn them, my girl, I promise you it will be the last thing you ever do."

"Is that a threat?"

"Merely a vow. I don't even know why I'm telling you all this, except to warn you away."

"But Sola, the Maker doesn't change people's hearts with ... with biobombs and uprisings. It's going to take time for people to see. It's a different kind of change."

"What do you know about change? You haven't changed. Do you not hate me more now than you ever did?"

Oriannon tried to get away from the one true thing Sola had said, tried to back away from the woman's vise-like grip, but Sola just would not let go.

"Please don't do this, Sola. I'm begging you. Your revenge is only going to make things worse. It's only going to cause more killing."

"Oh, I don't know." Sola's voice grew cold and stiff. "I think it'll make me feel better."

Oriannon swallowed hard, trying to think of something Jesmet would say in this kind of situation. But since she could not imagine him arguing with a blind woman on a cot in a cell deep inside a Troikan warship, the examples she had to draw from wore a little thin. Sola's eyes filled with tears that ran from her cheek to Oriannon's.

"Sola," she told her, almost feeling a twinge of pity, "I can think of a lot of other ways to feel better."

"You say that because you have choices. I don't. This is all I have left. This is all that's left for me to do, and I will do it. This is not by chance. It's my destiny."

"No, it's not. I can't believe you're saying this."

"And I would not have, until you saved my life and dragged me into your ship. You should never have done that. You should have let me drop to my death before I realized how blind I was."

"Maybe that's not a bad thing to know. Jesmet would say we're all blind until we hear his Song."

As if to remind her, Oriannon felt the warmth of the Stone in her pocket.

"There you go again!" answered Sola. "How do you always know what your precious Jesmet would say, unless you're making it up in your head?"

At first Oriannon wasn't much inclined to answer truthfully. What if Sola actually took her word for it? What then? But in the end she slipped the Pilot Stone out of her pocket and held it up close, where Sola could feel it on her face.

"This is how I know. I hear his Song in this Pilot Stone. And even if you don't believe it, I don't care. It helps me, and it shows us the direction to go. It showed me and Margus and Wist. And that's all I need to know."

"Let me see that." Sola released her grip on Oriannon's neck and grabbed the Stone.

"Not everyone hears it," Oriannon warned her. "I didn't at first."

"If I can't hear it, it's a useless rock and you're making it all up to suit yourself. Something you can collect and put on your shelf. But ..."

Her voice trailed off at that point, and Oriannon could tell the Stone had come alive once more. Ori saw the glow even through Sola's clasped hands. Worried that their captors would notice, she covered Sola's hands with her own, but still it shone brighter and brighter as the Song welled up like a flood that could not be stopped.

Finally she gave up. Well, it was Jesmet's Stone anyway. If he chose to show its power to these Troikans, that was his problem.

First, though, they would have to pry it from Sola Minnik's illuminated hands. While Sola could not have seen that, she might have felt its warmth as she held it closer to her face.

"So ..." asked Oriannon, "do you hear it?"

Sola nodded slowly, turning the Stone in her fingers over and over.

"Faint," she whispered, and all the acid had drained from her voice. "Very faint. I've never heard this kind of music before. It's ..."

Now she choked over the words and suddenly handed it back to Oriannon.

"It's too strange." She held a hand to her forehead as she stood without a word, wincing, as if the Song itself had caused her pain.

But now the Stone had awakened in a new way, even more than when it had helped them navigate. It vibrated even more deeply, with tones so profound Oriannon could feel them in her chest like a symphony, and Sola reached out her hand too.

"What is it doing now?" asked Sola.

The musical vibrations reached a point where Sola had to hold her hands over her ears, though Oriannon doubted that would help. She slipped the Stone back in her pocket, but the Song continued. She looked out through the force field. Rovl sat at his station, holding his ears and looking frantically around the control room. He spoke to someone on a com and ran out.

"Oriannon!" Now Sola stood as well, still holding on to her ears. "You've got to ..."

Her voice trailed off in the sudden silence, and she lifted her hands from her ears. Even without seeing, Sola must have sensed something else had happened. She lifted her hand slowly past the point where it would have collided in a shower of sparks with the force field.

"Hello?" she poked her head outside.

Oriannon held her back for a moment. *What had the Stone done, and how?*

"Sola, wait." But she was just as curious to see what was going on as Sola apparently was to hear it.

"There's no one out here, is there?" Sola whispered.

"I don't see anyone, but that doesn't mean anything. I'm sure Rovl will be back any minute."

Sola spun to face Oriannon, throwing off her hand.

"Your rock," she hissed, hopefully not loud enough for the monitors to catch. "Your rock did this, didn't it?"

Oriannon wasn't sure how to explain what she didn't understand herself.

"It wasn't the Stone," she explained. "Stones can't do anything except be stones. It was the one who gave it to me."

"Now you're playing with words." Sola backed out of their cell, and a shadow of her old smile crept across her face. "I'd like to see what else that rock can do."

"No, Sola." Now it was Oriannon's turn to grab Sola's attention. She grabbed the collar of her tunic, and Sola gasped in surprise.

"What are you doing?"

"Making sure we understand each other." Oriannon kept her voice low. "You have something you need me to keep to myself, and I have something I need you to keep to yourself. So I keep my mouth shut about the biobomb if you keep yours shut about the Stone. Do we have a deal?"

Once again the old Sola smile crept around the edges of her lips, and she leaned a little closer.

"Why, Oriannon Hightower, that's exactly what I would have done if I were in your position, which thankfully I am not. I'm proud of you."

"But do we have a deal?" Oriannon insisted. She did not want to talk about this again, nor did she want to spend any more time this close to Sola Minnik. Most certainly she did not want Sola saying she was proud of her.

"We do." She pushed Oriannon's hands away and straightened the collar of her tunic. "And we understand each other perfectly. Perhaps more than you know. Now, I'm going to stretch my legs if you don't mind."

"I don't think that's such a good idea, Sola."

"I am not going to cower in this beastly cell any longer than I have to. You see yourself that there's no one out there to stop me."

"For now. I don't know what happened to them, but ..."

But Sola would not be stopped from wandering around the empty control room, as if she was out for a stroll. Perhaps she was simply proving a point as she waved both hands uncertainly ahead of her — that she could leave the cell if she pleased. But if anyone was going to get into trouble, it would not be Oriannon.

Even so, she worried about what she had just said — the deal she had just made with Sola.

On the surface her promise seemed crazy, ludicrous. Obviously she could not sit back and let Sola Minnik just walk into the Troikan Council chambers and commit such a horrific crime. Obviously she could not stay quiet and just let it happen.

But that's exactly what she had promised to do, and as she watched Sola walking about the control room, Ori had the strangest feeling she had done the right thing. She wasn't sure where it came from, just that it was and that it would somehow work out. She could break her word by letting someone know of Sola's plans — and risk bringing down the wrath of the Troikans on them both. Or she could keep her word by remaining silent — and walk away with blood on her hands. Beyond those two horrible options, she saw no other way out.

"Ow!" Sola yelped as she ran into a low counter, tumbling sideways and crumpling to the floor. "You didn't tell me that was there, you idiot!"

"You didn't ask me." Oriannon was tempted to add "you idiot" but held her tongue. Her father would not have approved, though Oriannon thought Sola earned that for walking around an unfamiliar room without being able to see. And for what? Just because she suddenly could? Oriannon didn't see the point.

"Well, then come help me up!" Blind or not, Sola still hadn't lost her ability to boss people around. "I think I twisted something."

Oriannon seriously considered ignoring Sola and crawling back under her sheet to hide. But no matter how much she detested the woman, she couldn't bring herself to turn away. With a sigh she walked across the room and took Sola's hand.

"There, see?" Sola nearly smiled up at her. "I knew you'd help me. You're just too nice of a girl."

"But I'm not too nice to let go." Oriannon released her grip, allowing Sola to balance on her own. "And you've been twisted for a long time."

"Oh, very good." Sola leaned on the nearby counter for balance. "You're getting better at that sort of thing. I've trained you well."

It took all of Oriannon's willpower not to shove Sola right back down onto the floor where she belonged, just to show her she could not keep the upper hand any more. But suddenly the door to the control room opened behind them. Oriannon didn't have time to turn around before a shock hit her in the back and she fell face-down to the floor, stunned. She'd been hit by a Troikan weapon of some kind, and she was unable to move or speak. Troikan voices surrounded them.

"Rovl!" shouted one of the other two Troikans in Rovl's working group. "How did they get out?"

"I have no idea. It must have been some kind of malfunction." Rovl bent to examine them and gently rolled Oriannon over on her back. Since she couldn't even blink her eyes, they watered profusely, and her entire body twitched, burned, and itched. It was almost more than she could stand.

"I'm sorry," he whispered. "I know it's unpleasant, but it's only temporary."

The words surprised her as much as the way they were spoken. She could see Vel and Trys examining the door to their cell, working a switch on and off, powering the force field up and down several times. Finally they turned back to look at Rovl, their arms crossed.

"There's nothing wrong with this force field," declared Vel. He wore a frown on his face like a badge of honor, the same way Oriannon had seen him from the start. A circular tattoo on his cheek began to swirl as he advanced on Rovl. "I don't believe there was anything wrong with it before."

Vel apparently held the most seniority—if tattoos were any measure. He carried the most by far; what she could see of his arms and hands was completely covered with geometric patterns. They moved like waves or snakes and changed color and direction as the confrontation escalated. Trys claimed nearly as many, though not quite as colorful. Rovl, whose chin and neck were decorated, rose to his feet to meet them.

"Vel, Trys, you've got to believe me," he began, but the others cut him off with a look of rebuke that seemed to snap Rovl's head back. His friends offered no mercy, just as they had offered Oriannon and Sola no warning before the stun gun attack. Oriannon followed the argument from her place on the floor.

"No, you listen." Vel pointed straight at Rovl, and his top lip curled in a challenge. "We took you into this troika because they said you were one of the best com technicians anywhere. We brought you in because we thought we could trust you. Well, a witless mistake like this could get us all killed, and I'm not going to let that happen."

By this time Vel's tattoos had changed to a vivid purple and yellow, and they lit up his chalky gray skin.

"I'm telling you ..." Rovl worked his jaw with some effort, but did not look as if he could move his head, though he struggled and shook. "I didn't slip, and I didn't fail you. You can look at the security cam records if you don't believe me. When I left here, the force field was up. I swear it was up."

"Maybe he's right, Vel." Trys shifted on his feet and seemed to soften a bit. "Let's just get them back into the cell before anyone else sees what happened. The longer we talk, the more chance someone will find out, and if that happens—"

"Don't push me!" Vel now turned on both of them with wild eyes. Oriannon expected a brawl right there in the control room. "Both of you! I know what can happen better than either of you."

"No push, Vel." Trys held his hands palm-forward in surrender. "Don't get so upset. All I'm saying is we should put the prisoners back right now before anyone else finds out. We'll have Rovl erase the monitoring records, so no one will know."

"Hmm." Vel considered the suggestion before finally backing down, though the frown never left his face. When he finally nodded, Rovl slumped as if he had just been released from a physical hold, and he rubbed his neck as if it had been twisted.

Vel held up his hand. "I still don't know why we were stuck with babysitting these prisoners all the way to the Gamma." He narrowed his eyes and steeled his voice. "A lesser troika should have been given the task."

"We follow directives," answered Rovl, as he gently helped Oriannon to her feet.

"You've got that part right." Vel shot back. "But I'll tell you something, Rovl. We have more important things to do too. And if you can't keep up with Trys and me, believe me, you can be replaced."

He stepped over and grabbed Oriannon himself.

"And you're too dainty, Rovl," he gruffed as he yanked Oriannon by one shoulder and her hair, showing his Troikan strength. Though she would have screamed in pain, she could still not even open her mouth. "Maybe that's your problem. You just mess around too much."

"Wait a minute, I—" Rovl sounded as if he would defend himself, but Vel didn't give him a chance.

"Let's get them back in there. Don't forget to power up the force field this time."

Oriannon felt herself dumped without ceremony on her cot, and heard Sola's body thrown down the same way. She started to feel more tingling in her fingertips, and she began to tremble. With a huge effort she tilted her head around so she could breathe, and saw Rovl standing in front of the cell's opening as the force field sprang back into place. He frowned and shook his head before turning away, oblivious to the deadly danger lying in the cot only a couple of meters away from him.

29

As they approached their destination, Oriannon found herself sleeping more and feeling less and less certain of her plan. Was acting like her servant the right way to keep Sola close by?

She shivered in her bunk, knowing what Sola had in mind—and what Sola had hidden in her body. Worse yet, no solution had yet presented itself to her.

Did I make a mistake, Jesmet? she asked. But Jesmet never answered, at least not the way he had back on the shuttle when visions had so clearly steered her into this maelstrom. She waited, bringing back to mind everything Jesmet had told her. That was all she had to go on now—just the remembering.

That will have to be enough, she told herself. What else did she have but the steady reminder of the Stone, the longing for home, and the remembering?

She looked out through the force field to see Rovl sitting alone, working on a monitor with a projected image over his head. Rovl glanced up from his work and caught her eye. She blinked her eyes shut in an instant.

"We're getting close," he told her.

She waited a moment before opening her eyes again, and she checked quickly to make sure Sola was still snoring.

"Is that—?"

"I can tell you now that you're looking at a close-up of two hundred twenty-one combined asteroid planets and way stations compressed to within two hundred meters of each other and linked with ten thousand kilometers of cables and high-speed transit tubes. Home. The Gamma. The centerpiece of Troikan culture, justice, and law."

"But why?" She asked what she had been wondering ever since she'd first heard of the Gamma. "Don't you have your own planet?"

"We did once. But when our star went supernova generations ago, we lost our home planet and decided to rebuild our world from scratch. The only problem is, all of it has been stolen from different peoples—stations, outposts, planets."

That explained a lot.

"And then with the help of your scribes, we discovered a much more efficient way to gather additional territory—much quicker than dragging asteroids over great distances by space tugs. Now we simply breach each piece to the Gamma, using the scribes' collected mental energies. Once the real estate arrives, it's blended into the Gamma through the technical genius of the Troikan people."

He threw his handheld across the room in obvious disgust.

"Pardon me for not being proud of the way we've built our empire," he told her. "But you'll have a chance to see it for yourself in the morning."

It was the first time he had talked to her like that, and it startled Oriannon to think he might really mean what he said. Certainly he would not have mentioned anything of the sort with the others around. Or perhaps they already knew his opinions.

"Why?" she asked. "Why are you telling me this?"

The tattoos on his neck swirled with emotion as he took a deep breath.

"You don't know what it's like to be part of a troika the way I am, mind-controlled by Vel and Trys every day, every night." He looked around carefully, as if they might be interrupted at any time. "Conquering planets is one thing, but when so many people are treated as if they're in the way, just to be disposed of . . ."

His voice grew husky with emotion as he shook his head and went on. "I know what we're doing, and I can't do it anymore."

Oriannon didn't know how to answer him. He returned to his work as she studied the vast floating image of the Gamma — much larger than she had expected, intertwined with structures of all kinds. She recognized several structures of Coristan design, but many were unfamiliar. Several Coristan ships were tied to the outer edges, and she wondered if they were the ships that pursued them when they first left Corista.

"I'm sorry," she finally told him. "So we're almost there?"

"Five hours, twelve minutes, and . . . fifteen seconds." He nodded. Maybe he was embarrassed about what he'd said.

"Rovl?" she asked, and he looked up again. "May I ask you something else?"

He looked around again, but he finally nodded.

"When they take us in," she asked, "will you make sure I go with her no matter what she says? No matter how much noise she makes? I really need to be with her."

He shook his head slowly, then shrugged.

"Don't know why you'd want to do that," he answered. "She doesn't have long to live. People in her position — people who fail — are usually executed. The Council's only seeing her as a courtesy."

"But they've already asked me to come with her. You heard them."

"Sure, I heard them. I just think you might have a better chance if you distance yourself. That's what I would do. They might not know yet who you really are, or what you've done."

Ori caught her breath and tried not to let her surprise show. Who she *really* was? Did he know?

"Please ... if you can." She surprised herself with the boldness of her own words, but he surprised her even more by agreeing.

"If that's what you want. But listen. All this? The way we steal way stations? It's not what I would have ... you know, not what I would have done."

He stuttered to a stop, probably realizing he was saying more than he should say to a prisoner. Oriannon understood and didn't press him for more. As she watched, the view of the Gamma grew larger and changed perspective.

"One other thing, Rovl." Now she knew she was pushing her luck, and she knew he knew. "Is there anything you can do to save the people on Asylum 3?"

"Don't ask me that again." He frowned and looked away. "I've already said too much."

●●●

Five hours, twelve minutes, and fifteen seconds later Sola was up and pacing—as she had been for the last hour. Doubtless she heard the busy work of the three techs, as well as the constant com traffic and chatter as they neared the Gamma. Oriannon sat on her bunk, checking the chrono on the wall and listening. Another flurry of calls came in, and Rovl turned to the others.

"We've got problems with Asylum 3."

"What kind of problems?" asked Trys. As far as Oriannon could tell, he gave Rovl the hard tasks, while he chatted on their com line and took credit for the work.

"I don't know. Nothing like what we've experienced before. It appears the way station is on its way, but we've lost contact with the landing party."

"But you said it's coming?"

"Due in just a few hours, about the same time we are. They brought it a few thousand klicks away from the Gamma and are powering it in with tugs, just to be safe."

"Then don't worry about it. You know how subspace com links garble over long distance."

"But— "

"Come on, Rovl. Don't we have enough problems of our own without worrying about everybody else's? We need to get back to this landing checklist."

So they did, and their com line awoke with increasingly urgent voices calling them for power-surge checks and nav coordinates, data unpacks and system fixes. Apparently the whole ship relied on Rovl, Vel, and Trys to solve their technical problems.

"Do you understand what they're doing?" asked Sola, resting on her bunk. "They haven't brought us any food lately."

Oriannon couldn't believe Sola would be thinking about food as they neared the Troikan Gamma and what awaited them there. But she did her best not to let her voice betray her emotions.

"I think they're busy with other things," she told Sola.

Besides, Oriannon imagined the condition of two Coristan prisoners was low on the Troikan's priority list—compared to bringing in an asylum station and adding it to the Troikan empire. She watched the flurry of activity on the other side of the force field, trying to keep her mind off biobombs and dying, and rested her hand on the Pilot Stone for some measure of comfort. She drifted between prayer and restless sleep until Vel's booming voice woke her with a start.

"We're there!" he announced. "Hang on!"

Blinking lights overhead and a nudge told them they had dropped out of their cruising speed, most likely to dock with the giant home-built "planet."

"Did you feel that?" asked Sola, sitting up. Oriannon felt the shift in gravity too, and she gripped the side of her bunk to keep from falling as internal grav plates compensated. Sola didn't wait and jumped up to stand in front of the door with her arms crossed. Oriannon watched Rovl and his two co-workers who were busy with landing checks and other duties passed down from the main guidance center. None of them paid their prisoners any attention.

"I'm waiting," she reminded them, sounding peevish. Even then they ignored her for several more minutes, until another Troikan with dark blue coveralls and a full complement of tattoos stepped into the control room.

"The Coristans." He motioned with his head. "They're summoned."

Oriannon stood and faced Sola, holding her back from the door and keeping her voice to a whisper.

"Please don't do it," she said. "You can still change your mind."

"Leave me, fool." Sola's voice cut through the tension as she shoved Oriannon straight into the force field, which briefly sparked before it was turned off and Oriannon stumbled backward into the larger room. Rovl picked her up from the floor.

"Thank you," Oriannon was barely able to mumble before Sola set up a loud protest.

"I refuse to have this girl along with me! The Council doesn't know her, and I simply won't have it."

"You have no say in the matter," replied Rovl in a matter-of-fact voice. "The Council asked specifically for her, so I'm taking you both."

"No!" A fresh wave of fear washed over Oriannon when she realized she wasn't the only one being dragged into Sola's suicidal plans. And she hadn't yet figured out a way to neutralize the bomb.

But now she had no choice. Rovl steered them through the ship's brightly lit corridors, passing scurrying Troikans in blue coveralls, all busy securing their ship. Oriannon assumed they were docked somewhere in the Gamma project, linked to the heart of the Troikan world where the Council met.

"You are taking me directly to the Council chambers, I assume?" asked Sola.

"That's right. The Council chambers recently moved to a new meeting place, since they acquired better facilities in a new way station."

Sola seemed deep in a memory and didn't respond as he helped her step through a series of three air locks, each one popping their ears. They finally reached the outside hull of the ship and stepped into the Gamma project.

They mounted a moving walkway, connected to the ship's main entrance and held on as the walkway accelerated through a clear plexi tube. A draft hit Oriannon, and she shivered. She looked at the dark expanse on one side and the busy cluster of small planets and way stations on the other.

"Is this—?" she gasped, and Rovl nodded.

"The Gamma. Space stations, way stations, small asteroid colonies, planets ... all linked together like a giant web. All brought here to give the Troikan people a place to live together."

Sure enough, clear tubes, similar to the one they were in, linked other pieces of this giant configuration. She saw many Troikans as they passed from one domed station to the other.

But unlike the diverse crowd of people she witnessed on the asylum stations, she and Sola were the only Coristan faces she saw in the entire collection; the only ones not covered in living tattoos. She looked down at her bare arm and rubbed the goosebumps. Rovl looked down at her as well, and nodded slightly.

They traveled through another dome and down into the central courtyard of what had once been an asylum station, where workers on lev platforms were modifying wiring and plumbing. Rovl pointed them out.

"It doesn't take much to link into the Troikan system," he told them. "Only minor modifications are needed to adjust for a more Troikan atmosphere, and to bring all the communications systems together."

Oriannon slowed down to look around as he walked them through a crowded central plaza toward three glass elevators.

"When was the last time you were ... home?" she asked.

"Three months, and I haven't seen this part yet. It's what you used to call Asylum 1. Recognize it?"

"We didn't get a chance to visit it." Oriannon's heart sank, and she could say nothing else as they continued on. Though she had never been to this way station, she recognized the distinctive ancient Coristan flavor of white marble columns and elegant, flowing arches. On this level, elegant inlaid stone floors made their footsteps echo to the tall ceilings, perhaps twenty meters overhead. She hoped the Troikans appreciated all of this, and she wondered if they noticed some of the smaller details, like the carved Trion stars at the head of the columns — the symbol of Corista, and the symbol of Jesmet.

"It's very pretty," commented Rovl. "The Troikans are great admirers of foreign architecture, art, and music."

"Religion?" she wondered.

"That too. They ... I mean, *we* take the best of all worlds, and bring it here. Even matters of faith."

Perhaps. But he would not know what it all meant. From this far out in the system, the Trion would only shine distant and cold, and they would not look at all the same as they did from Corista. Jesmet's Songs and the Stone, which she still carried in her pocket, might seem only an amusing addition to their collection of conquered philosophies, though she hoped it would be more. The elevator continued to rise.

Asylums 2 and 5 would soon join the Troikan architecture, and then Asylum 3, swept clean of its original inhabitants. Where were they now? She wondered how long they could survive, conveniently stranded on an ice planetoid or wherever Vel and Trys decided to send them. If nothing else, Oriannon would have a moment to tell the Troikan Council what was really happening, before ...

She gritted her teeth, remembering Sola's plan.

"Are you all right?" asked Rovl, and she quickly regained her composure.

"Yes."

The elevators opened to an upper terrace level, laced with indoor plants that cascaded off the walls and painfully reminded

Oriannon of home. The Troikan Council chambers had been placed in a high-ceilinged former library, occupied by studious scribes only weeks earlier. Rovl paused before the doors long enough for a newly installed eye scan to do its work. Twin hand-carved doors slid aside as a soft tone indicated they should enter. Oriannon let her hand rest on the edge of the rich dark pluqwood, once imported from the highland forests of Corista, where viria songbirds filled the sharp, fragrant air with their own special music. But the wood reminded her that she was too far from home, and her time was running out. Rovl waited for them.

"Come," he told them with a curt nod.

Sola paused to press the heel of her palm to her left cheek before clearing her throat and stepping inside.

The five-minute fuse had been set.

30

"Come in, come in!" One of the three well-dressed Troikans waved to them from a seat behind a richly carved ironwood table—an artifact from the pirated way station library. The three—a lanky man on the end and two women next to him—appeared pleased to receive visitors, and their tattoos seemed to fly from one person to the next, like a captive bird flittering from perch to perch. The designs varied from simple swirls and lines that followed the contours of their limbs to serpents that morphed into fanciful winged creatures.

Oriannon's throat went dry, and she stared at the man while Rovl introduced them. It was the same man she had seen in the transmission speaking with Vel and Trys!

"You wanted to see the Coristans," said Rovl, his eyes fixed on the tile floor at their feet. Perhaps this was part of the protocol.

"Yes, thank you," replied the woman on the end, nodding slightly. "You will wait at the door, please, but do not leave the room."

Rovl did as he was told, leaving Oriannon and Sola to face the Council alone in the former Coristan library, cleared of its ancient books. Oriannon estimated they had four minutes left, and her heart raced as the woman in the middle seat spoke up.

"So good to see you again, Sola." The woman smiled as if greeting an old friend instead of a condemned prisoner. "How many months has it been? Well, several. Sorry to hear of your accident."

Oriannon had definitely not expected pleasantries. The councilor went on.

"After your unfortunate failures to gain control over the Owling population, we were disappointed to hear that your career would be cut short this way."

"Is that why you brought me here, Ploril?" Sola finally spoke up, showing her old venom. "To tell me what I already knew?"

"Sola, Sola." Now Councilor Ploril smiled and leaned forward over the middle of the table. "I always feared it was a mistake to work with you. Please don't prove me right again, in front of your friend."

"Friend?" Sola seemed to grit her teeth together. "She is . . . she was the last ruler of Corista."

Coming from the mouth of Sola, the words sounded officious—a little too eager to please—as their remaining time shrunk down to just over three minutes. None of the Council showed any surprise. The man studied his nails, looking bored with the entire meeting.

"We know that," said Councilor Ploril. "Oriannon Hightower of Nyssa, we're very pleased to have you visit the Gamma project, which is growing all the time. You might like a tour later. Our antiquities and museum staff have requested that you speak with them—perhaps explain to them how your planet was once governed."

Oriannon blinked in shock. Here they stood—a rebel assassin and the so-called last ruler of Corista—and this councilor was inviting her to give a speech. The councilors waited for her to say something, but she was counting down the remaining minutes of her life. Two and a half minutes left. What could she do with such a small amount of time? What would Jesmet want her to do? She wrestled with the words that would not come.

What's the worst thing that could happen? she asked herself.

"Actually ..." Oriannon cleared her throat and planned out her last words. "I would rather tell you about the plans my Maker has for you and your people."

"Oh, really?" Councilor Ploril leaned forward with interest. "Have you come to discuss religion with us? I just adore foreign religions. So fascinating. They're a hobby of mine."

"Not religions." Oriannon shook her head. "I mean your only hope, the Maker's Song."

"Only?" The Councilor's smile faded slightly. "That sounds rather exclusive. A little narrow-minded, wouldn't you say?"

"Not narrow-minded. Wide open. The Song was my mentor, and he was executed because of me. But he didn't stay dead, and I've been sent to tell you about him so you can find hope too. It's not religion, but ..."

This isn't going to work! Oriannon clenched her hands as she realized how badly she had failed, and her insides knotted up. Ninety seconds remained. She didn't have enough time to explain Jesmet's Song, or what it could mean to the rulers of the Troikan Empire. They weren't taking her seriously, and their time was almost up.

There was one thing she could do. She dug into the pocket of her tunic and pulled out the Stone, warm and glowing. Perhaps it didn't matter how treacherous these councilors were, or how ruthless. They had never seen the power of the Pilot Stone.

"Look, I don't know if I can explain it." Oriannon coughed to clear her throat. "So I'd like you to have this as a gift. It's a Pilot Stone, and the Maker sings his Song through it."

The lanky man at the end of the table burst out laughing, but clamped a hand over his mouth when Councilor Ploril gave him a stern look.

"Councilor Tau, please."

So that was his name. Vel and Trys had never mentioned it; just called him "sir."

"Excuse me," he told her, bowing his head slightly and twirling his hand for her to go on. "I've just never heard of such a thing. Proceed."

So Oriannon handed the Stone to Councilor Ploril, who smiled her thanks as tattoos washed across her face.

Thirty seconds.

"I'm so pleased to have a souvenir from your planet for our antiquities museum," she told Oriannon. "But my, it's quite warm, is it not?"

The Stone began vibrating, and the Maker's Song could be heard plainly, though still in the lower register where it seemed to vibrate the chest more than anything else. The third councilor on the end stood up with a look of concern on her face.

"Rovl! Have these two been screened? What is that thing?"

"I assure you they have, Councilor Osmos!" Rovl stepped up to the table. "We knew of the rock, but we thought it was simply a primitive talisman of some sort. It's inert. Just a rock."

Ten seconds.

"Then what's going on here?" asked Councilor Osmos. "What's that . . . that music?"

"I'll tell you what's going on." Sola stepped forward with a grim smile. "When you die here, your people will see that Sola Minnik of Corista wasn't powerless and disgraced after all. You can't kill me the way you planned! *This* is my destiny!"

Five seconds. The councilors stared in confusion at Sola, who stood with her arms outstretched. Councilor Ploril couldn't seem to decide which was more frightening; the glowing, humming Stone in her hands, or the clearly disturbed blind Coristan woman standing before her. Oriannon closed her eyes and prayed that the Maker would allow her death to be swift and painless.

Only nothing happened, except the passing of another ten awkward seconds. The councilors rose to their feet. The Stone powered down again, and Sola frowned and slowly drew down her hands. Perhaps her counting had been off by a few seconds?

Still nothing happened, and the terror and frustration at her failure was plainly written on her face, almost as vividly as a Troikan tattoo. After another minute, the biobomb had not exploded, and finally Oriannon breathed out with an obvious puff of air.

"Yes, well ..." Councilor Ploril looked at her with a mixture of confusion and amusement as she took her seat once again. She did not know how close she and her Council had come to breathing their last. "That was a most peculiar display. Normally I would demand an explanation, but in this case it appears to be a moot point, and frankly I don't really care. Sola Minnik is condemned."

The other two nodded their agreement as Councilor Ploril turned to face Oriannon.

"On the other hand, I should like to hear more about this mentor of yours, Miss Hightower. Perhaps later. For now, Rovl, would you please escort these two out immediately? Oh, and please make certain Sola doesn't harm herself before she is executed. She appears quite unstable."

"No, wait!" Oriannon now had another chance with these three. Her heart still raced, and she took a deep breath. "Did you know that the people of Asylum 3 were not taken back to Corista as you ordered?"

All three looked at each other with varying degrees of concern. Oriannon thought Councilor Tau choked just a little.

"How do you know such a thing?" asked Ploril after a pause.

"It's a long story, but Rovl isn't responsible. Vel and Trys were trying to look good, and they dumped the people on an ice planetoid."

Councilor Ploril looked to Rovl.

"I assume you will deny this charge?" she asked. "You know we have strict procedures for dealing humanely with settlements when they're absorbed. You all know that."

But Councilor Tau wouldn't allow Rovl to answer, and he raised his hands for silence.

"This is more than enough drama for one day. We'll deal with this, Rovl. You have your instructions. Leave us immediately, and take the Coristans with you. We'll be in touch shortly."

"But this is a serious charge!" said Ploril. She looked at Tau and was about to say something else, then seemed to change her mind.

Meanwhile Rovl did as he was told, dragging them both outside to the empty hallway. The door closed behind them, and he let Sola stumble to the side in shock as he faced Oriannon.

"What were you trying to do there?" he asked her, his eyes wide. "Have me killed?"

Oriannon tried to keep from shaking. He had no idea they had nearly lost their lives.

"No," she told him, "I thought they might be able to do something about Asylum 3 if they really cared. They might be able to help all those people before it's too late."

"If this is true, they may already be gone." He shook when he spoke, and it could have been any mixture of anger and frustration. He paced in a circle around her. "The landing detail should have been in contact with us long before this."

"Meaning ...?"

"Meaning they haven't followed protocol. Asylum 3 hasn't arrived the way it should have."

"So you're saying there's a chance the people might still be alive?"

"I don't know. All I know is something is just not right. Trys and Vel wouldn't let me follow up before I brought you here."

"I don't understand." She crossed her arms. "Why not?"

Rovl shrugged. "When things don't go right, Vel and Trys look for a way to pin it on me. But it doesn't matter; it's probably too late for those people anyway."

Ori paused before answering, still thinking back to what had nearly happened in the Council Chambers.

"I don't think it's ever too late," she told him. "Not for me, not for you … and not even for Sola."

Sola just leaned against a nearby wood-paneled wall, her head in her hands.

"All right." He sighed, glancing at Sola. "I'll take you to a safe place. But look. There's nothing I can do about her. And really, you have no idea what you just let loose in there."

"I think I do."

"No, you don't." He lowered his voice to a whisper. "I'm talking about the kind of corruption that goes all the way to the Council. Did you see how Councilor Tau reacted? I've heard rumors, but that confirmed it for me."

"They're not rumors. I heard Vel and Trys talking with him when you were gone." She swallowed hard, glad to finally tell him. "I just didn't know who he was before now."

Rovl shook his head. "So you just placed yourself in a lot of danger. And you brought me into it as well."

"But Councilor Ploril— "

"Ploril can't help you. She means well, but Tau controls her. Neither can Osmos. She's too weak. You should never have brought up Asylum 3 with Councilor Tau in the room."

"I'm sorry," Oriannon pressed her lips together so she wouldn't cry. "I had to try."

"Well, I'll say one thing for you: You may be crazy, but you've got a lot of guts. And I may still be able to shield you. Come with me."

He started to pull her toward the elevators, but she dug in her heels.

"No, please, Rovl. I can't hide. Sola's condemned. You have to find me and Sola a ship."

"A ship?" He seemed to consider her idea for a moment, then shook his head. "You don't know what you're asking. Listen, I think you still have a chance. Not a big one, but a chance. But if you run with her, you'll have zero chances. They'll hunt you down."

"I think they're going to hunt me down too, after what I just said. Where do you think I have more of a chance? Out there, or in here?"

He tried to interrupt, but she wouldn't let him.

"Or are you going to let me be brushed away," she said, "the way you let it happen on Asylums 1, 2, and 5—"

"That's enough," he snapped, his expression clouding over.

"I'm sorry." She wished she hadn't mentioned the way stations. "I know it wasn't your fault."

"But it is." He paced back and forth, brushing a hand back through his short hair. "It was. I knew it was wrong, and I didn't say anything."

"And now?" she ventured yet another question. "What are you going to do now?"

What few tattoos he had swirled in confusion across his neck and shoulders, as if matching his turmoil. Finally he knit his hands behind his head and nodded.

"All right." He lowered his voice, beckoning her to follow. "Now I know for certain you're crazy, and maybe I am for helping you too. They'll kill me, but ... I'll try to find you a way out."

"And Sola," she added, close on his heels. "We have to bring Sola."

He shook his head in confusion.

"I still don't understand the connection between you two. You're not her servant. And what was she doing in there?"

"It would take too long to explain." Oriannon stepped over to Sola and took her by the arm. Eyes glassed over, Sola hardly seemed to know where she was.

"But it had something to do with your Stone," he asked, "didn't it?"

"In a way."

With Sola between them, they started down the hallway toward a transport tube. Oriannon looked over at Sola, whose lips moved silently as she stumbled along. The hard part would be keeping her from making a scene as they tried to steer her toward one of the exit tubes.

"My destiny!" mumbled Sola, tears flowing down her cheeks. "I don't understand. They told me it couldn't fail."

"Your destiny isn't here and neither is mine." Oriannon did her best to keep Sola moving. "Our destiny is Jesmet."

Sola only shook her head and seemed to grow more agitated, so Oriannon lowered her voice and hoped Sola understood.

"Listen to me," she whispered. "Rovl is going to help us. Do you hear me? He's going to help us get off the Gamma."

"No." Sola shook her head, but she seemed to awaken from her daze. "What if I—what if it's delayed? We don't have a chance."

Rovl looked at her and furrowed his eyebrows.

"Do you know what she's talking about?" he asked.

"You don't want to know." Oriannon kept close to Rovl as they neared a crowd. He didn't press the matter as they dragged Sola along and wound their way through the crowds to a nearby tube.

"Rovl, why are you doing this?"

He shook his head as they hurried between and around other Troikans on the moving sidewalk. "I'm not sure I can tell you yet. But maybe someday you could introduce me to this mentor of yours. First, I have to tell you—"

He stiffened at the sight up ahead of something or someone moving against the current of people.

"Tau's men," he said quietly. "I think they would rather we not share how much they violate Troikan law. There really is a protocol for conquering way stations."

The words had no sooner left his mouth when the crowd in front of them screamed and ducked. Oriannon felt the chill of a paralyzing beam graze her shoulder.

"What are we doing?" Sola protested as Rovl pushed her over the railing. He had no time to explain as they jumped across the sidewalk headed the other way, and then to the catwalk on the far side. "You must tell me what we are— "

"Stay down and run!" shouted Rovl.

"Here," yelled Oriannon, grabbing the blind woman's hand. "Just hold on to me."

"But— "

They managed to slide and tumble back down the slope of the catwalk to the tube opening as Troikan disruptor beams tore at the floor behind them, flinging shattered tiles in all directions. Rovl took a hard left turn and dove through a door to a utility corridor, a low-ceilinged alley lined with high pressure lines and power cords. They would have to make it to the end of the corridor—or be caught in the middle with nowhere to hide.

"Can we make it?" Oriannon wondered aloud as they ran single file for the longest fifty meters of her life. She would have carried Sola if it would have done any good, but she settled for pulling Sola's arm, practically out of its socket.

"Tau's men?" Oriannon gasped at the end of the tunnel. "They're that desperate?"

"It seems you may have been right about your slim chances." Rovl grunted as he desperately tried to force open a frozen access hatch. "And now we're locked in. I'm sorry."

As Rovl continued to wrestle with the handle, he barely avoided another disruptor blast.

"Rovl!" cried Oriannon, flattening herself as best she could against the side wall of pipes. She pushed Sola's face to the wall too, framing the woman's nose between two pipes.

Rovl, however, turned to face their pursuers—holding out his hands in surrender for a moment ... before crumpling to the floor.

What in the world? Another beam slammed into the door only centimeters above his head right where he had been standing. As if he'd choreographed the move, Rovl kicked the now-shattered door off its hinges and rolled to safety beyond.

"Follow me!" he cried, and what else could Oriannon do? As another disruptor beam sent sparks showering all around them, she pushed Sola ahead and scrambled through the door. Once they'd made it to relative safety, Rovl slammed shut the shredded remains of the door — not that it made much difference — and casually dusted off his shirt as he stood.

"Just a minor system malfunction," he told a passing man, who looked at them with wide eyes. "We'll have it fixed in no time."

Rovl pulled Oriannon and Sola by the arms and tried to blend into the tide of Troikans milling about a broad plaza. Incredibly, Sola still said nothing, but allowed Rovl to lead her. Again, this part of the Gamma looked quite familiar.

"Did we lose them?" Oriannon wondered, looking over her shoulder as they hurried into another tubed walkway.

"I'm not sure," answered Rovl. "But don't look back."

She didn't, but she couldn't help noticing where they were.

"You're taking us back to your ship." She gripped Sola's hand and wondered how they could get off the moving walkway. "Rovl, you're not helping us escape. You're taking us back."

"Would you please just trust me?" he asked them, never letting go of Oriannon's arm. "I've put myself on the line here. Now do what I say or go back to the Council."

As if she had a choice. Oriannon took Sola's hand again, and they continued through the boarding area to the large Troikan ship. Rovl breezed by the few maintenance workers as if he knew what he was doing. They heard shouts from behind them. Oriannon looked over her shoulder and caught a glimpse of one of their pursuers.

"This is not good," mumbled Rovl as they darted aboard and hurried down one of the main corridors, then up a service ladder to the next deck. Rovl might know every square meter of this ship, but they couldn't keep running.

What was he thinking?

"It's up here just a little ways!" he told them. "The evacuation deck."

Oriannon saw a red emergency flasher on the wall and painted red stripes on the floor leading them to a landing that opened onto a row of some thirty round hatches. Each one featured a prominent red lever with multiple warnings and pictorial instructions for the ship's life pods.

Once again, their pursuers had nearly caught up to them. Rovl paused for a moment on the edge of the landing behind the shelter of a wall.

"We're not going to make it, are we?" For a blind woman, Sola Minnik had a strange ability to see what was going on around her.

"It's only five meters across the landing to the life pod doors," Rovl told them. "I'll hold them up in the corridor, and you two run for it."

"Not this time." Before they could stop her, Sola yanked her hand free and marched straight toward the noise of the pursuers. At the same time she called back over her shoulder.

"Go catch your destiny, Oriannon Hightower. I know what mine is."

"No, Sola!" Oriannon screamed.

But Sola was past listening. She blocked the incoming corridor, her arms open wide.

"I have a biobomb!" She announced in her loudest voice. "If you touch me or hit me with any of your weapons, it's going off, and you don't want to see that happen!"

For a moment, Oriannon considered staying right there and surrendering with Sola. Surely the bluff couldn't work, and she knew Jesmet wanted them to stay together. But before she could move, Rovl grabbed her by the arm and dragged her across the landing to the nearest escape hatch. Alarms and warning voices screamed the moment he jammed down the lever. A rush of air swept them off their feet, and they landed on their backs in the basin of a tiny escape pod designed for perhaps ten or twelve passengers. Oriannon pulled herself into a navigator's seat in a small out-facing viewport, below which had been mounted a rudimentary control stick and several simple digital indicators.

"There!" cried Rovl, pointing to a single red button below the indicators. "Press it now!"

Oriannon looked back through the open rear port to see Sola still standing there with her hands outstretched, screaming something about taking them all down with her.

Oh, Sola. It could have been different.

"Oriannon!" Rovl repeated himself. "Please—*now!*"

So Oriannon leaned into the button, which slammed the hatch shut behind them and launched them away from the larger ship—and the rest of the Gamma. She gripped the control stick as powerful G-forces pressed her hard against the back of the navigator's seat. Rovl was thrown to the back of the small, padded passenger area as they shot away.

"Where are we going?" At three and a half G's, Oriannon's face felt as if it was melting back into the seat, making it almost impossible to talk.

"Away," answered Rovl, his voice distant over the roar of boosters. "Just away."

31

Getting "just away" from the Troikan ship was good, but would not be good enough for long. A few minutes after Oriannon and Rovl rocketed away from their pursuers, Rovl crawled forward to steer them in an actual destination.

"Let me see what I can do," he told her as she handed over the control stick and slid over to the other seat. She couldn't decide if they should be celebrating their escape, mourning the loss of Sola, or dreading the uncertain path ahead. None of the three options seemed right, and she could not shake the feeling that she had somehow betrayed her pledge to stay with Sola. But what could she have done differently?

Rovl adjusted their course, tapped on one of the indicators with his finger, and fiddled with a call button on the com. Neither Oriannon or Rovl said anything for several long minutes. She felt for the Pilot Stone in her pocket, then sighed as she remembered in whose hands she had left it back on the Gamma.

"By the way," he finally told her, still focused on the way ahead, "you did the right thing back there. I know it was hard to leave her. But I've never seen anybody do that kind of thing before, the way she did. Have you?"

"Once." Oriannon turned around in her seat to gaze through the rear port as the sprawling Gamma project slowly disappeared from view. "Only once."

Rovl certainly deserved to hear her stories about Jesmet. She hoped they would have time as they traveled far away from the Gamma. But for now the silence of the life pod seemed comforting as they hurtled through unfamiliar space. The only sounds were the faint hiss of life support and an occasional beep from the simple guidance system, along with a low, musical hum that grew steadily louder. Rovl looked at her curiously.

"That musical sound," he said, tipping his head to the side. "Hear it? I don't think it's the ship."

She listened for a while longer to be sure she wasn't imagining it, then smiled. How could it be?

"It's Jesmet's Song. I thought … I thought I needed the Stone to hear it."

They both listened to the distant echo of Jesmet's music, clear and distinct even this far out in space. The melody flowed and rippled around them as if their tiny craft was immersed in a mountain stream flowing with living water. If anything, it sounded even clearer than when Oriannon had actually held the Stone in her hand.

"So …" He squinted at his instruments again. "Does this mean you know where we're headed?"

Oriannon listened and nodded. She pointed ahead, through the forward viewports.

"We're headed in the right direction," she said. "To the place where you were going to bring Asylum 3."

Rovl understood she meant the place where the way station should have rematerialized into regular space from its journey through the Breach—a safe landing spot only a hundred thousand klicks from the Gamma. As he'd said before, it would be towed the final distance to the megacity.

"You sure you want to go there?" he said, still gripping the simple steering handle.

She nodded yes as they continued on, and she crawled back to watch the Gamma grow smaller and smaller. As it did, however, another tiny shape appeared from far behind them. Oriannon caught her breath, watching its faint glow.

"Rovl," she told him, "there's something back there. Can we speed up?"

"I see it." Rovl glanced over his shoulder and frowned. "I should have known they would follow, even though I was hoping they wouldn't. Nothing we can do about it, though, because this life pod has only one speed: slow."

"You think they'll catch us?"

He paused, rechecking he instruments, then sighed.

"At this rate, almost surely yes."

Oriannon studied the growing shape, wondering what would happen to them both if they were recaptured. After all this, would Jesmet let it happen?

"Think of it as a sixty-two minute joy ride," Rovl told her. "We're going out in style, so I guess it didn't matter which direction we chose."

He paused and shook his head before going on. "I would have liked to have met this mentor of yours. Now ..."

Oriannon wasn't ready to give up this easily. Not quite yet.

"How far to Asylum 3?" she asked.

"Three minutes and ... a few seconds," he replied, tapping a digital readout. "But really, it doesn't make much difference whether we're overtaken by a Troikan ship or we dock at a Troikan way station. Either way, we're done."

The way station, though still distant, loomed directly ahead and grew in size each second. Soon, Oriannon could make out at least a dozen space tugs attached to the outside of the large asteroid colony. The tugs pushed it slowly on its intended course toward the Gamma, where it would add nicely to the Troikan living space.

Meanwhile, the long, silver Troikan cruiser closed the gap from behind at an alarming rate.

"Still want to try to dock at your asylum station?" Rovl asked with a sigh. His face had fallen into a look of resignation. "There's really not much point anymore."

"Yes there is, Rovl. Please trust me. We need to try."

"Well, their com must still be offline; I haven't been able to reach them. It's odd, but, at this point, it doesn't matter."

"What about ..." She nodded toward the back of the life pod. "... them?"

"Oh, they've been hailing us for the past several minutes." He pointed at a blinking red light on his console. "I've just been blocking that frequency. You want to hear some angry Troikans?"

"No, thanks." Oriannon never stopped praying as the way station grew larger and larger ahead of them, while Rovl ignored the large Troikan cruiser that drew up directly behind them.

"Rovl, what will they do to you?"

Rovl smiled but kept his hand on the controls.

"You don't want to know. But I'll tell you this much: They're never going to make me do the kinds of things I used to do. I'm done with destroying the lives of people I've never even met. The Troikan Empire can get along with me from now on."

Oriannon swiveled her head from front to back, watching their progress as they approached Asylum 3. A tone sounded on their control panel, and Rovl wrinkled his eyebrows in concern.

"One strange thing follows another." He pointed up ahead to where the way station now nearly filled their view. A beam of light broke the darkness as a landing bay slowly opened. "It's either for the ship behind us, or it's for us. I guess it depends on who's in control of the doors. I'm going to say it's for us."

Without slowing, he steered straight for the bay, while the sleek Troikan ship crowded in only several hundred meters behind. Oriannon held on to a hand grip as they headed in.

"I'm surprised," said Rovl. "They haven't— "

He was interrupted by two tremendous thuds, one right after the other, slamming into the back of their pod and rocking them sideways. Rovl wrestled the controls to correct their course, while Oriannon did everything she could to hang on.

"Grappling hooks!" he yelled. "Grab the O_2 masks and give me one. We might still make it inside!"

That sounded optimistic, as they had only two ways out of the tiny craft—the rear entrance they came in, or through the second hatch directly overhead. Either way looked impossible.

By this time they had managed to reach the loading dock, coming in much hotter than they normally would have. Oriannon could see the lights of the way station streaming in through the forward viewport. The back end of the pod strained and groaned, and she knew they would have only seconds before they were yanked right back out by the two cords the Troikans had attached.

"Hang on to me." Oriannon grabbed him around the neck with one arm as she clutched her own O_2 mask. The instant their pod came to a grinding standsill, Rovl yelled, "Now!"

When Rovl hit the evacuation button, the hatch jettisoned and they popped out of the opening, sucked out with the air in the craft into the vacuum of space. Rovl's mask snagged on something and ripped off. Oriannon held him tightly as they tumbled into a grav zone and their pod was ripped out from under them. Yanked backward by two enormous grappling hooks, the pod boomeranged back out through the giant bay doors as Rovl and Ori tumbled in slow motion to the floor.

But the bay doors still gaped open to empty space. Fearing she might be pulled back out as well, Oriannon hooked her foot on a steel eye bolt in the floor, the kind used to tie down visiting space vessels. Rovl found a similar handhold, and she gulped a lungful of O_2 before pulling off her mask and giving Rovl a turn. He yelled something at her, but it was instantly swallowed in the vacuum. The floor shook beneath them.

Why did we come here? Oriannon wondered. As the giant outside doors rumbled and closed like interlaced fingers, she lay on the floor and listened for the wonderful hiss of breathable air flooding back into the Asylum 3 landing bay. Rovl groaned and rolled over, still gasping. With the air came the first sounds as well.

The giant bay doors locked together with a satisfying thud. Motors and compressors whined and strained to bring back a breathable atmosphere. Several buzzers sounded in the distance. But sweetest of all was the sound of voices singing the far-off music of the Stone, almost like they'd heard earlier.

Only this time they heard it much closer and in person. Jesmet's music!

Rovl struggled to his knees, clutching his chest as he set aside the breathing mask. He must not have heard it yet.

"We've got to get up," he told Oriannon, who was scrambling to her feet as well. "They might come right back in here."

Oriannon stood and listened, letting the melodies wash over her all over again.

"It doesn't matter anymore if they're out there," she finally answered. "Don't you hear it?"

Rovl paused and wrinkled his forehead, and he looked around the landing bay with a puzzled expression.

"I thought I was just remembering the music from before," he whispered. "I'm not, am I?"

Oriannon shook her head and led him by the arm toward a tall set of double doors that opened to the way station interior, each marked with a large 03. It didn't surprise her when the doors pulled away with a *schuss,* and they were met by her mentor.

"Jesmet!" She forgot all about the pursuing Troikan vessel when she saw him standing in front of them. He looked comfortable in his forest-green mentor's robe with his beard neatly combed—but with the angry red burn scars still painfully visible. His eyes penetrated Oriannon's soul, the way they once had when she and

Margus and all the others used to sit in his orchestra class, learning to play his wonderful, peculiar, difficult music.

"It's wonderful to see you, Oriannon," he told her with a smile. He stepped into the landing bay to give her a warm hug before holding her out at arm's length. "After all you've been through. It almost looks as if you've grown several centimeters."

"So ..." She hesitated. "This isn't one of those visions? Not that I would object, because I could use a good vision right now. But—"

Jesmet laughed long and low.

"Why don't you ask Rovl?" he suggested. "He can tell you whether this is a vision or the real thing."

Rovl hung back a bit, as if he didn't quite know what to make of Jesmet. He winced when he brought a hand to his side.

"My bruised ribs tell me this is real. I'm not sure I can trust my eyes. And ..." He studied Jesmet a little more closely. "How did you know my name? Do I know you?"

The smile never left Jesmet's face as he held out a hand in greeting.

"Not yet, Rovl. But that's going to change."

Oriannon stepped closer to them, feeling like a hostess introducing her guests.

"Rovl, you said you would like to meet my mentor someday. I didn't think it would be so soon. This is Jesmet."

"The one who was executed," Rovl whispered, accepting Jesmet's handshake.

"Not one of my top ten experiences," Jesmet slipped an arm around each of their shoulders and turned back toward the door. "I wouldn't recommend it to most people."

"Oh, Jesmet, I—" Oriannon halted in her steps, afraid to tell him what had happened on the Gamma, and especially about leaving Sola. A flood of emotions washed over her, and she didn't know where to start. She had so much to tell him—not all of it good—and so much to ask him ... about Margus and Wist, about Iakk ...

"I know all that." He nodded, and surely he knew what she was thinking. "We do have a lot of catching up to do, don't we? I'll fill you in on all the details."

"I didn't stay with Sola," she whispered.

"But you did! You did everything you could, right to the end. It gave her a chance to show you something better than herself."

"Wait." Rovl shook his head in confusion and looked over at Jesmet as they stepped through the main doors together. "This is too strange. You weren't back on the Gamma, were you? You couldn't have been, yet you know everything that happened."

"Something like that, Rovl. But I have to say, I appreciate what you did for Oriannon, and for everyone who calls me their mentor. You're very welcome here."

Rovl looked past Jesmet to the inside of the station, where music spilled toward them through a short corridor. No one could look at the mentor without feeling the music.

"I'd like to believe that," he said, "but you have no idea what I did to the people of Asylum 1 and 2, and—"

"And what you might have done to the people of this way station?" Jesmet finished the horrible sentence. "I know all that. About you and Vel and Trys, and about Councilor Tau. But please, come inside, Rovl. Things have a way of working out, and you did the right thing by coming here."

Oriannon still kept her eye on Rovl.

"You took a chance with me, didn't you?" she asked. "Thank you."

He shrugged.

"I told you, you were right. The Council would never have let you go, and I just couldn't go along with things the way they were anymore. I figured it was worth a try."

"And now you see that it was." Jesmet told them as they walked down a softly lit high-ceilinged corridor. "But you, Miss Hightower.

I must say that if I were grading you on your attitude these past several weeks, we would have quite a bit more work to do."

Oriannon knew what he was talking about, and it brought color to her cheeks. At the same time, his words didn't sting as much when she felt the warmth behind them.

"You were quite right, though," he added, "about changing the Troikans from the inside-out. Wait until you see what happens now that Councilor Ploril and the other Council members have the Pilot Stone."

He laughed at his own announcement.

"Life is going to be quite different on the Gamma project. I promise you that." He looked at them both, stopping before they entered the main arboretum. "Just like it's been different here on Asylum 3 for the past few days. We've purified the water system for one thing. The scribes are actually waking up. They're beginning to see through the fog they created for themselves."

Oriannon smiled at the thought of seeing Cirrus Main back in his right mind. Perhaps Iakk would be back to his old self as well.

"Everything changes from the inside-out," she said.

"But we're not going back to the Gamma?" asked Rovl, worry slipping across his face again. "Are we? You know I can't exactly do that, because—"

"No, no, Rovl," Jesmet assured him. "Don't worry. We've picked up the people we needed. We're actually changing course and turning back to Corista again, though it will take several weeks at the speed we're going. However, I know you'll like it there."

They stepped into the plaza. Oriannon saw a celebration under the beautiful giant Trion sculpture, where scribes who had never known Jesmet now cheered him as their guest of honor. It looked as if they'd been waiting for him to enter.

"Corista?" wondered Rovl. "Is it safe?"

"With the new government, it will be. And besides ..." He looked at Oriannon and rested a hand on her shoulder. "Oriannon will have a chance to make good on a promise she made. A promise to someone she loved."

THE SHADOWSIDE TRILOGY
TRION RISING
2
ROBERT ELMER

1

Read an excerpt of

Trion Rising,

Book 1 of The Shadowside Trilogy.

I thought you said you knew how to fly this thing!"

"I did. I do. Trust me."

Easy for him to say. Oriannon could only grip her stiff bucket seat with both hands and count down the final seconds of her young life. She cringed at the buzz of a high-pitched warning.

"On present course, nine seconds to impact," came the metallic warning voice. "Eight seconds ..."

Ori wondered how she had let Margus Leek talk her into sneaking aboard the little two-seat interplanetary pod. It was fast, but built for speed and certainly not comfort. If she stretched her arms even a little she would elbow the pilot.

"Relax, Orion." Margus Leek yanked the joystick to starboard, and their pod brushed by the antenna of a rather large telecommunications satellite. "I grew up flying these little things."

"Tell me why I don't feel any better." Oriannon tried not to scream as they buzzed by another piece of space debris—an old fuel tank—leaving it spinning in their wake. "And my name isn't—"

"I know, I know. Sorry. You don't have to tell me. It's Or-i-ANN-on." When he smiled, she could almost see his eyes twinkling through his scratched sun visor. "Oriannon, Oriannon. Don't know how I can forget a VIP passenger like the esteemed and honorable Oriannon Hightower of the Nyssa clan."

"It's just Oriannon, okay?" she told him. "Forget all the other names."

He laughed as they dipped below an orbiting solar collector, close enough to read the warning label on the underside. She closed her eyes and wondered what it would be like to grow up without all the baggage that came with being an elder's daughter. If her father wasn't an elite member of Corista's ruling Assembly—

But the impact buzzer sounded again, and she snapped her eyes back open.

"Whatever you say, Just Oriannon." Margus smiled again. "And don't worry. I'm watching where we're going."

Could have fooled me, Ori thought.

Now Margus readjusted his nav-system by passing his index finger across a colored grid screen and tapping in several coordinates from memory. The move doubled their speed and set them on a direct course to Regev, the largest of their world's three suns. Anything not strapped down, including Ori's lunch sack, crashed into the back of the small cargo area behind their seats.

"So how about a tour of the Trion?" asked Margus, sounding like a tour guide.

As they picked up even more speed, Ori frowned and twisted the family ring on her finger—the ring with the tiny, brilliant blue corundum stone set in the distinct diamond shape of Saius. As the second largest but most intense of their suns, the real Saius now filled her eyesight even more than it had back on the planet's surface.

Unfortunately, she could also smell overheating deflectors, like burning rubber. Did he really have to jerk them around so much? This time the impact alarm insisted they veer away from a restricted zone.

"Immediately!" screeched the buzzer voice.

"What's that all about?" asked Oriannon. Margus silenced it with a tap to the flashing amber screen.

"No problem, Your Highness," he told her just before they flew straight into a blinding white light and every alarm in the pod went off at once.

"Margus!" Oriannon held a forearm to her face, but that did not help her as they tumbled out of control in a maelstrom of warning lights and screeching alarms. So this was how her life would end? She broke out in a sweat and gagged at the nose-burning smell of fried electronics.

"Do something!" Oriannon cried. She coughed and held on as the inside of the pod warmed to sizzling. In the blinding light she couldn't even make out Margus sitting next to her.

"Just a sec," mumbled Margus. And as quickly as the light had overpowered them, it suddenly blinked out, leaving them spinning slowly, silently, and in the dark. A lone alarm buzzed once then died to a pitiful whimper.

"Are you going to tell me what just happened?" Ori slowly lowered her arm and blinked her eyes, but the horrible flash of light and heat still echoed in her eyesight. It would take several moments to get used to normal space light once more. Margus shook his head and tapped at the control panel in front of him, as if he were trying to wake it back up. A few of the dials flickered, but not all.

"Weirdest thing I've ever seen." He looked around and behind them. "I think we got caught between two of those big solar reflectors, and— "

"And what?"

"And, uh, it's probably a good thing we didn't stay back there." He jerked his thumb and tapped the instrument panel once more. "Looks like it cooked us a little."

A little? Ori swallowed hard, wishing she could just stop this ride and get out right there.

"Look, Margus," she finally whispered, choking back the bitterness that curled her tongue. "I don't know what we're doing here, and my dad's really going to be upset with us when we land. *If* we land. We've got to turn around right now."

"That's the one thing we can't do." Margus was sweating under his silver flight helmet visor too. "We can't go back that way. Better just enjoy the view. There's the Trion, see?"

The Trion—which meant "three lights" in the ancient Coristan tongue—was made up of three suns. Regev, a red giant, never blinked as it cast a perpetual rosy glow over the brightside of Corista. This rosy glow was offset by the white-blue of Saius, a much brighter and more intense flame. Between the two suns, the Brightside of Corista never saw darkness. Heliaan—the smallest, distant yellow sun some people missed—stayed in the background. Together the three suns joined to create the flickering violet hue of the pretty Coristan sky, though it had turned darker the higher they climbed.

But right now Oriannon wasn't impressed. She peered up through the clear plexi bubble over their heads, the only barrier between them and the cold vacuum of space and the searing light of one of those space mirrors.

"You sure we can't just go back?" she asked, shaking off her jitters.

"I'll get us back, Your Highness." By this time he'd removed a panel and was yanking out circuits. "Just have to override a couple systems, and we'll be good to go. My dad showed me how to do this once."

"While you were up here?"

He paused a moment before answering.

"Uh, no. Back in his shop. But it should work."

So he wrestled with the controls as they bounced from one space mirror to the next, ducking behind them to avoid being fried all over again. Margus touched one wire to another, showering sparks in his lap but firing the ship's thrusters as they glided—the long way—between the orbits of their home world and eleven other distant moons, all circling the big planet.

"I never knew there were this many of these mirror things up here." Ori braced for the next deflector bump.

"Must be hundreds of them," Margus said as he nodded. "I just don't get what they're for. There's something strange about all this."

Strange wasn't quite the right word. But all Oriannon could do was look out the window as they dodged the curved mirrors, each one many times bigger than their little pod. She couldn't pretend to care about the stunning view Margus had promised before they took off on this horrible ride. But if she cared to look, Oriannon would have seen the lush green landscape of Corista below, bathed in the trebly bright light of their three suns.

In fact, if she had cared to, she could recite every detail of the landscape. Sometimes her eidich's memory came in handy, if she could just put aside all the mental baggage that crowded her brain with bits and details, faces and names, trivia and conversations that would never go away.

The Plains of Izula reminded her of a quilt her grandmother Merta had once showed her, decorated by patchwork fields of grain and orchards of every colored fruit a person could imagine: trees loaded with golden aplon, deep purple pluq, and her favorite, the lip-puckering orange simquats. And when she finally looked down, she couldn't help catching her breath at the forest green, myrtle green, emerald green, fern and sea green, lime green, moss green, deep cobalt green, viridian-that-matched-her-eyes green, olive, and everything-in-between green. Here it stretched all the way to the horizon, which wasn't far in this tiny, well-watered garden planet, Corista.

And there! In the Highlands, not far from the boundary between light and dark, was Seramine, perched like a jewel in the jade crown. Seramine, the capital city, her city. Were they finally getting closer? Even at this height she could imagine how the bright windows of grand whitewashed palaces and halls seemed to catch blue and red rays of sun, winking back at her. Did they know she was up here watching?

Once more, they bumped off the back side of another orbiting mirror, sending them spinning into the clear. Oriannon instinctively gripped the handle next to her seat, ready for anything.

"Sorry." Margus pointed ahead. "But see? I think we're all clear now."

"Wonderful." Maybe she didn't sound as enthused as he would have liked. "I'm still thinking about what my dad's going to say."

"I thought you said he was always too worried about Assembly stuff to pay much attention to you. Is he really going to worry about one little borrowed pod?"

"You don't know my dad. And the pod—are you sure you can land this thing now?"

She adjusted the headset of her comm and went back to peering out through the hard-shell bubble—just before a new screech of warning alarms pierced the tiny cockpit.

"So it needs a little maintenance." Margus shrugged and replaced a circuit panel, bringing back the lights while spewing a plume of smoke at her feet. Oriannon could only hold her hands over her head and close her eyes. She hoped it would all just go away, and soon.

But once more the pod jolted and lurched to the side. And as Margus grappled with the controls, they once more spun out of control, falling like a delicate cerulean flower petal through the edge of the atmosphere. Even without looking she could feel the heat radiating from the bubble above their heads, but this time the fabric of her silver coveralls kicked in with coolant that flowed through its built-in blue tubing. If they were going to die in this little pod, at least they would die comfortably.

"I think," she moaned, trying to ignore the butterflies in her stomach. "I think I'm going to be sick."

"You might want to hold off on that a few minutes, Your Highness." Besides that infuriating grin of his, he could also sound infuriatingly cocky. Maybe that's why she liked him, though she'd never admit it. After a few minutes the shuttle spun a final time, then rocked from side to side like a hammock, before the scream of wind around the cockpit told Oriannon they'd dropped back down into Corista's violet atmosphere.

"Forty-eight thousand klicks," announced Margus, as they swooped ever lower, leaning dangerously to the side. And now he could have almost passed for a Coristan shuttle pilot, instead of a fifteen-year-old impostor who had hijacked the little pod for a silly joyride. "Forty ... no, wait."

He tapped on a dial with the palm of his hand. That dial wasn't working, either.

"Margus—"

"No worries." Didn't he ever worry about anything? "We don't really need that thing. It's just for show."

"I don't believe you, but listen—"

He looked over at her with his eyebrows arched, waiting for her to finish.

"Thanks." She finally got the word out.

"What, for getting you into trouble or for almost killing you?"

"No." She shook her head. "For not giving up."

He shrugged. "No wor—"

"Don't say it." She interrupted him. But it didn't matter now as they finally slipped into a landing pattern, a lineup of incoming shuttles and pods—each separated by only a few meters and held in place by point-to-point tractor beams. Oriannon wished she could slump just a little lower in her seat so the pilot in the larger shuttle behind them wouldn't recognize her. But she could hear every word that now crackled over the comm line, which seemed to work.

"You're out of order, Bravo One-Nine," came the voice over the comm. That would be the guy in the shuttle. And it sounded just like someone complaining that Margus cut into the lunch line at school.

"Sorry," Margus responded through his own headset. "We've got mechanical problems. Need to touch down right away."

"Stand by," came the voice again, and a moment later the shadow of the much-larger ship hovered over them, and they felt the lurch of a grappling pad pulling them up.

"Hey, ah ..." Margus got back on the comm line. "We don't really need a tow."

We could have used one a long time ago, thought Oriannon.

"Relax," the voice told them. "We'll have you back to port in just a minute."

Or ten. Either way, Oriannon held her breath until landing thrusters screamed and she felt a comforting *thump* as they finally landed, upside-down, in the midst of Spaceport Corista. While the engines wound down, a beehive of workers in blue coveralls bustled around the ships, attaching power cables and fluid exchangers, rolling up with floating lev-carts full of tools.

"So how do we get out of here without anybody seeing us?" she wondered aloud, raising her voice to be heard over the scream of still more engines.

"Too late for that." Margus hit the canopy control so it lifted clear with a whoosh of air. "Follow my lead."

"That's what got us into trouble in the first place," Ori mumbled, but she climbed out after Margus, and they hopped down to the tarmac. Her knees buckled for a moment as she readjusted to the planet's light gravity.

"Coming?" Margus already had a step or two on her as they hustled past dozens of parked shuttles, pods, and cargo ships. They nearly made it to the hangar exit when one of the workers caught up with them.

"You! We didn't get your flight plan download." A tall Coristan with typical olive-colored skin and typical sunshades tapped his clipboard. "In fact, looks like you were flying through a restricted area, and I don't even have an original flight plan for your unit. It's still in the maintenance pool."

"I know." Margus had to crane his neck to look up at the worker. He inched toward the exit as they spoke. "We just had it out to test the systems."

"You know that's not how we do things. But, hey— " The worker crossed his arms and looked them over a little more closely. "Aren't you Supervisor Leek's kid?"

By this time Oriannon was ready to melt through a crack in the concrete floor.

"Uh . . ." Margus had to be looking for a way out too. "We were on assignment from the Assembly."

Oh, Margus, she thought, *anything but that.*

And sure enough, the worker threw his head back and laughed, long and hard.

"Nice try." He finally stopped laughing long enough to notice Oriannon, and it probably didn't do any good that she tried to look away. "You'll come with me to the office, and we'll . . ."

His voice trailed off, and he stared at Oriannon's hand. Her ring, actually.

"Like I was saying . . ." Margus tried to explain once more, but this time the wide-eyed worker waved him off.

"I didn't realize," he muttered, backing up a step. "Sorry to bother you. You know the way out?"

Margus looked at the guy with an expression that said *Huh?* But Oriannon knew exactly what had just happened. She answered for the both of them.

"We know the way. Thanks." And she didn't waste any more time chatting. But a quick glance up at the corner of the huge hangar area told her what she was afraid of: A small, grapefruit-sized security probe hovered like an eye in the sky, its red light telling her that it had not missed a thing. In fact, the small silver sphere had probably recorded every word of their conversation with the maintenance guy.

"That was cool!" whispered Margus as the double doors slid open for them. "What did you do, some kind of mind control?"

She fingered the ring. "Something like that."

Only problem was, she knew that what had spooked the hangar worker wasn't going to impress her father.

And the trouble, she told herself, *hasn't even begun.*

Forbidden Doors

A Four-Volume Series from Bestselling Author Bill Myers!

Some doors are better left unopened.

Join teenager Rebecca "Becka" Williams, her brother Scott, and her friend Ryan Riordan as they head for mind-bending clashes between the forces of darkness and the kingdom of God.

Dark Power Collection

Volume One

Softcover • ISBN: 978-0-310-71534-4

Contains books 1–3: *The Society, The Deceived*, and *The Spell*

Invisible Terror Collection

Volume Two

Softcover • ISBN: 978-0-310-71535-1

Contains books 4–6: *The Haunting, The Guardian*, and *The Encounter*

Deadly Loyalty Collection

Volume Three

Softcover • ISBN: 978-0-310-71536-8

Contains books 7–9: *The Curse, The Undead*, and *The Scream*

Ancient Forces Collection

Volume Four

Softcover • ISBN: 978-0-310-71537-5

Contains books 10–12: *The Ancients, The Wiccan*, and *The Cards*

Echoes from the Edge

A New Trilogy from Bestselling Author Bryan Davis!

This fast-paced adventure fantasy trilogy starts with murder and leads teenagers Nathan and Kelly out of their once-familiar world as they struggle to find answers to the tragedy. A mysterious mirror with phantom images, a camera that takes pictures of things they can't see, and a violin that unlocks unrecognizable voices ... each enigma takes the teens farther into an alternate universe where nothing is as it seems.

Beyond the Reflection's Edge

Book One

Softcover • ISBN: 978-0-310-71554-2

Eternity's Edge

Book Two

Softcover • ISBN: 978-0-310-71555-9

Nightmare's Edge

Book Three

Softcover • ISBN: 978-0-310-71556-6

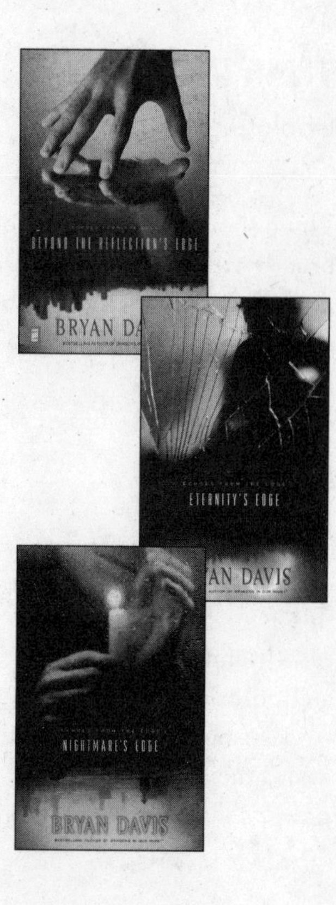

Book 3 coming soon!

Pick up a copy today at your favorite bookstore!

Visit www.zondervan.com/teen